Love's Legacy

Adam J. Ridley, Blake Allwood

Blake Allwood Publishing

Printed in the United States of America

Box Elder, SD

E-book ISBN: 978-1-956727-12-8

Paperback ISBN: 978-1-956727-13-5

AMZ Paperback ISBN: 979-851220-88-30

Library of Congress Control Number: 2021920776

Content Warnings

Attempted Murder

Gunshot

Violence

Death or Dying

Join Blake's email list to get advance notice of new books and receive his occasional newsletter:

www.blakeallwood.com

MM Romance
By Blake Allwood

Transitions Series
Aiden Inspired
Suzie Empowered (MF Romance)
Bobby Transformed

Chance Series
Love By Chance
Another Chance With Love
Taking A Chance For Love

Romantic Series
Romantic Renovations (1)
Romantic Rescue (2)
Romantic Recon (3)

Melody Series
Melody of the Heart
Melody of the Snow

Road to Rocktoberfest Anthology
Changing His Tune - 2022

Coming Home Series (2023)
A Long Way Home
Family Home
Down Home
…and many more

Novellas
Tenacious
Moon's Place

Romantic Fantasy
By Adam J. Ridley

Big Bend Series
Love's Legacy (1)
Love's Heirloom (2)
Love's Bequest (3)

The Witch Brothers Series
Emerald Earth
Diamond Air
Ruby Fire
Sapphire Water

Acknowledgements

A special thank you to

Bryan Seranas – Developmental Editor

Jo Bird – Line Editor

Renee Mizar – Developmental Editor II

Ann Attwood – Final Editor

A special thank you goes to all my friends and family who supported me, I couldn't have done it without you.

John Gilchrist

for his work on the family tree and being a great Beta-reader.

And of course, a big thank you to my husband who encourages me to keep going down these rabbit holes never knowing where I might end up.

1

Flex

THE ELECTRIC PULSE SURGED through me as I touched the handle of the motel reception door. "What the hell?" I said to myself, then shook my head when I touched the handle again. This time there was no shock.

"Must be static electricity," I said, and although my heart was beating significantly faster, I ignored it and pushed through the door.

I walked into the front room and turned back to see if maybe there was some explanation, but there was none I could see. I was about to say something to the front-desk person I'd heard come in behind me, but when I turned around and saw the man behind the desk, the same electrical sensation that'd hit me before surged through me again. Just this time, it was more... intense.

The man looked to be in his mid-twenties. He was short and lithe, with long lashes accentuating gorgeous brown eyes that would've made any female model jealous. His arms were strong and muscular from what appeared to be work-related exercise, and not time spent in a gym.

He looked up and smiled, which made his entire face glow and my knees go weak. "How can I help you?" he asked. I froze for a moment and subconsciously reached up and rubbed the place above my heart where the electrical discharge still stung a bit. Finally, I came to my senses, and told him my name.

"I'm Flex... um... Fletcher Henry. I'm traveling with Eric Anderson," I said. "We should have adjoining rooms."

The man typed in our names and then smiled. "You have the honeymoon cottage. Is that good news? Should I be congratulating you?"

I laughed. "No, we didn't just get married. That's why we wanted the rooms to be separate. We're friends from years back. We ran away from home and wanted to visit Big Bend before it gets too hot." It wasn't a complete lie.

"Well, Mr. Henry," the man said in a sexy, southern drawl that put images in my mind of hot cocoa being stirred. "Your accommodations are ready. I hope you and Mr..." He looked at the computer. "You and Mr. Anderson have a good time here in Alamito."

I winked at him before I knew what I was doing. "You can call me Flex," I said and blushed... I was not the type to flirt, but something about this man triggered me.

I pulled the rental car over to the cottage, and Eric and I began to unload. The place was as cute as it could be. Like the rest of the motel and campground, you could see distinct signs of renovation. The interior was what you'd expect to see on an *HGTV* series. It was modern with clean lines, and the bedding was obviously new and looked particularly chic.

I turned toward Eric and shrugged in surprise. "I guess we won't be roughing it after all."

Eric smiled and agreed. The two rooms were separated by a door. When the cottage was being used as a honeymoon suite, one room could easily be used as a living room and kitchen, and the other a master bedroom. As it was, Eric and I flipped for the bigger bedroom, and he won. I didn't mind though, the reviews for the room had said the hideaway bed was as comfortable as the main bed.

We went back to the car and unloaded each of our dogs. Puddles, a poodle, of course, belonged to Eric. I had the rambunctious Jack Russell, Ace. We were lucky, because Ace and Puddles enjoyed each other's company, and got along very well.

"I'll take them out," I volunteered, and grabbed both dogs, putting them on their leashes. I headed out the door before Eric could comment.

As I walked them across the courtyard, Ace immediately spotted a chicken pen, and began pulling me that direction. I was intrigued enough that I decided to let Ace lead us over and check it out. As we neared the chickens, Ace began lunging at the pen. I pulled him back and began to rein him in, when I heard barking at my back.

Before I could turn around, Ace darted toward the barking. Unfortunately, between him and me, his leash got caught against a rusty fence pole, that was just sharp enough to snap it.

When I finally managed to turn around, a Chihuahua was bounding toward Ace, and by the time I got to them, they were sniffing each other. The Chihuahua's lips curled back, his hackles raised, and I could tell the little dog wasn't friendly and was more likely than not going to bite Ace. I hurried over just as the owner came out of her camper screaming, "Lucca, Lucca." The dog turned to look at her owner as I grabbed Ace up and turned to pick Puddles up as well, just to make sure neither dog got attacked before the Chihuahua's mom got to him.

"I'm so sorry," the woman exclaimed. "I opened my door to put some things in my car, and she dashed out."

"No worries," I assured her, holding up the broken leash. "This got cut on a piece of rust." She smiled as I introduced myself.

I was just about to leave, when I heard Eric call, "Is everything okay, Flex?"

"Yep," I said over my shoulder, letting Puddles down, so I could hand her leash to Eric.

When I faced the woman again, her expression had changed completely. She looked at me in disgust. "You need to keep your dog *contained*," she huffed, then headed back to her camper.

"What was that about?" Eric asked.

"I'm not sure," I shrugged. "But I'm guessing she thought we were a couple."

"Well, we aren't, but we could've been. Guess she's the anti-gay *not* welcome wagon, huh?"

"Guess so," I shrugged again, and we walked back to the cottage.

We'd only been back a few minutes when the phone rang, and the handsome man I'd first met behind the desk when we arrived, said, "Mr. Henry. I'm sorry to bother you, but we've had a complaint about your dog. Can you come to the front desk, please?" I answered in the affirmative, but I was already angry enough to spit nails, even before walking out of the room.

I knocked on Eric's door. "Hey, can you keep Ace? I have to go deal with the bigot. She's trying to get us kicked out of the motel."

"Seriously?" Eric asked in surprise.

"Apparently," I said, then headed toward the office.

When I got there, the disgruntled old woman was stomping around in front of the main desk, waving her hands and basically having a hissy fit. She stopped when I walked in, and put her hands on her hips, tapping her right foot.

"Mr. Henry, thanks for coming," the man said, with some hesitation.

"What seems to be the problem?" I asked, turning my own glare at the woman.

"Um…" the man began, but was interrupted by the woman.

"You know what the problem is, your dog was off his leash and tried to attack my dog."

I was shocked by the blatant lie, and I had to catch my breath before I responded.

"Don't you mean, your dog was off her leash? You admitted to me that you let her escape when you were loading your car. That's when she rushed *my* dog. You and I both know, the only reason my dog was off the leash is because when he turned to meet your terror, his leash snapped."

The woman crossed her arms, and I could tell she was about to call me a liar, or possibly worse, so I interrupted her as I turned toward the young man. "I think we all know this isn't about our dogs," I said, then looked her square in the face. "This woman was quite pleasant to me until my friend Eric came over. She thought we were a couple, and as a result, she decided to use this farce as a way to get rid of us."

I could tell I'd hit the nail on the head by the way the woman flushed. She dropped her arms, but knowing she was in an impossible situation, she crossed them again and turned away from me to stare at the guy behind the desk.

I noticed the man's jaw was locked, and his expression became angry. Despite the pleasant greetings when I'd first arrived, I had to assume he'd side with the woman, so, I waited for the words that told me I needed to leave. Instead, he looked at me, and said, "I'm deeply sorry, Mr. Henry. If I had known this was a homophobic stunt, I wouldn't have bothered you. Please, apologize to your friend for me as well."

Both the woman and I stared at the young man in shock. I turned to leave without saying a word. I didn't have the words, really. We were in West Texas of all places, so I didn't think anyone would be defending the rights of a gay person, no matter how in the right we were.

2

Mitch

BEFORE MR. HENRY LEFT, I was already dialing the number of the park across the street. "Yes, is Lia there? Hi, Lia, this is Mitch Armstrong at the Alamito Motel. I'm good, thanks. Hey, I have a camper who needs another place to park tonight. Do you have room? Perfect, I'll send her over."

I looked at the woman standing across the desk, and ignored the fact that she appeared to be so angry, her face looked like it could explode. "Mrs. Stanfield, I've already warned you to stop being nasty to the other residents, and I told you that if I had to say something to you again, you'd be asked to leave. I'm afraid lying about a guest who literally just got here, because you don't like his or her lifestyle is simply the last straw. As you heard, Lia said they have room across the street at the Events Campground. You can pull your camper over there."

The woman stared at me for a moment, before the tears began to fall. "But all my friends are here. The Events Campground is nasty."

I ignored the crocodile tears. "I'm sorry, but again, I did warn you."

I turned to go into the backroom, almost afraid of what damage the woman would do once I left, but fortunately, when I came back out, she was gone. About an hour later, I saw her camper leave the motel and pull in across the road.

I figured there was going to be hell to pay. Mrs. Stanfield was one of eight widows who lived here full time. When I inherited the motel from my grandfather, they were some of the campers who rented from him. I'd allowed them to stay on the ridiculously low-cost rent he'd charged, which honestly didn't cover the cost of utilities, but there was more than money involved when it came to these things.

The eight women were more than a handful. They tended to be busybodies who poked their noses in everyone else's business. Luckily, I only had to chastise them occasionally when they crossed a line. *Usually*, I just found their antics amusing.

Mrs. Stanfield had gotten worse over the past year, however. It wasn't only the usual annoying things the women tended to do. One evening, during the weekly Bunko game they held in my kitchen, Mrs. Stanfield had gotten upset with one of the other ladies, and pulled her hair. Of course, the other woman was livid and slapped her. I walked into the kitchen just in time to see Mrs. Stanfield pull her fist back and nail the other woman right in the nose. I yelled before the punch landed, and shocked Mrs. Stanfield enough that there wasn't much weight behind the punch, but still, things had gone too far. When the other ladies left, I asked Mrs. Stanfield to stay back and told her to find another campground.

She'd cried then too. Unfortunately for her, I learned long ago not to be influenced by crocodile tears. My mother had been a master at using them to get her way.

When she left, I thought I'd seen the back of her, except that the other ladies, including the one who'd been attacked, came and asked me to reconsider. Of course, I had, and here we were once again. *No good deed goes unpunished,* I thought, but at least the grumpy old coot was now someone else's problem.

3

Flex

I GOT BACK TO the cottage and knocked on Eric's door to retrieve Ace. "How'd it go?" he asked.

"You won't believe it, but the guy actually took our side. I'm going to guess this could get him fired, though. I doubt the owner will be thrilled that he took my side over a damsel in distress."

Eric frowned sadly. "I hope not. It sucks when people doing the right thing get punished."

"Yeah, I agree. I'll go back down there later and check on him."

"Good idea," Eric said. "When do we need to be out at the ranch tomorrow?"

"We're expected by ten in the morning. The real estate agent is supposed to be there by noon, but I wanted to get a good look at the place before she arrives."

Eric looked at me. I'd never been particularly good at hiding my emotions, and I figured he could see the grief and sadness warring inside me, but Eric was a sensitive guy. Instead of pressing the point, he nodded knowingly and turned to his side of the suite.

"I think I'm going to turn in early. I'm exhausted after last week and the trip down from Oregon. I'll catch you around eight. That should give us enough time to eat, then get to the ranch."

I nodded. The ranch was about a thirty-minute drive from Alamito. I was tired too, so I decided I'd get Ace fed, then head back to the office and speak to the poor man behind the desk, to see if there was anything I could do to help save his job.

I left the cottage just as the old woman I'd had the run-in with rounded the corner in her camper. She locked eyes with me and flipped me the bird. "Wow, that one's a piece of work," I said out loud.

I waited until she pulled out of the parking lot, then walked over to the office.

I found the man thumbing through paperwork. He didn't look concerned, so I hoped maybe things weren't going to be as bad for him as I'd thought. When I entered, he looked up. I could see the weariness in his eyes before it was hidden by a genuine smile.

"Hello again, Mr. Henry. What can I do for you?"

"I... I'm just checking on you, actually. I hope you didn't get in trouble defending me from Mrs. Evil Britches."

The man chuckled. "I didn't get in trouble. In fact, since I own the establishment, there really isn't anyone to get in trouble with."

I was shocked by that fact. "Wow, really? You don't look old enough to own a business," I blurted out, then turned red in the face. I'd never been good at catching myself before I said stupid stuff.

He laughed, "My grandfather left me the motel in his will, along with enough money to do some repairs. I was going to renovate it and sell up, but I admit, I've gotten rather attached to it since I moved back last fall."

I quickly ran through the timeframe in my mind, and thought out loud, "So, you've been here for almost a year then?"

The man looked up, and the weariness seemed to settle on his face again. "Yes, it doesn't seem that long, though. There's still so much to get done."

"From what I've seen, you've done an incredible job. The cottage is beautiful."

That brought a smile to his face. "It was my first project. I wanted a comfortable place for newlyweds to escape to. As you know, since you're here, there isn't anything around for miles. Every town, even those in the middle of nowhere, deserves a nice place to... honeymoon," he said, and the sweet smile turned a bit mischievous.

The look, although fleeting, was delicious, and my nasty mind thought of a variety of ways I'd like to get that smile back on his face.

"Well, Mr..." I looked at him and shrugged. "I'm sorry I never got your name."

"My name's Mitch Armstrong," he said, causing that same strange electrical current to course through me, that had when I first arrived. What was it about this man that made me feel so... weird?

"Mr. Armstrong, it was nice of you to come to my aid earlier. I'll be honest, I wasn't sure that would be the case. I was all prepared to leave, but I was equally prepared to leave a nasty review for you online."

The man laughed. "I bet you would've, not that it would've mattered, since I'm pretty much the only motel around. But," he quickly back-pedaled. "we do what we can to make things nice for folks, though."

"Well, what you did mattered a lot to me and to Eric. Although, he's as straight as an arrow." The man looked at me again, this time with a bit of curiosity that he let go, without asking whatever it was on his mind.

"You thought we were together, didn't you?" I asked, wanting to find out more about the man, but not knowing how to ask without appearing nosy.

He continued smiling as he nodded. "I know you said you were friends, but that's usually how gay folks talk about their lovers around here."

"Are there many gay people around here?" I asked skeptically.

"More than you'd think," the guy said, with no malice in his voice.

"I wouldn't think Alamito would be a very gay-friendly place."

The guy nodded again. "It wasn't when I was growing up, but after the Supreme Court made their marriage ruling, even the churches seem to have found other things to go after. We've finally just sunk into the routine of the community."

There I had it, he was gay, but even with that information, I had to push further. I just had to. "So, you're gay too?" I asked, waiting, not sure how he'd respond.

"Yep," he said. "Been out since I was sixteen. I left here when I was eighteen, and swore nothing short of gold and silver would get me back. Seems I wasn't as stubborn as I thought. All it took was inheriting an old motel that was about to fall apart."

"I can imagine how awful it was. My grandparents lived down the road. Not too far from the national park. I spent my summers here, but we really never came into town unless my grandma needed supplies. For the most part, I just spent the whole summer riding horses and doing every possible chore my grandparents could think to give me."

Mitch chuckled with recognition. "My grandpa owned the motel, and my mom and I lived with him. I've been cleaning sheets since I was old enough to walk."

I was chuckling then myself. "It seems we both had grandfathers who thought an idle mind was the devil's playground."

"Well," Mitch replied. "He sure told me that enough. Good thing my mind was never idle very long, so I guess the devil has left me alone."

"Yeah, I'm pretty sure I was safe too... at least while I was here during the summer."

Mitch looked at me. "So, why didn't you stay at your grandparents' place? Not that we aren't happy to have you," he quickly added.

"Well, that's a long story," I said, and the sigh had the young man looking at me with sympathy. "My grandpa died about five years ago, and my grandma long before that."

"I see," he said. "I'm sorry for your loss. Even though my grandpa was a mean ol' bastard, I loved him and I miss him something fierce."

I nodded in agreement. "Yeah, mine was mean as well... what do y'all say out here? He was mean as a snake." I chuckled at the saying. "But, he never hesitated to tell me how much he loved me. Even after I came out, he said it was weird and he couldn't understand why anyone would want to touch a hairy man, when you could snuggle up to a pretty woman, but the next words out of his mouth were that it didn't matter what he thought. It only mattered that he and my gran loved me, no matter what I wanted, no matter how weird it was."

I smiled, but the backs of my eyes were stinging with unshed tears. It had been a long time since I'd come out to my grandfather. But, that simple, matter-of-fact love that he'd shown at that moment still burned a brand on my heart. Like Mitch said about his grandfather, I missed mine something fierce.

I knew I needed to change the subject, so I didn't end up bawling my eyes out and embarrassing the shit out of myself.

"Are you the one who did the desert gardens?" I asked.

The smile that'd never left Mitch's face beamed then with pure happiness. "Yep. Felt like the old place needed a little sprucing, and I couldn't afford to put in a bunch of non-native species, nor could I afford to irrigate them if I did. Most of the plants came from around the property. I just had to reposition them."

"I saw some of those cacti. I bet that was... precarious."

Mitched laughed. "You have no idea. Those cactus thorns go through leather like it was silk. I had to remove most of the thorns to move them. What you saw is the new growth. Most of my cacti were quick to regrow the thorns. I guess it is their only protection, but dang, I hoped I wouldn't see them again for at least a couple years."

I smiled, and was enjoying the passion he was showing for his gardens. "I already took a ton of photos and posted them on Facebook. My mom loved them, and since she pretty much hates everything to do with this area, her compliment is something you should be proud of."

The conversation stalled, and I realized I needed to let him get back to work. I turned to go, and Mitch quickly asked, "How long are you going to be in the area?"

"Just a couple of days, then I have to fly back to Houston to manage some business stuff. Eric has to get back to Portland too. He has classes on Tuesday."

"Is he a student?" Mitch asked.

"No, he's a teacher at a high school there. Although I have no idea why. We both hated high school. I guess the guy is a glutton for punishment."

Mitch chuckled. "Yeah, I sure wouldn't want to do that. I got my degree in business management and thought I'd be running a large corporation in Houston. My gramps clearly had other ideas," he said, as he gestured around the room.

"So, would you like to come by for dinner one night?" Mitch was blushing, which made him even cuter. It seemed impossible, considering how cute he already was.

"Sure, we'll be back tomorrow night. Why don't we go somewhere for dinner."

Mitch just smiled and looked at me like I was a simpleton. "Honey, there is nowhere to go in this one-horse town after lunch. Kimmie's is only open for breakfast and lunch. If you want dinner, it's pizza, or one of us will have to do the cooking."

"Oh," I said. My face turning red now. "I can't put you out like that. Unfortunately, I can't really leave Eric, since he came on this trip for me."

"No problem, I assumed he'd join us. I don't mind cooking. It'll give me something to do besides slave behind this desk, or deal with grumpy old women."

I smiled. "Okay, if you're sure. Can I bring anything?"

"No, I have everything we'll need. Do you prefer steak or chicken?"

"Both," I said, and he laughed.

"Sounds good, then I'll just let inspiration guide me."

"Um, I'm guessing we'll be out at the ranch until four or five. Can we plan to be at your place by six-thirty or seven? I'm sure we'll both want a shower before we eat. It's dusty and dirty out there, and I haven't been in the house since my grandparents died. It's probably pretty nasty."

"No problem. See you at seven, how's that?"

I grinned. I was secretly jumping up and down inside at the thought of him inviting me over for a meal, even if Eric was going to be with us, which was probably best, because the crush I was developing on this man was intense. I was sure I'd be trying to attack him before we cut into the steak or chicken.

"I'll see you at seven," I managed to say, and walked out of the office.

As Eric and I sat at the diner waiting for the waitress to deliver our breakfast, I couldn't help but feel nervous. Eric noticed and decided to push. "So, spit it out. Why do you look like you have a kidney stone with spikes like one of the cacti out there?"

I chuckled. Eric always had a way of making me laugh, even when I didn't feel it. "You know I haven't been there since they died," I said, and Eric just nodded.

"Are you worried one of your cousins will be there?"

"Nah, I think they're all back in Houston licking their wounds. Truth is, I doubt I'll ever hear from them again. Rubin and Jessie are both jackasses and always have been. I'm sure they bought into my aunt's whole *he's gay so he doesn't deserve it* bullshit, but Effie..." I just shook my head.

"Did he ever talk to you in court?"

Effie, or Edward, was the only cousin I liked. He always came to the ranch for the summer with me. Even though my mom was the oldest, Aunt Rebecca had her kids young. In fact, she had Rubin and Jessie before she graduated high school. My mom and dad didn't get married until she was twenty-three, and then I didn't come along until a couple of years after that. So, the only one of my cousins I was close to was Effie, who got the name because I couldn't say Eddie when we were little. He was my best friend and had been my entire life.

"No," I said. Even I could hear the sadness in my voice. "He never showed up. He wouldn't have inherited anyway. My aunt was using the argument that the property deserved to stay in the family. Rubin was the oldest grandson, and he already had heirs, so according to her, he should be the one to inherit."

All that trouble, despite the fact, my grandparents' will was iron-clad. My grandfather said the land belonged to his eldest daughter's first-born. That's how the ranch had passed down through the generations, and that was how his will was written in 1985 before either of my aunts had kids. Then, when I was born, he amended it with my name.

Aunt Rebecca argued that the property had been passed down to the eldest son for generations, and since her son was the oldest, he was the rightful heir. She even used the excuse that I was gay, so I wouldn't be able to produce offspring, and if I did, they wouldn't be legitimate."

"God, your aunt is a bitch," Eric said, shaking his head.

Just then the little old lady who was our waitress showed up with plates of food. I could almost hear her wanting to tell us young'uns to watch our language, but she bit her tongue, and even managed a smile before she walked away.

Both Eric and I almost rolled out of our seats laughing. It was a minor miracle the waitress hadn't gotten onto us.

By the time we left, I felt a bit better. Eric said he would drive, knowing I'd want the time to prepare myself, before we arrived at the ranch.

As we drove, I watched the landscape around me.

Eric's comments mirrored my own thoughts. "This part of Texas is so rugged and desolate, almost foreboding... but it's also beautiful, different than the rest of the country."

"All that sort of describes the people out here too, huh?" I asked.

Eric was a lover of all things history. He smiled. "That's true! Stubborn too. Hell, it seems most of the land out here has been in the same family since it was settled. That's unusual in itself."

"Did you ever hear about how my people settled here?" I asked him.

"A little," he replied. "But, remind me. I'd like to hear it again."

"Well, you know my great-great-great-great-grandfather settled here after the Civil War. He was captured by a Comanche raiding party, though, and ended up marrying an Apache woman they held captive as well."

I knew Eric had heard all this, but it was cathartic to tell it again, almost like we were reliving our summer childhood memories as I recited the old tales.

We rehashed the stories of my ancestry, stories my grandfather used to tell as we sat on his big front porch following dinner, and before we went to bed.

"My first ancestor ended up acquiring over forty-five thousand acres before he died at the ripe old age of a hundred and two. But, in later generations, the government took over half the land away when they built the park. That and, well, the Indian and Confederate soldier thing is why our relationship with the feds has always been strained."

When Eric corrected me about the state of Texas taking the land, not the US government, I looked at him before shaking my head. "You're enjoying this too much," I said, chuckling. "I do love that you're still interested in all this, though."

"It's fascinating, you've got such deep roots in this part of the world. That sorta fascinates me. Hey, last time I asked, you were going to try to get accepted into your tribe. How did that go?" he asked.

I shook my head. "I couldn't prove it, because my ancestors weren't on the native rolls from the early nineteen hundreds. And because they were never part of a reservation, there's no way to prove they were native."

I was deep in thought about my ancestral heritage, when I felt Eric slowing down. I looked out of the window to see my grandparents' driveway coming into view.

I sighed, and Eric reached over and patted me on the shoulder. I smiled to reassure him I was fine.

When we pulled up to the old house, it appeared to be abandoned. My aunt's attorney had asked permission to lease the property to one of my grandparents' caretakers, to ensure none of the tourists coming to Big Bend vandalized it. I agreed it would be a good idea and the judge granted the approval. Supposedly, we were going to meet with that caretaker today.

I'd been around rentals, and had seen the damage renters could do firsthand. I could only hope the damage wasn't so bad we couldn't sell the place. I'd talked to my mom, who even refused to come back to the property to take the things she was given by my grandparents. She hated it here, and told anyone who'd listen that she'd said, when she left, she would never return—and she never had.

When Aunt Rebecca challenged the will, my mom just put her arms around me, and said, "If the property wasn't worth millions, I'd tell you to give it to the bitch and let her rot on it." But, unlike my mom, the ranch meant more to me than just a piece of property worth millions. It was where my people were from.

I could immediately see some much-needed maintenance had been put off. The old windmill my grandfather was so proud of had several fans missing. It whirled haphazardly in circles, making a horrible squeaking noise as it did. The old fences around the garden were lying on the ground, and the weeds and cacti inside the fences had grown tall enough to house at least a hundred rattlers.

The house was in better shape, but it still needed a coat of paint. We stepped out, and before we could get up to the house to knock, an old man came onto the porch with his hand shielding his eyes from the sun.

"Well, if it ain't little Flex, all grown up," he said, his toothless smile spreading across his face.

"Jimmy Bean Stewart, is that you?" I asked, shocked to see him. "Damn, man, aren't you like two hundred fifty years old or something?" It had been my grandfather's favorite way to greet Jimmy, and I couldn't help but repeat it. Jimmy slapped his knee, and before I knew it, he'd engulfed me in a bear hug. I'd swear the man was so skinny, you could feel his bones rubbing together from the hug, yet as the air was squeezed from my lungs, I could tell he was still strong as an ox.

He looked warily over at Eric, before recognition struck him. He stepped back, and exclaimed, "Is that Eric the Attacker?" Eric had spent summers here after his mother passed away. My grandpa had been taken with Eric, so if gramps wanted me to do a chore, he gave Eric an equally difficult one to gnaw on. As a result, we knew pretty much every one of grandpa's ranch hands.

Eric smiled as wide as Jimmy did, and the old man grabbed him into a hug as well. Next thing I knew, the door to the house swung open, and out came Jimmy's wife, Emma Jean. She was not someone to mess with. The woman had never hesitated to whoop my behind. I was as afraid of her as I liked her husband, but the old woman stood on the porch, hands on her hips and a smile as big as Jimmy's.

"Well, it's about time you boys got here." She looked at me and over to Eric. I wasn't sure she recognized him, but it didn't matter. All boys were the same to Mrs. Emma Jean. "If you'd have gotten out of bed and come on down like a civilized person,

I'd have cooked you a good home-cooked breakfast, but since you meandered around all day, all you're gonna get now are some sandwiches for lunch."

I walked up to the porch and pulled my old caregiver into a hug, which she returned with gusto. When I pulled back, she was swiping at a tear. I tried not to notice, because I wasn't at all sure, even though I was over six foot tall and had about a hundred pounds on her, she wouldn't still try to whoop me if I embarrassed her too much.

We went into the house, and I was pleased to see it was spotless, probably even better than when grandma lived here. My granny was an outdoorsy woman. She was always happier shoeing a horse than cleaning a house, but Emma Jean had the place spick-and-span. "You've kept the place beautiful, Mrs. Emma Jean, my grandma would be proud."

"Child, your grandma wouldn't have even noticed," she said, and we all laughed.

Jimmy chimed in, his face sad. "Your grandpa asked that we keep the place up until you could claim it, but none of us knew your aunt would throw such a hissy fit." Emma Jean harrumphed and turned toward the kitchen. Jimmy watched her go and looked back at me.

"I'm awful sorry about the condition of the place, but I've done got too old to tend to all the things that need tending. When we volunteered to stay here to keep the place up, your

Aunt Rebecca never told us that we'd be needing to pay, but we wanted to stay, so we did."

Emma Jean came out of the kitchen with a jug of tea and several plastic glasses full of ice. As she set the tray down, she gestured for us all to sit around the table. "That hateful woman didn't do nothing but take our money. Didn't send a thing back to cover the expenses of the place. So, we had to cover the cost of the repairs on stuff too."

Jimmy sighed. "That's why the place is a mess."

Both Emma Jean and Jimmy sat quietly, neither making eye contact with me.

"She didn't tell me anything and the attorneys wouldn't let me ask," I said. "I had no idea it was you here on the ranch. I just figured it was one of the younger guys my grandpa hired shortly before he died."

Jimmy harrumphed. "Those worthless jackals ran off the day your grandpa stopped payin'. They had no loyalty to him *or* the place."

"I wish you'd have told me you'd stayed," I said. "You shouldn't have used your own money to take care of the place. If I'd have known, I could've gone to the judge on your behalf."

Both of them looked at each other and back at me. "Rebecca told us that we weren't allowed to speak to you, because of the lawsuit. I guess she thought it was a way to make some extra money before she lost that silly fight."

I was so angry, I could have knocked a hole in the wall. That evil woman really did take advantage of them.

I shook my head. "I'll see to it that you're reimbursed for what you spent. If we get the place sold, I'll repay you from that."

Both Jimmy and Emma Jean stared at me like I'd grown horns. Finally, Jimmy asked, "You're gonna sell the ranch?"

I looked down at my hands. "I'm sorry, Jimmy, I can't stay here. Even if I wanted to originally, there is so much bad blood in my family now, it wouldn't do to try to hang onto it. Besides, I don't know anything about managing a ranch this size."

The silence hung in the air for several long minutes, until Emma Jean broke it. "You don't owe us a thing, Flex," she said. "We wanted to stay, and we don't blame you for selling neither. This ain't no place for a young man." Jimmy nodded, the sadness never leaving his face. He was trying to make it easier on me.

"You know every fence would need mending, and there ain't been a cow on the property since before your grandpa passed. Emma Jean is right, we can't blame you for selling."

I reached over and grabbed each of their hands. "You have always been the best..." I hesitated and smiled at Emma Jean. "Well, when you weren't spanking me, that is."

Emma Jean laughed hard. "Boy, I only paddled you one time, and it was after you broke all my canning jars back behind that shed. You're lucky I got to you first, because if your granny had found you before I did..."

All four of us shuddered a little at the thought. My granny had no tolerance for messing around. I'd never thought of it that way, but maybe Emma Jean was right. Since she got to me first, I probably avoided a much more eventful punishment.

I comforted them and thanked them again. I told them Eric and I were going to go out and take a look around, and try to get an idea of all the work that needed doing. Jimmy stood up and put his hat back on. "I'll take you around. We've been having trouble with rattlers this year. Probably 'cause we don't got no hogs up around the house like we used to. So, you'd better let me take the lead. Besides, I know what is needin' work better'n anybody," he said.

I stood up and cleared my throat. "I have a realtor woman meeting me here around noon. If you don't want her coming in here, I can just take pictures. Mostly, she needs to see the property, so she can give me an estimate."

Emma Jean stood up, and in her no-nonsense way said, "Ain't no reason why she can't just come in. If she's coming at lunchtime, she can have sandwiches with us too. I'll see you boys around then." She turned then, and disappeared back into the kitchen.

I felt like a piece of coal in a kid's Christmas stocking. I'd had no idea it was Jimmy and Emma Jean looking after the place, or I'd have come out before thrusting a realtor on them. Once again, I had to fight off a feeling of hatred for my selfish aunt.

Jimmy excused himself to go use the bathroom before we went on the damage tour. When Eric and I were alone, I asked him to remind me to call my attorney when we got back into cell coverage, so I could ask what happened to the rent money the bitch collected. I knew I'd be on the hook for paying it back either way, but if I could force a little out of the old bag that stole it from them in the first place, it would bring me a great deal of joy to do so.

The property wasn't in horrible shape. The barn was still usable, but needed repairs. It had originally been an adobe structure, and parts of it still were. It was the old dairy parlor and where they kept the horse tack.

In the twenties or thirties, they'd built a larger wooden structure my grandpa's dad had purchased from some catalog. It was a traditional barn with two stories. My grandpa would complain when I was a kid that most of the barn was useless, since they didn't store hay as they did up north, so the whole second story was pretty much wasted space. The main level was still pretty good. The century-old timbers were sturdy, despite their age. There was little rain in these parts, so even though the timber-lined roof had been replaced long ago with tin, and several of the tin sheets had been blown away, there was little to no wood rot in the entire building.

Of course, we saw at least four rattlers as we walked around the building, and I wouldn't have been at all surprised if there weren't at least ten times that somewhere around the barn. My grandpa told me years ago that he hated hogs with a passion, but anyone with any sense knew if you didn't want rattlers up near your house, at least here in West Texas, you'd better have a few hogs around.

I once told my teacher what my grandpa had said and the man argued with me that hogs didn't eat snakes, that it was an old wives' tale. I was back at my grandpa's farm the next summer when I witnessed the truth firsthand. A huge rattlesnake was crawling across the pasture toward my granny's chicken pen. The hogs had the run of the fenced-in area that surrounded the barn and pen. I was sitting up in one of the cottonwood trees looking down at the snake as it made its way across the area, fascinated as any young boy would be with a snake that big about to take out its prey, which in this case, was my grandma's prize hen. Even with my eagle's vantage point, I didn't see the hog coming, until she was on the snake. In two bites, the rattler was decapitated, and she spent the next fifteen minutes or so eating the snake from head to toe. When she finally left, I climbed down and went over to see where the carnage had occurred. The only thing the sow had left was the rattler's head. Everything else, including the rattle, was gone.

The old chicken pen was riddled with dry rot and needed to be torn down. There were other sheds around the property in various states of disrepair. The sheds that had been built in the adobe style before the 1920s could be salvaged. I assumed the property would probably continue being used as a cattle ranch. What the heck else could be done with it?

The realtor arrived just as we were coming back up from the tour. When I told her there were rattlers, she just shook her head and said she would look at pictures. Jimmy went inside the house to give us room to talk, and I was glad he did, because what she told me made my stomach fall to my feet.

"The buildings will probably be torn down by the new owners anyway. There are only two kinds of people looking for property this size. The very wealthy who'll build a new fancy home to look out over the landscape, or another rancher in the area who wants to expand their holdings."

I sighed. I couldn't imagine over a hundred fifty years of history being wiped away just like that.

"It's a nice size parcel, even for these parts. I doubt we'll have any difficulty selling the property," she said. She said she didn't need to see the house and left the paperwork for me to look over.

I put the paperwork in the back seat of the car, so I could read it later when my emotions had settled down a bit. I felt like I was not only betraying my grandfather, but every one of my ancestors who'd lived on and managed this land. I couldn't even allow myself to consider an alternative, though. What the hell would I do in the middle of nowhere. Hell, they didn't even have internet or cell phone coverage out here.

There was no way in hell we were ever going to leave the property until we ate Emma Jean's sandwiches, which considering the very limited supplies in this area, were surprisingly good. When both Eric and I kept praising her, the old woman blushed. Finally, Jimmy told us to shut up before we gave her a big head, and he wouldn't be able to sleep in the same room as her tonight.

I asked Jimmy if the old GMC pickup truck of grandpa's still worked. "Yeah, of course it does," Jimmy replied. "Just got to use the choke." He stood up and walked with us out to the old pickup and started it for me. I was glad he did. Starting the old thing was like watching a well-choreographed dance.

"We're gonna go around the property along the old fence lines. If we don't return within an hour, come find us," I teased.

"This ain't the first time you took this ol' thing for a drive, I'm sure you'll do just fine." Both Eric and I looked at Jimmy wide-eyed.

"What?" he asked. "You didn't think we knew you'd snuck off to go skinny dipping down at the river?" Eric and I both hooted with laughter.

"No, we didn't know. We thought we got away with it."

"Pshh," he replied. "Why do kids always think they're the only ones to go skinny dipping. Y'all just be careful and watch where you step, them snakes are bad this year."

There seemed to be plenty gas, and the snake comment convinced us both that we'd rather ride, bumpy as an old truck that had long ago lost whatever suspension it had. I had forgotten how beautiful the property was. There was an old peak granny used to call the volcano. I remember climbing it with my dad when I was little. That was before he'd gotten sick. My mom was mad as a wet hen when she heard he'd taken me up the cliffs. She had refused to come for a visit, but my dad wanted me to experience where I had so many roots. Mom told me years later that he'd arranged with my grandparents to have me out during the summers from then on. My dad died when I was nine from throat cancer. He was a serious smoker all my life, and probably long before I was born. I had a hard time remembering him, but seeing the old volcano always brought back his memory crystal clear.

The access to the river was blocked these days. The park had found several people using the pass as a way into the back-country and had blocked the entrance we used to use to get to the river. There were two parks around Big Bend. One was a national park which was bigger than the state of Rhode Island. The other was a preserve, which was owned by the state of Texas. Even though the state took much of our land in the nineteen twenties, we'd fought a court battle regarding the land that butted up against the Rio Grande.

My great-grandparents had entered into a cooperative effort to conserve the area around the river, instead of losing it out-right to the parks. My family also had the original settlement with an adobe structure on this section of the land. It had be-longed to my ancestor who'd originally settled there. With our history, as well as the legal quagmire we threatened to pursue, the state agreed to a settlement that allowed us to keep the land.

At the same time, this section was also kept as a quazi-conservation area.

We rounded an area that doubled back onto another road that led back to the house. I put the old truck in park. This was the highest point on the property. It butted up against the old volcano, and you could see almost everything for miles, including the house and barn in the distance. When we were kids, Eric, Effie, and I would ride our horses out to this bit of the property almost every day, except Sunday, when we weren't allowed to do such things. Eric sighed beside me.

"I wish this was all closer to Houston," he said.

"Why?" I asked.

"Cause if it was, I'd talk you into keeping it."

I nodded. "Yeah, I'm sure my mom would've wanted it if it had been closer to civilization. Oh well, it is what it is."

The property was teaming with wildlife. Black bear, elk, deer, and mountain lions all lived here unencumbered. My family never really did much about them. My grandpa always said the land belonged to the animals as much as it did to us. We were all using it, but none of us really owned it.

I always assumed that was from our native teachings. As far as I could tell, all of my ancestors had been stewards of the land, and as a result, the wildlife continued to thrive here. There was a family legend that said my great-great-grandpa teased President F.D. Roosevelt that the only reason the new park would ever have wildlife was because once everyone stopped trying to kill them, they'd migrate from our property to restock the park. However, there was no evidence FDR ever made it to the park, or to my family's ranch.

I parked the truck back next to the barn, where it had been when we took it out. We both got out gingerly, making sure we stayed in the open spaces to avoid any potential rattlesnake strikes. "I remember there being snakes when we were kids," Eric exclaimed. "But I don't remember having to watch our every move."

"Yeah, me neither. Makes me miss the hogs." Eric didn't even look at me. He was too focused on the ground, to ensure he didn't accidentally step on one of the lethal creatures.

We hugged both Jimmy and Emma Jean, and I told them I'd see them again soon. I gave them my phone number, and told them to call me if they had any problems. They gave me their number as well, and I was shocked to find out it was still the same as my grandparents' number. "I can't believe they let you keep this," I said.

"Honey, there are very few people out in these parts. It makes it easier to keep the same number, so if anyone needs to reach you, they'll have it memorized. Everyone still thinks of this as the 'Ol Madison place.'"

We drove back mostly in silence. I thought Eric was just as upset by the lack of activity on the ranch as I was. The place had been bustling when we were children. Because of the size of the property, there were real live cowboys managing the cattle.

They came and went, but they were a big part of the momentum of the property nonetheless. There were several long-term cowboys on the place as well. Jimmy was one of those, but not the only one. I could remember at least three other men who worked on the ranch.

At one time, there'd been a long structure on the property where all the men could sleep, and right next to it were a few cabins where families of the cowboys or seasonal workers stayed. Sometime in the 1980s lightning struck one of the barns, and before anyone could put out the flames, all the buildings had burned to the ground. After that, grandpa let families bring trailers onto the property, on the understanding that they had to remove them when they left, or they would forfeit their last three months' pay. Of course, my grandpa paid in arrears, so it worked like a charm.

I looked over at Eric, who was falling asleep in the passenger seat. "I forgot to look at where the old trailers used to stand. Do you reckon there are still any hookups there worth using?"

Eric just shrugged. "Can't see why not."

"I don't reckon it matters," I said, noticing I'd slipped into my southern accent. "The realtor thinks they'll probably tear everything down anyway."

"That sucks, Flex," Eric said, and I had to struggle to keep myself from breaking down.

"Yeah," I whispered, then let myself fall silent.

"Did you ever think about keeping the place?" Eric asked.

I sat back against the seat, and thought for a few moments, before replying, "Yeah, at one time I thought I'd move to the property, and let my grandparents teach me about ranching. Unfortunately, my hormones always got in the way." I chuckled at the memory. "I was nineteen when my grandpa asked me to consider coming out, since when he was gone, he'd be handing the reins to me. I really did try to make that work in my head, but every time I went out dancing and a pretty man would..." I looked at Eric and blushed. "Well, you know."

Eric burst out laughing. "When they wet your lizard?" he said almost gleefully.

"Shut up, Eric!" But, we were both laughing so hard, I doubt he heard me.

When he calmed down, I looked over at him. "I thought I had a lot more time. Grandpa was a mountain of a man, even when he died, he looked like one of those bodybuilders you see on TV."

I stared straight ahead, not really seeing the landscape any longer. "If I'd known, I'd have let the lizard go dry."

When we arrived back at the motel, I yelled, "shower," before Eric even thought about it. "Oh, *shit*, I forgot to tell you, Mitch, the motel owner, offered to fix dinner for us. We're meeting him at seven. Is that okay?" I asked.

"Yeah, sure, I need that shower, and I'd like to take a quick nap. I'm still jet-lagged from all that traveling."

"That sounds perfect. I'm going to get my shower first, then I'll take the dogs out. Hopefully, we won't have the same experience we had last night."

"I don't know why you're complaining. Sounds like you might get a..." Eric hesitated, a wicked grin spreading across his face. "A wet lizard out of the deal."

"Shut up," I said, looking around to make sure no one heard him.

It didn't take me long to shower. Mostly, I wanted to get the dust off me. When I was done, I took a quick walk and sat down under the pergola designed for spectators to watch the sunset.

I didn't see Mitch come up behind me, until he cleared his throat. I looked back and couldn't help the happy skip to my heart. God, the man was beautiful. "Oh, hi, Mitch. How are you?"

"I'm good, you?" Mitch replied.

I turned back toward the west and told the truth. "I've been better."

Mitch came and sat on the bench with me. "Hard day, huh?"

"Oh, you could say that."

"Wanna talk about it?" he asked.

"Probably as much as you want to hear about it," I laughed.

Mitch didn't respond, instead, he just sat staring ahead like I was.

Finally, I sighed. "I didn't realize my aunt's tenants were a really sweet couple who helped raise me during the summers.

So, when I went to the ranch and saw them, I had to explain that I was going to be selling their home."

"Yeah, that is a shitty day," he said, and I nodded in agreement.

"Tell you what, I've got the front desk closed, and I've just finished feeding the chickens, so I've got a little free time, and more importantly, I have a bottle of Jack back at my place. If you want, I can pour us both a shot or two to take the edge off."

"Shit, that sounds great," I said. "Let me put these brats up, and I'll meet you... wait, where is your place?" I asked.

He just chuckled. "I live in the ranch house behind the office. You can just walk around the office and you'll end up on my front porch."

"Perfect," I said, and I waved at him as I hurried to rush the boys back to the cottage.

I dropped the dogs off, and when I opened Eric's door to put Puddles in his room, I could already hear him snoring.

I wrote a quick note to tell him I'd gone over to Mitch's early for a drink. *Come over when you wake up*, it said.

I found some tape in my carry-on bag and taped the note to the back of his door. I fed Ace, made sure he had clean water and headed out as fast as possible without looking like an idiot, or the desperate person I really was.

4

Mitch

AFTER MOVING BACK TO Alamito, I mourned the fact that I was pretty much giving up any hope of ever finding a man. Sure, there were gay guys in town, but none of them were my type—not even close. Jake, an old hippy who'd moved here in the sixties, was quick to tell me he liked the guys, and I had to make it clear I wasn't looking for the daddy, or in his case granddaddy types.

Of course, that also ruled out Dan and Bob, who were a couple in their forties, but who also made it clear they were willing to consider a third.

Lukus, well, he was less gay and more asexual. He'd told me early on, he was a gay man, but that he was happy just being by himself. I once asked him if he ever went to town to find a boyfriend, and he just laughed at me. "Nope, I'm done hunting for a man."

I wasn't. I never had been. I wanted a boyfriend, but unfortunately, I had to settle for the occasional drive to Marfa, Alpine, or when I was really desperate, El Paso. The problem was those weren't really places to meet guys looking for a long term relationship. Those were flings at best, but mostly they were just hookups.

When Flex and Eric came into my office, my gaydar went off immediately. I figured the two must be a couple, so I kept my flirting to a minimum. As fate would have it, the old bag had inadvertently brought us together, and hearing that Eric was straight, well, that made Flex a possibility.

I knew I was shamelessly flirting with him by inviting him to dinner, but he was so handsome. Tall, dark... as cliché as that was, he sure checked all my boxes. You could see the man had a little Latin in him. The dark hair and lightly tanned skin with rich brown eyes seemed to confirm that. I salivated as I thought about how much fun it'd be to play around with that tall swimmer's built frame of his. It'd also be nice to have a guy I was attracted to have at least some connection to this area, now I'd come to think of it as my home, not a place to run away from, like I had when I was a kid.

I knew his friend Eric was here with him, so I didn't try to exclude him, but I sure wouldn't mind getting Flex alone for a while. I shrugged that off and invited him to dinner.

The next day, when I saw him brooding on my sunset bench, I couldn't help but go over and see what was up. Really, I was happy for any excuse to spend more time with him. I could immediately tell he was upset, and I genuinely wanted to soothe the tension I saw in his face. The offer of a drink was altruistic for sure, but I thought there could be a lot of ways, besides just the alcohol, to ease the tension.

"Damn, man," I said to myself. "Have a little human dignity. He's just had a bad day." I obviously needed another run to the city. I was becoming as creepy as ol' Jake.

Flex came up to the house shortly after I'd entered my kitchen, pulled the Jack down and found a couple glasses. My grandpa had been a recovering alcoholic, so back then there was never any alcohol in the house. He'd sobered up before I was born, but not before he pushed my mom away.

I didn't know much about my grandmother, other than she died when mom was a baby. My grandfather ended up nursing the bottle, until my mom was well into her teens, which was probably the main reason I came along so early.

Anyway, after I inherited the motel and ranch house, I was cleaning it out and found several shot glasses. I almost tossed them, before I had the sense to look them up. They were all pre-prohibition shot glasses from a variety of different distilleries around the country. The most expensive could fetch over fifteen hundred dollars, while even the cheapest I found was worth over sixty-five.

I'd long ago put the most expensive ones in a safety deposit box in Alpine. I kept the less-expensive ones, though, and used them myself, thinking that was what my ancestor would've preferred, instead of me sticking them on a shelf to ignore.

When Flex came in, I gave him my Jack Daniel's shot glass, taking the Hoffman for myself.

"Thanks for the drink," Flex said, then downed the shot I'd poured him. "Oh, that hits the spot."

"*Really* bad day then?" I asked.

The guy chuckled. "Well, it's been a bad several years, but today was certainly one of the worst. Nothing like a bad family seed to fuck your world up."

I nodded. I knew way too much about that. "My mother is our bad seed. Best meth addict this side of the Davis Mountains."

"Oh, ouch. Yeah, mine is an evil aunt, who thinks everything my grandparents ever owned is hers by right. Did your mom fight you for the motel?"

I almost spat the whiskey I'd just drunk out through my nose. "Um, no! There was no fight. She hates it here. She hated my grandpa, and now she hates me, because I moved back here. But that's okay. It's best that she stays away."

Flex sighed. "Well," he picked up the shot glass I'd just refilled. "Here's to avoiding!"

"Here, here!" I said, and we both sucked down our shots.

"Well, that's enough negativity for the night. Any good news?" I asked.

"Not much that I can think of, except you're cooking dinner tonight. That's about the best news I've had in a week."

"Don't say that until you've eaten my cooking. Besides grilling meat, I have two things I know how to cook, chicken enchiladas and Ramen noodles."

"So, which one is on the menu tonight?"

"You're lucky, I made a run to Alpine earlier in the week. I have the ingredients for enchiladas."

Flex laughed. "Good, I was going to have to take over your kitchen if you said Ramen. What can I do to help?"

I thought about saying he could just hang out, but I'd rather have the sexy man busy, instead of staring at me while I cooked. "Why don't you cut up the onions, while I start cutting up the chicken."

"Wow, you know how to cut up chicken? That's at least the start to fifty other recipes," I said, being just a little snarky to lighten up the mood a bit.

"Yeah, but if you start cooking, people will begin to expect it from you. I've never liked being stuck in a kitchen. I prefer to be out working on the buildings, or in the gardens."

"So, what did you do before you became a motel owner?" Flex asked.

"While going through college, I worked in construction. My company was in El Paso, but we worked in Mafia, Alpine, and even did a little work in the national park."

"Do you miss it?" he asked.

"The construction? Yeah, sort of. I like the freedom of working with my hands every day, instead of crunching numbers behind a desk, or dealing with customers, especially the really squirrely ones."

"Like the lady yesterday?" I asked.

"Exactly like the lady yesterday, and unfortunately, there are several more where she came from."

"Has she given you any more problems?"

"No, and surprisingly, neither have her friends. If anything, it's been quieter than it's been since I took over from my grandfather."

"Hum, you probably scared them. This place is about one-hundred-percent better than the RV park across the road."

I just laughed. "Well, it wasn't when I took over. In fact, it was probably a good deal worse, truth be told. My grandfather hadn't really done much with the place in years. I think he'd have closed it if it hadn't been for the old ladies who'd kept him company. They may be annoying, but they were good for him when he was alive."

"Are you going to let Miss Thang come back then?"

"No! I most certainly will not be letting her back. She pushed me too far, and if I let her get away with it, again, I'll lose all control."

"I don't envy you. I doubt I'd be very good at the diplomacy part. I tend to be someone who speaks his mind, then thinks after."

"Yeah, that wouldn't work here." I chuckled. "So, what do you do for a living?"

"I'm a business analyst at a company in Houston."

"Wow," I said. "That's, um, interesting."

Flex laughed. "Yeah, about as interesting as watching grass grow, or in your case cacti."

"Sorry, that wasn't very nice of me. I just didn't think of you as someone who'd sit behind a desk wearing a suit and tie."

"Yeah, it's not my first choice either, but I worked for my mom in her florist shop during high school and even through college, so after I graduated I wanted a change. I took the first job that was offered to me, and it does pay well, so there I am."

"You didn't like the florist shop?" I asked.

"The florist was fine. The working for my mom was the part that needed to change."

"Oh, I get that. I can't imagine it really. I tried working for my grandpa one summer, and by the time the summer was over, we were both ready to kill each other. I did manage to get a lot of improvements done, though, while I was avoiding him."

"I'm sure."

He handed me the onions, a little spark passing through me as our hands briefly touched. I cleared my throat, and began the process of making the enchiladas.

Flex watched me with fascination. Finally, he asked, "Are you this methodical in everything you do?"

I looked up at him, confused at first, but when I turned back to the counter, noticing I had everything laid out and premeasured, I chuckled. "Well, this is how they did it on the Food Network show I watched to learn how to cook it."

Flex just smiled and nodded. I hated when I gave away my secrets too early. I did like organization, and although I wasn't naturally inclined that way, after living with my grandfather, who was a slob, and my mom, who was an addict hoarder, I'd learned long ago, it was best to keep things in their place. You couldn't control what life threw at you, but if you were prepared, most of the time you could deal with it.

"Unfortunately, it's just me running this entire place, so I've had to learn to be pretty organized." That wasn't a total lie. I did need to be organized, but I was beginning to feel like I was oversharing, and that tended to be one of my greatest downfalls when meeting a new guy.

"Anyway, when do you think you and Eric will be headed back?"

"In a couple days. I needed to make sure my family ranch was still standing after the past few years of fighting for custody of it. Now I have to meet the realtor and sign the paperwork."

"Will you be coming back?" I asked, hoping I didn't sound desperate.

Just before he answered, I heard a knock at my door. I groaned inside, thinking it must be the older women coming for retribution, but instead, Flex's friend Eric stood at the door. I'd completely forgotten he was coming. That was how easily I lost focus. Just put a handsome man in my home and I was brain-dead.

I welcomed Eric and showed him to the kitchen, where I was almost ready to put the enchiladas together and slip them into the oven.

"Flex, do you mind pouring Eric a drink while I get these in the oven?"

Flex smiled and poured his friend a drink, using one of the other shot glasses I had sitting out. I almost said something since the one he'd chosen was worth about $250, but decided it didn't matter. At the end of the day, it was just glass.

5

Flex

ERIC, MITCH, AND I laughed until we cried. Mitch told us about his encounters with the local gay crowd in Alamito, describing the characters and their attempts to get into his pants.

I almost spat my drink out after Mitch demonstrated how an old hippy, who was bumping up against seventy, did the yawn and stretch, then slipped his arm around his shoulders. This was right before telling him he could take his dentures out before giving him a blow job.

You could tell the guy had a soft spot in his heart for all these men, but experiencing the hardships of being a gay man in a very rural small town had its adventures.

After we'd eaten, we all sat on the front porch and watched one of the most beautiful sunsets I'd ever seen. It was almost as if the porch had been built to perfectly capture that view. When

I said as much, Mitch just smiled. "My great-grandpa built this house. Of course, it was just a small adobe back then. Maybe two rooms. When my grandfather married, he added the rest. It's hard to say why it has such a good view of the sunset, but I like to think he did it on purpose."

"Has it always been a motel?" I asked.

Mitch shook his head. "No. Story goes that my grandmother refused to live out here unless she could find a job, and well, Alamito wasn't exactly bustling with life even back then, so he built the roadside motel and hired her."

I looked at him in shock. "That worked?"

"Clearly," he said. "We're here."

"People out here have colorful histories, don't they?" I asked, almost to myself.

"You have no idea. You should go sit at the general store sometime, and if you can manage to just hang out, the old men will start talking, and their stories are... well, let's just say they're full of stories."

"My grandma used to talk about the old men at the general store, and she didn't shed a positive light on them," I chuckled.

"Well, I was raised by one of the old men who liked to sit with that crowd, so that could be one of the reasons I have a more positive opinion."

"Probably so."

It wasn't very late when we left Mitch's place. Eric left a little early, saying he needed to check on the dogs, but I was sure it was to give me some alone time with Mitch. We cleared the table, and I helped fill the dishwasher.

When it didn't look like Mitch was going to make a move, I made my way toward the door.

Mitch followed me, and when I turned to say my goodbyes, the man stepped up to me, and slowly, giving me time to move away if I wanted to, kissed me. Gently at first. When I put my arms around him, he pulled me down to his level, and deepened the kiss.

When he stepped away, my head was spinning.

"That was nice," he said.

"Uh, huh," I replied, my brain a bit too scrambled to say anything else—not to mention the fact my crotch was a lot tighter than it had been a few minutes before.

"You wanna stay?" he asked.

I wanted to say yes, I thought I'd planned on saying yes, but for some reason, I said no. "I need to get back to Eric. I'll see you tomorrow?"

Mitch stepped back, the look on his face saying I'd missed my chance. Everything in my mind screamed to say, *"I've changed my mind, I'm staying,"* but the words didn't come out, and I turned and left.

As I walked back to the honeymoon suite, I shook my head. *Why the hell had I said no?* I'd looked forward to seeing the man all day. It was the *only* positive part of my day. When I turned the corner and saw Eric playing with the dogs, I realized he was my reason. I'd talked Eric into coming all the way to the middle of nowhere to support me through this. Ditching him for a quick roll in the hay was not my style—no matter how hot the guy was.

When I came up behind him, Eric looked at me in surprise. "No wet lizard?"

I punched him in the arm as I walked by. "Ouch, don't get mad at me 'cause you didn't get any!" he cried.

"Just shut up," I said, and sulked into the cottage.

We watched a stupid movie, talked about lost opportunities with lovers, and basically enjoyed our last night together.

"We should probably go to bed. We've got a busy day tomorrow," Eric said.

"Yeah, you want dog duty?" I asked.

"Sure, but you've got it tomorrow morning. I'm gonna sleep in."

"Sounds good," I replied, then started getting ready for bed.

I fell asleep pretty fast. I immediately realized I was in a dream, because the air around me had a sepia-colored look about it, like the old western movies my dad used to love watching.

I'd just walked into a saloon. Eric and another guy I didn't recognize were with me, and as we saddled up to the bar, the piano began playing behind me. I heard my brothers... yes, in the dream Eric and whomever the other guy was were my brothers, ask the barkeep for a whiskey. I nodded when the man looked at me confirming I wanted the same thing.

When I turned around to scan the crowd, I immediately saw the woman at the piano. She was pretty. Dark brown curls were tied high on her head, and she wore a dress that dipped way too low in front for her to be a reputable woman.

She turned and winked at me, and I smiled and nodded back to her. I wasn't much for loose women like this one, or otherwise, mostly I'd decided I didn't care much for the opposite sex.

When a crystal-clear tenor voice began singing, I looked up and to the right of the piano, and saw the most beautiful human being I'd ever laid eyes on. It wasn't until just then that I noticed it was the motel owner, Mitch, that I was looking at.

His eyes met mine as he continued to sing. I recognized the song Shenandoah, a song I hadn't heard until the war between the states broke out. I hadn't heard it sung since the war, even though we'd been stationed at Fort Davis for years after the war.

Wow, I was taking this dream a little too far, I thought to myself...

When his song ended, the man became shy and quickly disappeared. I knew then and there, I'd never settle until I had that man in my bed.

The scene changed then, and we were facing each other in what must've been one of the rooms above the saloon. The music was still going on below us. The man, who looked like Mitch, came toward me, no longer looking shy like he had when the song had ended. When he got to me, he smiled. The smile was pure feline and sent shivers down into my soul.

He dropped to his knees and began to pull by pants down when I heard something ringing in the background. I tried to focus back onto the beautiful face that was kneeling before me, but the ringing wouldn't stop. Finally, and unfortunately, I was awake.

When I realized it was my blasted phone that was ringing, I reached over and picked it up. "Hello…" I answered, still mostly asleep.

"Good morning, sunshine," the voice on the other end of the line said. The sound of the voice sent childhood memories running through my brain, and I immediately knew I was talking to Emma Jean.

"Mrs. Emma Jean, what time is it?" I asked, the sleep apparent in my voice.

"High time a man of your age should be up. By now, you should've had the cows milked and be headed to the pasture."

"Um, ma'am, we don't have any cows at the motel."

"That's why you should've stayed here, I could've gotten you up at a respectable time, instead of you lying around all morning."

I leaned up, and after rubbing the sleep out of my eyes, I glanced at the little clock on the dresser. Five o'clock in the morning. Geez, that was early.

"What can I do for you, Mrs. Emma Jean?" I asked, remembering to keep my manners in place, even though calling someone this early was pure evil.

"After you and Eric left yesterday, I went up to your grandpa's room and rummaged through some of his papers. I'd forgotten, what with all Rebecca's shenanigans, but he had some things he asked us to give to you after his death. I found them and laid them out for you. Do you think you could come pick them up before you leave?" she asked.

"Yes, ma'am," I replied. "I have a meeting with the realtor this morning. I'll come out after that."

"Will it be lunchtime again?" she asked.

I chuckled, despite myself. "Yes, ma'am. I'll try to be out there before noon."

"Oh, good, I'll cook you a proper meal this time. Will Eric be joining you?" she asked.

"No, he has to get to El Paso to catch a flight. It'll just be me this afternoon."

When she hung up, I lay back down and tried to go back to sleep. Unfortunately, now that I was awake, it appeared I was *really* awake. Damn, I hated my rancher's brain. My mom told me when I was a kid, it was genetics that caused me to wake up early and not be able to fall back to sleep. I'd taught myself to sleep later, but if anything woke me up, I was never gonna get back to sleep.

I got up, careful not to wake Eric, or cause Puddles to go nuts. Ace just looked at me from his little bed in the corner. I slipped on my running clothes, and decided to make the most of the morning. I figured I'd have less chance of running into a sidewinder if I stuck to the main road, and since the sun was coming up, it wasn't very likely that I'd miss one as I jogged by.

I ran up into town and then through the empty streets. One thing about these little West Texas towns, they didn't open at the crack of dawn like they probably used to, and they rolled up the streets in the evenings. So, if you wanted to run through town getting your morning exercise, there was no traffic to stop you.

I managed to get a full hour's run in before I got back to the motel. I was just about to run past the motel ranch house when I felt, more than saw, Mitch sitting on his front porch. Like my body was on autopilot, I turned and ran in his direction, instead of back to the room.

"You're up early," he said, as I reached his porch.

"Yeah, got a ridiculously early phone call this morning. Couldn't go back to sleep," I said, as I leaned over to catch my breath. I intentionally pushed the image of him kneeling in front of me out of my head. No good would come of me remembering the dream, unless I wanted to come off as a total perv.

"Want some coffee or water?" Mitch said, as he watched me leaning over.

"I haven't run for the past few days, and it catches up to me if I don't do it every day. I don't think I was made for running."

"It looks good on you," he said, and I looked up to see his eyes move down my legs, then back up to my face. My skin felt prickly under his perusal.

"Yeah, to both," I said, more to distract myself from that sexy look. I'd spent a good portion of the previous night thinking about what I'd like to do to that body of his, and it didn't pay to go back down that road this morning.

Mitch smiled and got up. When he came back out, he had a platter. In the fashion I'd already seen in him, it was perfectly arranged with a glass of water, a cup of coffee, and anything I'd want to put in it.

"You're a good host," I said, as I sat in a chair next to him on his porch.

He put the tray on a little table between the chairs and sat down. "I've been trained from birth," he said. "It's part of being in the hospitality business."

I drank the water first. As always, I enjoyed the way my body hungered for the refreshment of a cool glass of water after a run. Then I leaned back and let the beautiful morning air wash over me, before I drank the coffee.

"Do you ever think about going back into construction?" I asked.

"I think about it sometimes, but I'm probably going to keep this place going, at least for the foreseeable future."

I nodded, and after adding creamer, took my first swig of the bitter coffee. "Mmmm, why is it that first drink of coffee feels so good?" I asked, as I leaned back in the old rocker.

Mitch chuckled. "Caffeine is my drug of choice as well," he said. "It's a lovely hit, especially when you're up earlier than usual."

I turned to look at him. "Why are you up so early?" I asked.

He smiled, and memories of that seductive smile I'd seen in my dream came to mind, causing me to involuntarily shudder. "I was rather distracted by a handsome man last night. I woke up thinking about him, and couldn't go back to sleep."

Dude you have no idea, I thought, as the blood drained from my face and collected in my groin. "I regretted not staying the minute I said no," I admitted.

"I understand why you did. Your friend is here."

"He's leaving today," I said, and the admission caused butterflies to swim around in my stomach.

Mitch smiled. "I'm guessing a repeat date might be in order then, huh?"

I nodded, then drank down the rest of the coffee and stood up, ready to head for the safety of the cottage. If I stayed on the porch any longer with Mitch, I was going to attack him right here in public. Alamito might be a little more progressive than I thought, but I doubted his neighbors would be open to a fully-fledged sex scene on the Alamito Motel's front porch.

"I'm gonna get my shower, then head to breakfast at a little café I saw in town. Wanna join me?" I asked.

"Sure, but the food tastes like rubber. How about I cook breakfast?"

I turned around and looked at him. "I thought you only knew how to make Ramen and enchiladas."

He chuckled. "Well, I do have a few breakfast skills too. After all, every gay man should have the ability to feed his man after a night of passion, right?"

It was too much. "Probably right," I said, then ran away like a scared child.

That kind of sexual innuendo never really seemed to work for me, *until now*. It was like something was in the air, playing with my emotions.

As I rushed back to the room, I couldn't help but think about how his perfect features matched with his short muscular frame and beautiful workman's hands perfectly.

I shook off the whole, *something in the air* thing, by admitting the pressure was probably greater, since I was definitely going through a dry spell. I hadn't dated much since my last break up—not that it was all that bad. I'd been dating the guy for about six months when we both decided the only thing we had in common was our love of men.

He broke it off, but I knew it was coming, and I was happy to be done with the relationship. I thought I'd be back out on the scene right away, but then work got busy, and the lawsuit was finalized between my aunt and me, so I hadn't been out with a guy since then.

Apparently, that was too long, because I could literally rip this motel owner's clothes off right in the public eye.

I let the water pour over me in the shower, and allowed the images of the sexy man filter through my mind, as I stroked my cock. My mind returned to the scene in my dreams, but this time, I allowed the image to go further, imagining the full lips of the motel owner moving down my body. I rubbed my nipples, and stroked myself faster and faster. When I came, it was to visions of his luscious lips around my cock. I was glad I came in the shower, because I came so much, I'd have had to use a couple towels to clean up.

Eric was still fast asleep when I crawled out of the shower, so I dressed, then jogged back up to Mitch's house. I brought Ace with me this time to make sure he had his morning constitutional. I doubted the highly organized man would allow me to bring him into the house, but I figured I could just tie him to the porch while we ate.

When we got to Mitch's porch, I could smell the bacon cooking. "Hello," I called out.

"Come on in," he called.

"Hey, I have my dog with me. Is it okay to tie him up out here?"

"Just bring him in," Mitch responded.

"You sure? I didn't want to leave him behind in case he ended up trying to wake Eric."

"No, it's fine, we had a beagle until shortly after my grandfather died. In fact, I think I kept his bed. I'll go see after I'm done with the bacon."

I brought Ace in, and after releasing him from the lead, he immediately went around the room doing his usual checking out the place.

When he came to Mitch, he looked up, and his little tail began wagging. My little manipulator had learned long ago that his cute face and sweet little tail could win him the hearts of most people, given enough time.

Mitch was no exception, and after putting the bacon aside and pulling the pan off the stove, he leaned down and began ruffling up the fur on my dog's head.

Ace leaned into him, thoroughly enjoying the attention.

"You're good with dogs," I said.

"You act surprised," he chuckled.

"Well, you are really organized and don't have a dog, so I assumed you might not like them in your space."

"I grew up with dogs. Snoops, my grandpa's last dog, was the one I grew up with. It was just so hard to let him go, and I haven't had it in me to adopt another one. Your little terrier here might be the thing I need to get motivated to try again."

Mitch went straight to a hallway closet and pulled down a perfectly clean old dog bed. When he laid it down next to the table, Ace climbed in, scratched around for a moment, and lay down like he owned the place.

"He's home pretty much everywhere we go," I said.

"That's good," Mitch said. "Snoops hated to be away from home, and when we had to take him to the vet, he'd puke in the backseat at least twice before we got to Alpine."

"Oh, that sucks," I said.

"It did, but I still miss him, puke and all. What's your puppy's name?" he asked.

"Ace. I had a crush on Ace Young when he competed in Idol."

"Really?" Mitch chuckled. "I crushed on him a little myself."

"Can I do something to help with breakfast?" I asked, quickly stopping us from getting back onto that subject.

"Nope, I have the biscuits in the oven, bacon is fried, and I just need to cook the eggs. How do you like yours?" he asked.

"Hmmm... scrambled, I think."

Mitch washed his hands and began cracking the eggs into a bowl.

"How long have you known Eric?" he asked.

"We went to school together in Houston. We've been best friends since elementary school."

"Awesome, I didn't really make any long-term friends in school. Mostly, everyone knew my mom was an addict, and ostracized me because of it."

"Ouch, that sucks. Do they still treat you like that?"

"No, all my classmates moved out of town the moment they graduated. All thirty-three of them."

"You graduated from a class of thirty-three?" I asked, shocked.

"Yep, we had a big class that year."

"You've got to be kidding me. My high school graduating class was over three thousand."

"Sounds horrible, but you did manage to get a loyal friend out of the deal, that was something."

"Yeah, Eric is my best friend even now. His ex-wife was a beast. I still don't know what he saw in her, but she's the reason he ended up in Portland."

"Is it hard being that far away from each other?"

"Yeah, we used to see each other every week, at least. I think that's one of the reasons the beast needed to get him away from Houston. I was competition."

"So, his wife didn't like you?"

"She liked me as much as she does anyone. What she didn't like was anyone who competed with her time with Eric. The woman is a total piece of work."

"Sounds like it," Mitch said, with just the right amount of sympathy.

"He also has a job as an adjunct professor, something to do with transitioning his students from high school to college. Eric is a total history geek."

Mitch laughed. "He has the look about him."

"Yeah, history professor, right?"

Mitch nodded as he pulled the biscuits out of the oven.

"It's ready, shall we eat?"

"Yes, please, this looks yummy!"

"Buffet style, bring your plate over and help yourself. Do you mind if I give your pup a little bacon?"

"If you do, he'll be in your lap for the rest of breakfast. I recommend you wait until we're done if you don't want to be pestered."

He nodded, and we both filled our plates.

Mitch walked over to where his MP3 was sitting in the window against a speaker system. I laughed out loud when Ace Young's voice flowed through the speakers, the first stanza of *Crushin' on You*.

"Too much?" he asked.

"No, it's perfect," I said.

Ace, the dog, got up when the music started, turning his back like he was ignoring us.

The music *was* maybe too much, I was already infatuated with this man, and the music from one of my favorite artists flowing over us caused my heart to do funny things in my chest.

We fell silent as the music flowed. When the song was over, soft jazz filled the background.

"I'm trying not to be corny and reach for your hand," Mitch said.

"You can be corny," I said, and reached over, putting my hand over his. "I like you, a lot," I admitted.

"I like you too. Too bad you aren't moving here. It'd be fun to see where this could go."

"I think we're going to have to settle for what we've got, I'm afraid. I have to meet with my realtor this morning to put the property on the market."

Mitch nodded. "Then let's take advantage of the time we've got." Mitch stood up and leaned down, kissing me on the lips.

He pulled me up and led me into his bedroom.

Clothes were flung across his room as we devoured each other. I fell on top of Mitch when we both landed in the bed, and rubbed my naked cock into his, enjoying the amazing feeling of him under me.

"Oh god, that feels so... oh fuck... that feels so good," Mitch stuttered.

I was biting his bottom lip, which didn't help his ability to speak.

"I want you so bad, Mitch," I managed to say between kisses. When he moaned, I felt my cock harden even more, and began kissing my way down his perfectly muscled slim body.

When I got to his sexy treasure trail, I licked the rest of the way down, and quickly sucked him into my mouth, when I reached his plump and fully erect cock.

He moaned as I pulled him deep into my throat. I sucked him several more times, each time building more and more pressure, until I could tell he was about to come. Edging him, I pulled off and watched with wicked pleasure as he all but whined when I let his cock fall from my mouth.

"You taste so good, Mitch," I whispered, before I used my tongue to explore other parts of his body.

His shaved balls surprised me. Most men I knew, who weren't used to frequent hookups, didn't bother with grooming. The smoothness of them sent chills through my body, and I licked and caressed the soft silky skin with my lips.

"Fuck," Mitch said, causing me to look up, straight into those beautiful brown eyes of his.

I moved back up his body, again showering each perfect inch with licks and kisses until I reached his mouth. He moaned around my tongue as I dry humped him, before flipping him on top of me.

If he was surprised by the act, he didn't show it. Instead, he began sucking on my neck as he took up the dry humping. God, how could his cock feel so good just rubbing up against me?

He sat up, then reached over to his drawer, and pulled out lube. He spread the lube on my cock and then lubed his ass before he began riding me, letting my cock push up against him, teasing his hole, but not penetrating him yet.

"I don't have a condom, but we can do this if you don't mind."

"No... no... I... I don't mind," I managed to get out.

Everything about this man turned me on. He was sure and confident as he took charge, riding me.

I could feel the explosion coming, and I looked up at him just as he reached for his cock and began jacking himself off.

When he threw his head back in a moan, I knew he was close too.

The pressure he applied to my cock as he slid up and down, increased, and I let out a loud moan as I pulled back and climaxed over his ass. Seconds later, he came, sending stripes of white cum across my chest and hitting my mouth.

When he looked down at me, he smiled. "Sorry that was so fast. It's been a while."

I smiled back. "For me too."

I reached over and swiped the cum from the side of my mouth, and was about to wipe it on my chest when I saw his eyebrow cock.

So, I licked my finger, letting my tongue swirl around the end, capturing every last drop of cum. When he shuddered, I knew I'd found someone with a cum kink. That was useful information to know, and I fully intended to take advantage again before I left.

He fell down beside me, and I cradled him in my arms, both of us drifting off in the afterglow.

I probably could've slept for an hour or so, had Ace not barked, waking us up.

Mitch jumped out of bed, grabbed a towel and sat next to me while he cleaned off.

"I'd like to do that again, maybe with a condom next time," he said, looking shy.

"That's a hell yes from me," I said, laughing. "How about now?"

I pulled him over me, and back onto the bed as he giggled and squirmed. "No, I have to get to work, and you said you have plans too."

"Yeah... damned realtors."

He kissed me, and said, "Check back with me when you're done with your day. Maybe we can do a repeat date and dessert!"

I was ready for dessert now. Instead, I threw my clothes on and rushed back to the cottage, knowing I would probably be late to meet the realtor. Eric was still asleep in the next room, so after grabbing another quick shower, I dressed, and rushed to the little restaurant in town where I'd agreed to meet her.

Unfortunately, even in my dead rush, I was still five minutes late.

The realtor was clearly miffed by my late arrival, which was strange since I was giving her a very significant listing. I guessed I was used to realtors in the city where they would bend over backward to get your listing, or sell you theirs.

"I'm sorry I'm late, I got caught up at the motel."

The woman didn't respond, instead, she simply handed over the paperwork. Her rudeness was almost enough for me to walk away, but I quickly remembered my hateful aunt and thinking it was best to move this property as quick as possible, I turned to the line where I was to list the property, and signed my name. The realtor had come highly recommended by my attorney, because in this area of West Texas, she had the most connections to people looking for large properties like mine. Otherwise, I could end up being saddled with a long-term listing, and the buyers would be likely to try to squeeze me.

"Do you need anything else?" I asked, trying to let the women know I was not pleased with her rudeness.

"No, I'll be in touch if we have any bites."

"Do you need my tenants' number?" I asked.

"No, if my buyer wants to see inside the property, I'll let you know, and you can set that up yourself. As I said, it's unlikely any of my buyers will want the buildings."

My stomach turned again at the thought. I didn't say good-bye, but left the diner with a feeling of dread. My ancestors had lived on the land for over a century, and here I was tossing the entire thing into the hands of a hateful human being and walking away. Even though it made me sick to think about it, I almost wished my cousins had won, then at least, it might have stayed in the family. Had they talked to me, instead of suing me, I probably would've talked to them about setting up a plan for them to buy it.

I shook my head, forcing those thoughts out of my mind. My aunt and older cousins had created so much ill will with the family since my grandparents died that I couldn't imagine having anything to do with them ever again.

That reminded me, I needed to talk to my attorney about the rent money collected while we were in court. Aunt Rebecca shouldn't have been collecting the money, since the ownership was in dispute.

I called his office, and immediately his assistant answered.

"Hello, Mrs. Cromwell, this is Fletcher Henry. Is Mr. McDonald available?"

"No, dear, he's in court today, can I help you?"

"Probably better than him," I said, causing the older woman to chuckle. It had only taken a few months before I realized that Mr. McDonald's assistant knew more about the cases than he did. She might not be an attorney, but the woman had a remarkable mind. "I was on the property yesterday, and found out my tenants have been paying rent to my aunt. Did we know that was happening?" I asked.

"Not that I know of," she replied. "If rent was being collected, that should've been put into escrow until the trial was over."

"I thought as much, would you look to make sure, and have Mr. McDonald give me a call when he can?" I asked.

"Sure thing, sweetie. How was the property?" she asked.

"Sad," I said on a sigh. "It's really run down since my grandpa died. I probably should've come out to check on it, but well, it was just too difficult seeing it without my grandparents there, especially while fighting my... um... aunt." Mrs.

Cromwell chuckled. I knew she had heard my unspoken descriptive word for her. I was really working hard not to call her a bitch. Mom had recently chastised me, saying it was too offensive to say in public... even though it was true.

"I know, honey," the assistant said, comforting me in her usual way.

"Let me know about the money. The couple that rented the place were friends of my grandparents. They shouldn't have been required to pay any rent. In fact, you might also let Mr. McDonald know they were spending their own money on maintenance as well."

"I'll let John know as soon as he's back in the office."

"Thank you, Mrs. Cromwell."

"Anytime, sweetheart," she said, and hung up.

I laughed, it was so common for me to call the office when I was upset, and by the time I was done with the phone call with Mrs. Cromwell, I always felt better. She really did have a special gift for working with people.

By the time I got back to the motel room, Eric was awake and eating a bowl of cereal.

"You weren't joking when you said you were going to sleep in. Hell, I've been up since five."

"Sounds like a personal problem," Eric said, his hair still sticking up on all sides of his head.

"Wanna go into town and walk through the shops with me before you leave?" I asked.

"No, not really. I just wanna veg a bit. I've got a four-hour drive back to El Paso, and then a five-hour flight back to Oregon. I think I'd rather just chill until I begin my long trek back."

"Cool, don't forget you have to drop me off at the rental car place in Alpine to pick up another rental. I also told Emma Jean I'd be out there for lunch, so I'm afraid your chill time is reduced to just under an hour."

"No problem. I'll go get my shower then. I'm guessing Emma Jean is the god-awful early phone call you got this morning."

"Yeah, you heard that?"

"Yep, I'd just gotten back in bed after taking a leak."

"At least you could go back to sleep, I was wide awake, but I did get to spend some quality time with Mitch this morning."

Eric stopped mid-stride and turned to look at me. "You got your lizard wet?"

"God, you are disgusting! Go get your damned shower!" I said, throwing a pillow and laughing at his retreating back.

s usual, I was sad watching my friend drive away. I missed the days when I got to see him on a regular basis.

I checked my rental car out, and headed straight for the ranch. I walked in right around noon, which saved me a tongue-lashing from Emma Jean.

She'd cooked quite the spread. There was a roast with potatoes and carrots, and homemade rolls, which were always my favorite thing the woman made. After we finished all that, and I was so full I thought I would pop, she pulled out her famous vinegar pie. I knew it didn't sound good, but I remembered as a child devouring them along with most of the ranchers. If we didn't get our hands on a piece early, we were, as Jimmy used to say, "Shit out of luck."

I dug into the pie, and the memories from my childhood flooded me. The pie had a tangy sweetness bursting with flavor, kind of like a cream pie, but different.

"Mmm, Mrs. Emma Jean, you outdid yourself. I haven't had this since I was a teenager."

"I remember you and Effie sneaking in before lunch and reserving your pieces."

I chuckled. "You were very generous to let us do that. The ranch hands would've taken us on for those pieces if they'd known."

"Please, they knew, they all adored you two boys."

"Maybe, but they sure loved their vinegar pie. Not sure who'd a won that one." Jimmy smirked.

Emma Jean looked nostalgic. "You get done with that pie and head up to your grandparents' bedroom. I laid the stuff on the bed for you to look through."

"Did y'all not move into that bedroom?" I asked.

Emma Jean and Jimmy looked at me like I was insane. "No way! That is reserved for the owners of the house. Besides, we both liked the first-floor bedroom. These old bones don't climb stairs like they used to," she said with a sigh. "I do manage to clean and air the room out at least once a month, though, but that's about all I got in me."

She shook her head as she gathered up the dishes and took them into the kitchen.

Jimmy watched her leave, and turned back to me, shaking his head. "It's hard ta get old, but it's harder to watch the life you love slippin' away. You know we were happiest when the place was busy. Both of us loved all the commotion. Emma Jean especially loved working in her kitchen. You know your granny wasn't much of a cook. She was more of a cowhand, and better at it than most of the men we hired, so Emma Jean owned this house. I think she mourns not having a dozen mouths to feed every day. I try to eat enough to keep her happy, but old age seems to have stolen my appetite." He looked at me, then smiled. "It made her happy to cook for you. Thanks for coming back so she could."

I nodded. "I wish she lived closer to Houston, I'd let her cook for me every day."

Jimmy almost choked. "No way you gonna get that woman within a hundred miles of that city. She's a desert girl that one is. We went to El Paso a few times, and every time she'd come home and need to take a shower, saying she had city grit on her." He chuckled. "No, this area is where both she and I will be 'til we're gone."

He thought for a moment. "I guess we're about the last of the old folks that used to live in these parts. Everyone's looking for city life these days. Ain't many people running cattle over the desert any longer neither, and I don't spect that'll change now."

The old man sighed and got up. "You better go on up there and go through those papers, before Emma Jean comes back in here and skins me for keeping you from it."

I smiled. "Jimmy, I appreciate y'all so much for keeping the place up. I wish I'd known what my aunt was up to. I could've made it easier on you these past few years."

"Aah, don't you worry none about that, boy. We wanted to be here, and it was worth what we spent on it. I just wish things'd worked out different, so you could've kept this place. I never did understand what was wrong with your momma and aunt. They neither one wanted to stay here, both ran out just as fast as they could. Then for Rebecca to turn on you like she did..."

Jimmy shook his head as he walked toward the door. He turned around before he left, and said, "You know your grand-pappy would've taken a belt to her if he'd been here to see it. I know he'd never have guessed it would turn out this way, or he'd have set it up different."

I just smiled. "Ain't no reason to cry over what is. We just got to get through it," I said, remembering almost the same words coming out of my granny's mouth when I'd get upset by something Effie had said or done when we were kids.

Jimmy must have recognized the saying also, because he smiled. "That's about right," he said, as he turned and walked out the door.

I climbed the stairs to my grandparent's bedroom, nostalgia sweeping over me as I went. I stopped to peer into the bedroom Effie and me, then later, Eric and I shared as kids. The room was the same, still the same bed and bedcovers that had been there all those years ago. What surprised me was how tidy the room still was, just like Emma Jean had planned on me staying. Maybe she had. I sort of wish I'd stayed the night at least once before I left.

I went into my grandparents' bedroom, and the sight brought me to tears. Oh, I missed them so much. My granny was such a character, full of life, spitting tobacco and drinking whiskey, like the men who worked for them.

My grandpa, of course, was the stoic one. He had a no-nonsense attitude with the men, kept the upper hand, and seldom smiled when they were working. I remembered my granny ribbing him over it, but he always smiled at her. They loved each other with their entire being, and that was what I missed the most, seeing how two people who were *so* different from each other, made a life *so* perfect together.

I got myself together, then went to the stack of papers Emma Jean had put out. I opened the envelope on top first and pulled out a ledger that described the final accounts at the ranch. Grandpa had sold the cattle about a year before he'd died, and invested the money. The account numbers and investment paperwork were all tidily put together.

It was a miracle my aunt hadn't gotten her hands on this. If she'd known about it, she would've figured out a way to get her hands on the money. As it was, they were all in my name, or jointly in mine and my grandpa's name, at least. I had no doubt she'd have forged my signature to get the money. I didn't put anything past that woman.

I'd have to check the balances, but unless they'd had a significant loss in the stock market, I had a substantial amount of money to work with there.

Next, I found a letter that my grandpa had addressed to me.

Fletcher, (He never called me Flex.)

You'll find I've invested your cattle seed money with the Alpine Trust. They've been good for me in the past, so I trust they'll hold onto and maybe even improve your money until you need it.

I wasn't able to keep the cattle going after I broke my leg, so I decided you were smart enough to invest in them again as you needed. You can trust the folks at Mills' Ranch up in Marfa to help you restock. Stay away from Strickland and Emmitt's ranches. The kids that took those ranches over don't give a damn about quality, and will stick you with cattle that ain't gonna do very well in these parts. If you ask Little Pete over at

Mills' to set you up, he'll do you right. Besides, I already talked to him and he agreed to help you find the best stock for the place, not to mention, he's the one that bought most of my stock anyway. The Mills' always did want our stock. We beat them out two decades running at the Abilene Fair and Rodeo. I'm sorry, but now that they got their hands on our cattle, you'll have a harder time winning in the future.

I could hear my grandpa's dry humor in that last paragraph. He'd have thought giving our prize stock to his competition a serious injustice to his descendants. I'm sure this was his way of punishing me for not coming back early enough to help him on the ranch.

You'll need to have Jimmy help you get back up and running. You'll need a few hands, but don't just hire anyone. These past few years, we've had a harder time finding reliable people. In fact, we had hands try to rustle the cattle at least twice these past ten years. Jimmy'll know who you can trust.

Son, I'm sorry I didn't do more to help you learn. After your grandma died, I sort of lost my way, and I regret that now. I should've told you about your heritage, showed you how the land can support you if you treat it right. I realize I let you down, that I let our family down. I'm sure they'll all give me a good beatin' when I go on up to see them.

Remember this, though, this land is yours, it's in your blood. Once you get your hands into the dirt, the place will tell you how to keep going. Cattle don't run heavy on our land like they do in the east, but if you remember to respect the land, it'll keep you solid.

You need to keep in mind, the land can only support a limited number of stock. Don't overgraze, or you'll undo the natural balance. I used to talk to you about that when you were young. Remember those talks, because that's the secret of this ranch's success that comes down through your ancestral line.

Listen to the land, listen to the voice of your people, and let them guide you. That's what I'd have tried to teach you anyway, but at least if I'd had time, I could've given you some short cuts and pointers along the way.

Your granny and I love you with everything in us, son. I know your cousins are gonna be sore at you that you inherited the place, but that decision was made long before you or they were born. Feel free to show them this letter if it'll help. If not, well, you can tell 'em I'm sorry, but it's how this ranch has been passed down over the years. You can also tell 'em that if their mama had shown interest, I'd have given it to her.

There are good people still scattered throughout these parts. I'm sure as soon as you're settled, they'll start showing up. Try not to turn away strangers. People come to this place when they're needed. They've always just been attracted to the place like that.

Kindness and hospitality have always been the foundation of the place. Keep that going and you'll be fine.

Again, I'm sorry for not doing right. Forgive me, and don't hesitate to lean on those who know the place and can help you find your footing.

Love,

Grandpa

I sighed, and felt the heavy weight of my decision to sell the ranch resting on my shoulders. I put the letter down, and could've wept at how horrible I felt inside. I didn't think I'd ever be done mourning my grandparents. They were my rock and foundation throughout my childhood. I collapsed onto the bed and put my head in my hands.

What am I doing trying to sell this place? I sat up and shook it off. I needed to call Effie and see if he wanted the ranch. I needed my ass kicked for trying to sell it. *What have I been thinking?*

I made a mental note to call my cousin when I got back to Houston, and finished going through the paperwork.

I opened historical documents that spanned back to the original land grant. Each one was like opening a treasure chest. I found the awards we'd won through the ages for the cattle, and documentation from Texas telling us they were going to take the land in eminent domain. Then there was the documentation from the court case showing the settlement. From what I knew about the area, the state had been ruthless taking the land from the local people, so the win for our family, if nothing else, was something to hold onto the property for.

The more I perused the family documents, the more resolved I became to keep the farm in the family. Hell, if Effie wasn't interested, I'd go look up some of our long-lost cousins and see if they were. I didn't have to live here, but I could make sure it stayed in the family.

When I came down the stairs, I felt like a different man. I'd made a decision to keep the property, and I'd never been surer of anything in my life.

I found Emma Jean and Jimmy in the living room and sat down in the old recliner across from them.

"I've decided not to sell," I blurted out.

Jimmy just smiled at me and Emma Jean winked. "Honey, we knew that already. You just needed to come to that realization," Emma Jean said.

"How did you know?" I asked.

Jimmy laughed. "This place is in yer blood, it's part a yer soul. Ain't no way you're gonna walk away from it, at least not by choice," he said on a sigh.

"I have no idea what I'm gonna do," I said. "I'll give Effie a call and see if he can come meet me. If I can't run it, I think he might."

"Don't let his mama get word a that," Jimmy said. "She'll terrorize the poor boy half ta death."

I nodded. "Well, I've got to get back to Houston to make some plans. I'll come back when I can, but I hope you two will continue with the place until I can get back?"

Emma Jean stopped knitting and looked over at me. "Son, we're here as long as we can be. You just have to remember the two of us are old and can't do what we used to. You need younger stock than us to help you with the place."

I smiled. "Not you, Mrs. Emma Jean, you're like the hills, they never get old."

"Psst," she exclaimed. "You got the tongue of your great-grandpa. That man could sweet talk a mountain lion. Even the hills wear down with age, sweetheart," she said, and resumed her knitting.

I chuckled, but I knew she was correct. I needed to get my act together while I still had the help I needed. Running cattle was not that profitable any longer, at least not like it had been. My grandparents were the last generation to make a good living doing that.

I needed to spend some time with my grandpa's books to determine if I could bring the ranch back or not. I knew my grandpa might never forgive me if I didn't, but if we were going to keep the ranch in our family's hands, I needed to employ something that would keep the lights on. Whether or not that was cattle, or something else, was yet to be seen.

After collecting as many of the recent ledgers as I could find, I stuffed them in the back of the rental, hugged Emma Jean and shook Jimmy's hand, promising again, I'd be back when I could, then I left for Alamito.

As soon as I got coverage, my first call was to Effie. "Hello," he answered. I could hear his two boys in the background.

"Hey Effie, it's Flex."

Effie fell silent. I knew this would be a surprise, since I'd ignored his calls and avoided him during the trial. In my heart, I knew he wasn't involved with his mom's legal shit, but my attorney had told me not to get involved with any of them, since it would likely hurt us in court.

"Hey, Flex," he finally said.

"Yeah, um. I wondered if we could get together when I get back to Houston."

"Are you at the ranch?" he asked.

"I just left there. I found some interesting things I'd like for you to see. Do you think you could meet me?

"Um, yeah, I'd like that," he said. "I really miss you, cuz."

"I know, I've missed you too. We can talk about all that when I see you."

"Yeah," he said.

Effie was never one for a lot of words. I'd pushed him out of my life after our grandpa died, and I could feel the tension between us, but if I was going to make this work, I needed him on my side.

"I'll text you when I get back in town, maybe this weekend?"

"Sure," he replied. "I have Friday and Saturday off. I'll have to bring the kids, though. I don't have anyone to keep them."

"That's okay," I said, wondering why their mom couldn't watch them, or for that matter, why he couldn't drop them off with his mom. Talking straight and direct like I'd have to would be harder with the kids around, but you had ta do what you had ta do. I was just happy he was willing to meet me.

The next phone call I made was to my realtor.

She didn't answer, so I left a message telling her I'd changed my mind.

As I pulled into the parking lot of the motel, I remembered I had a date tonight with Mitch. It seemed like my world had collapsed in on me since I'd left here this morning.

After taking Ace out for a long walk around the park, I lay down for a quick nap. I needed a distraction, or I was sure I wouldn't be any good for anyone tonight.

As soon as my head hit the pillow, I was fast asleep.

When I woke up, it was almost dark out. Shit, how long did I sleep?

I looked at the little clock, and it was half past eight. I'd been planning to meet Mitch thirty minutes ago. I grabbed my phone and texted him.

Sorry, fell asleep. I need a quick shower, then I'll head over if you're still up for company.

I wondered if you'd gotten cold feet. Yeah, come over when you can. I was just about to go downtown and get a pizza I ordered. I got an extra-large in case I heard from you.

God, that sounds really good. As long as you didn't put pineapple on it.

What, you don't like pineapple and anchovy pizza?

That turns my stomach. If you ordered that, I'll just go without.

It's meat lovers, no pineapple or fish, so you're safe.

See ya in a few!

I stripped and showered as fast as I could. I was excited to see the sexy man again. I couldn't wait until I could nuzzle my face into his soft neck, or kiss those beautiful long lashes.

Dang, I said to myself. You've got it bad.

Now that I wasn't selling the ranch, I'd have time to test out whether or not Mitch and I had a chance at more than a couple of hookups. Should I bring that up, or would it put him off?

I'd like the opportunity to get to know him better, but I could use some good sex tonight as well.

I'd just play it by ear and see how the night went. I could either tell him my news, or fuck his brains out and tell him in the morning. Spontaneity, that was what this situation would call for.

Mitch was just walking up the driveway as I came around the corner. "Perfect timing," he said.

"Did you walk up to the town?" I asked.

He nodded. "It's only a short walk, and I didn't want to have to make Lander drive over here just to drop off a pizza. He's been shorthanded since his son quit on him."

I just shook my head. "Y'all really do know everyone here, don't you?"

"All the full-timers for sure. It's a small town. Knowing what each of your neighbors is up to, especially if there's drama involved, is how we entertain ourselves."

I chuckled. "Well, sounds like I'm gonna get to learn more about that, since I've decided not to sell."

Mitch stopped and looked at me. "I thought you just signed the realtor's paperwork."

"I did, then I saw a letter my grandpa wrote me before he died. It was the clincher. I can't sell. That place is too much a part of who we are. I'm going to reach out to my cousin, and see if he wants to help me run the place. Last time I spoke to him, he said he wanted to. I'm not sure if his wife will agree, but if they're still on board, then that'll make this a lot easier."

Mitch took the pizza into the house and put it on the table. "So, you are gonna stay then?"

I sighed. "Yeah, I debated not telling you. I didn't want to chase you off until I'd seduced you again."

Mitch cocked an eyebrow in my direction. "Why do you think you couldn't seduce me if I knew you were gonna stick around?"

I shrugged. "I don't know. A lot of guys don't want their hookups to get any ideas about long-term stuff, you know."

"Not really. I'm not that big on the hook-up thing. In fact, I'd never do it if I weren't stuck out in the middle of the gay desert."

"Yeah, sorry... it's just my experiences with other gay men. It feels like they typically discourage any kind of commitment."

Mitch winked at me, and as he pulled plates and cloth napkins out and brought them to the table, he said, "I think you'll find I tend to be atypical in most ways."

He was correct. I could already tell this guy was atypical. Who used cloth napkins for pizza? Hell, who used plates for pizza? My experience was usually lean over the box, but Mitch was not the kind of guy to lean over a pizza box. He was more refined. Did I like that or not? Guess time would tell.

6

Mitch

FLEX THREW ME FOR a loop when he said he was going to come back to these parts. I already knew I liked him more than I had any guy in a long time, but I'd reconciled in my mind that he'd be gone by tomorrow, and I needed to be happy with that.

The thought that this could be more was both scary *and* exhilarating.

As we ate the pizza, I let my mind consider the opportunity.

"So, would you be living down on your grandparents' ranch?" I asked.

"I'm not sure yet. I just decided today, and it's all been so fast... Maybe," he said.

"But, it's possible your cousin could take the ranch over."

"If I'm lucky, that would be ideal," he said.

I inwardly sighed. Even if Flex stayed, it didn't seem like he wanted to. He didn't seem to see himself here.

We were silent while we ate our pizza. When we finished, I asked Flex if he'd like to take a walk.

"Um, won't we step on a snake?" he asked.

I laughed. "Unlikely. They tend to avoid crowded areas. We don't really see them in the town, unless it's early spring and they're coming out of hibernation."

"Well, I guess then..." he said hesitantly.

"You're gonna have to come to terms with the rattlers if you're to survive here."

"Trust me, I'm fully aware of that. I've dealt with the damned things since I was a kid. My grandparents' ranch is teeming with them. Maybe I need to figure out how to become a rattlesnake rancher. I've got plenty of those that are natural."

I chuckled. "Well, there are such things, but I don't know much about them."

"I need to go get Ace. Do you mind if we take him with us?"

"Nope, I don't mind at all."

Flex left while I cleaned up the dinner dishes, and tossed the napkins into the hamper. I was just finishing up when Ace came bounding into the house.

"Hey, buddy," I said, when I saw him.

Flex came in behind him, and I asked if I could give Ace a piece of sausage from the pizza we didn't eat.

"Just a little. He tends to get sick if he eats too much people food."

I winked at him and leaned down to give Ace the little treat. Ace was clearly food motivated, because the moment I gave him the sausage, he stuck to me like glue.

"He's a food slut," Flex said. "He'd dump me in a heartbeat if you had a piece of fresh meat."

"I dated a lot of guys just like him," I said, causing Flex to choke and laugh.

"I guess I've dated several like that myself."

We walked companionably toward town, and Flex let Ace have his lead, which meant he was darting all over the road in front of us. There was almost no traffic, so he had the run of the place.

"I'll admit, this does change things for me a bit. I like to take things slow. I wasn't joking when I said I'm not that into hookups."

Flex looked at me. I could tell he thought I was saying I wasn't interested in him.

"Yeah, I was afraid of that," he said.

"Well, I'm still interested, very interested," I reiterated. "Do you think there could be something more to this than hooking up?" I asked.

Flex shrugged. "Maybe. It's hard to say. I'm not even sure what my future holds, but I know I'm really attracted to you, more than I've been to someone in a while, but I need to be able to play it by ear. I'm not that big on long-term commitment."

I laughed. "Dude, I wasn't asking you to marry me. I just wanted to know if I needed to put the skids on, slow things down, so we could get to know each other."

"Definitely not," he said. "I don't want to slow nothing down." He moved in front of me, letting his hands slide down my arms, then back up. "I want to feel you under me, feel your body react when I kiss you, or suck on your nipples. I want you with every part of my being, and if this ends up going somewhere other than just being really great sex, I'm happy either way."

His words hit me right in the groin. "Yeah, I want all that too," I managed to squeak out.

We turned around at the same time and picked up our speed, headed back to my place. Poor Ace must have wondered what had happened to his walk.

"God, your body feels so good," I said, as I landed on top of him.

"Mmm," Flex moaned.

Things had moved so quickly this morning, I hadn't had a chance to taste him. I was so gonna remedy that this time. I rolled off him and turned to take his long cock into my mouth. I'd been impressed with his length this morning, and knew it'd be amazing in my mouth.

I licked his head, tasting the precome that had collected there, before sucking him into my mouth.

"Fuck," Flex moaned loudly. "Fuck, yeah!"

That prompted me, and I took his long cock deep into my throat. When I swallowed, Flex gulped and began fucking my mouth.

"Mmm," I moaned around his cock. Fuck, I loved the feel of a man taking me, shoving his cock inside me.

Before I knew what was happening, Flex shifted and took my cock into his mouth.

I pulled back. "Flex, shit... oh, fuck... that feels so..." My words were cut off when he shoved his cock back into my mouth as we sixty-nined.

I knew I was going to come if we didn't stop. Just having a tall, muscular man next to me was enough, but when you added his amazing cock, and the taste and smell of his masculine body, I could come just thinking about it, much less feeling him.

I was about to stop him when he rolled me onto my back, and lifting onto his knees, began fucking my face harder.

Oh, god, I couldn't think. The pleasure of his thrusts was more than my brain could handle.

Luckily, he'd stopped sucking me, so I didn't come too soon.

He was moaning as he face-fucked me, and my mind kept thinking what it'd be like to have that long cock fucking my ass.

He pulled off me and got on his knees, our eyes meeting.

"Can I fuck you?" he asked.

"God, please..." I said, my brain still too mushy to say more than that.

He smiled, a sexy, naughty smile, and said, "Did you get condoms?"

"I did," I said, and reached over to the bedside table, pulling an unopened box out and handing it to him.

"Extra-large, huh?" he said, making me smile.

"One of the biggest I've seen."

Flex wasted no time opening the box and pulling out a condom. He rolled it on, then leaned over and took my cock back into his mouth.

I squirmed at his attention, and moaned as he edged me again.

When I grabbed his hair to warn him I was about to come, he lifted up, took the lube from the table, and began to lube himself up.

"Can you do it doggie style?" he asked.

I nodded, still unable to make coherent sentences.

"Good. On all fours then."

I did as he instructed, and almost purred when his long sexy finger began to probe my hole. He kissed my ass cheeks as he pressed against the resistant guardian muscles. When I didn't loosen, he reached around me and began to jack me off.

When his tongue touched my opening, I almost jumped out of my skin. I'd watched this a hundred times on porn sites, but no one had ever done it to me.

Seconds after his tongue assaulted my hole, I understood why people did this.

"Oh, fuck. Fuck... that feels so... oh, my god..."

The sensation sent chills through my body.

"I had no idea this felt so... Oh, fuck, Flex, don't stop."

I was on the verge of coming, when Flex must've noticed, and knocked my hand away from my cock.

"Not yet," he said. "I wanna be inside you. I want to feel my cock slide into your tight, sexy hole."

"Oh, fuck," his words were almost as erotic as his tongue... almost.

When he used his finger to probe me along with his tongue, I must have loosened, because his finger went in without much resistance.

"You're so tight, so fucking tight."

I moaned as his finger began to stretch me. I wanted to make excuses about how long it'd been, but I couldn't speak, just experience, feel that glorious sensation of having my ass touched and licked.

When he slipped in a second finger, I arched up. "Oh, yeah... Flex... that's... that's... oh, fuck!"

Flex chuckled as he scissored me, nipping at my ass cheek as he did.

When he stuck his third finger in, I was ready, and fuck, I wanted his cock in me, not his fucking fingers.

"Now, Flex, fuck me now... stick your cock in..."

I didn't get the words out, because just as I did, he lined his head up to my hole, and let it slip inside.

"Aaah," I moaned incoherently.

When he slipped in further, stretching me in a painfully delightful way, I arched against him and pushed back. He was the biggest man I'd ever fucked, and yet, I couldn't get him inside me fast enough. Sweat broke out all over my body, sending tingles through me.

When I shoved back and felt his cock slide all the way in, I heard him moan, then curse.

"Shit, you're so tight, Mitch, you need to hold still or I'm gonna come in you right now."

That was what I wanted. I wanted him to fuck me and come inside me. I wanted to feel him shudder as the ecstasy washed over him, but not yet.

We held still for a moment, letting his excitement pass.

He leaned over me and kissed my back. When he straightened up, he began to rock into me. Slowly at first, trying to keep his orgasm at bay.

Then, he began to fuck into me. Harder and harder.

"Fuck, yeah... fuck, Flex, yeah, fuck me harder, *harder!*"

He moaned loudly as our bodies slammed into each other.

He'd been fucking my prostate ever since his cock had slid inside me. It was almost more than I could handle, and I knew if I even touched myself, I'd explode all over the bed.

Even without the stimulation, I felt my orgasm rising.

"Yes, Flex, fuck, I'm gonna…"

Before I knew it, Flex spasmed behind me, his orgasm overtaking him before mine, and as it did, he shifted and slowed down, and his cock slammed into my prostate, causing me to explode before I even felt it building.

"*Aargh*," I yelled out… as my orgasm overtook me.

Flex jerked one last time and pulled out of me, and as he fell to the bed, he pulled me down with him.

We were spooning, his cock still pressed up against my ass.

"That was so hot," Flex whispered into my ear. "You're so hot."

I moaned, my body still shaking from the intense lovemaking.

He curled his long muscular arms around me, and pulled me into him as he kissed my neck.

"You're so fucking sexy," he said.

I was surprised how easily I fell asleep, Flex curled up behind me. Usually, I had to have the fan on to drown out noise and the covers pulled down on the bed. Evidently, none of that mattered tonight.

7

Flex

I T'D BEEN A LONG damn time since I'd enjoyed a man's body as much as I was enjoying Mitch's. My ex had been... okay, but nothing as delicious and sensual as this. I reluctantly pulled my body away from his the next morning, and got up to take a shower.

When I came out, Mitch had already put the coffee on, and asked if I wanted breakfast.

"No, thank you. I don't usually eat breakfast. Coffee will be good," I said. "Besides, if I'm going to eat like I have the past few days, I'm going to have to get back into the routine of running."

Mitch laughed. "I'm guessing if you take over your grandparents' ranch, you'll never have to run to stay in shape again. That's some really hard work."

"Oh, trust me, I know, but how do *you* know? Did you work on a ranch?"

Mitch nodded. "Oh, yeah, my grandpa would pawn me out every chance he got. I usually helped when people were gathering cattle, or needed help with chores that were easily assigned to a teenager."

"That's good to know," I said. "I may need to lean on your skills once we get things moving again."

"Nope, I'm retired from that kind of manual labor. Nowadays, I'm a full-time hospitality executive."

I laughed. "We'll see," I said. I went over to where Mitch stood across from me and pulled him into an embrace, giving his ass a good squeeze. "Maybe I could figure out some trade to pull you back into the ranching business."

"Humm, that might be something that could be negotiated."

"Name your price," I said, as I ground my cock into his.

"Let me show you," he replied, and pulled me into a deep kiss.

"Mmm, we need to move fast," I said, as I kissed his neck. "My flight leaves at noon, and I still have to get to the rental place and drop off the car."

"I can do amazing things with fifteen minutes," he huffed, and dropped to his knees.

While still out of breath, I sighed and commented how I was gonna miss his incredible mouth.

"Good, I like to leave an impression," Mitch said, and winked at me.

I got into the car, opened the window, and willed him to kiss me again, just one more time. He complied, thank god!

As I drove away, I could still smell him on me. I hadn't been this ridiculous over a man... well, ever. I wondered if it was just all the emotions associated with dealing with my grandparents and the ranch.

Don't overthink it, I chastised myself. Just enjoy it. Why can't you just be a dude for a minute and not get all emotional over meeting a new guy? I'd swear, sometimes I thought I could write those sappy articles for one of the teen rags.

No matter how much I tried, I couldn't get the guy off my mind. I pulled into the parking lot of the rental place an hour later, dropped off my car. The little twink that drove me to the airport flirted like there was no tomorrow, causing me to chuckle. While I waited in the terminal, sipping a coffee, I texted Mitch,

What is it about being well-sexed that attracts other gay men? I haven't been flirted with in months. I'm gone less than an hour, and the twink that picked me up from the car place came onto me.

Nothing like a satisfied man to get another man's juices flowing.

You feeling satisfied?

Mmm, I could use a little more, but I'm good for a minute.

I smiled at the thought. I'd love to be back there to give him a little more, but life was getting in the way.

I was just about to put my phone away, when I got a call from my realtor. Big surprise, I'd left a message the day before, and she was just now getting back to me.

I answered, hoping to ensure the contract was canceled before she listed it.

"Hello," I answered.

The woman immediately laid into me. "Why did you make me do all that work just to change your mind? Not only that, I have a buyer on the line. He was going to drive down this weekend to look the property over, then he was going to give you a very good offer."

"I'm sorry, I'm not interested. Thank you." I responded.

When the words "You son of a bitch..." came out of her mouth, I hung up on her.

While she called me back repeatedly, I finished my email, sent it to her, and forwarded it to my attorney with a return receipt. That way, the beast couldn't say she never got it. God help me, at this point, even if I changed my mind again and decided to sell, I'd rather have Lucifer be the agent.

I followed up with my attorney, then telling him that I'd fired my realtor, and was going to explore keeping the property.

By the time I finished my conversation with him, my flight was being called. I put my phone on airplane mode and boarded. At least I had a few hours to decompress from this clusterfuck of a trip before I was home, then the drama of figuring out what I was going to do with my life would start, but for now, I could just relax.

As usual, Houston's Airport was a stream of activity. I didn't turn my phone on until I got to my car and was headed out of the airport and toward my apartment.

My phone started dinging. Fifteen messages from the realtor. I flipped through them, until I came to one from my mom.

"Honey, this is Mom. I just got a call from a man who said he wanted to talk to you about buying the ranch. I'm not sure why he didn't go through your realtor, or how he got my number, but anyway, I thought I should let you know."

That was strange. I wondered why he didn't just call me.

Once I got back to my apartment, I found my digital recorder and started documenting all the insane phone calls from the realtor, and sent those to my attorney as well. I'd learned from my experience with my aunt, you documented *everything* when something might come back to bite you in the ass.

I guessed I'd have to reinstate my retainer with him after all this. Lord, it was out of the frying pan and into the fire with all this crap.

I was exhausted, but before I could relax, I still had to take Ace for a walk, since he'd been stuck in that crate for so long. Before I could put his lead on though, my mom called again.

"Hi, Mom, what's up?" I asked.

"Hi, honey, how was your trip?" she asked.

"Emotional, draining. In fact, I was just about to take Ace for a walk, then get ready to go to bed."

"That's good, dear," she said. "I wanted to tell you that the man I left a message about, he stopped by my house today. He was insistent that you call him back immediately."

"Mom, you should've told him to leave. I've canceled the realtor. I'm not selling."

My mother was quiet for a moment. "Well, honey, I can't say I'm surprised, but are you sure? That old place is cursed."

I laughed. "Mom, just because you hated it doesn't mean it's cursed. I used to love it there."

"Yeah, but no one keeps cattle in the desert any longer. There just isn't any money in ranching."

"I know, Mom, I'll have to figure something else out. Right now, I need to rest, and if that man shows up, or calls you again, you tell him we're not interested. Call the cops if you have to."

"Okay, honey," she said, a little too sweetly. I knew my mother like I knew the back of my hand. That woman was not done with this conversation, but this was the *sweet mom* tactic. It always predicated the *concerned mom* tactic, which was closely followed by the *mean mom* tactic. It wasn't like I could avoid them, but I'd come to learn over the years how to navigate my mom's manipulations. At least she couldn't paddle my behind any longer.

After I got back from our walk, I decided I could live without my shower and fell into my bed, and was asleep before my head hit the pillow.

I couldn't remember when I'd slept that hard, or dreamed so clearly.

The dream started ominously. I could feel something was off.

The darkness was as black as crude oil and the stars weren't out. I knew this was a dream, because in the real world, the stars on the ranch were so bright, you could almost see your way around without a flashlight.

I could feel that I wasn't alone. Something slimy and malicious was there with me, something unnatural, something that didn't belong there. I walked toward the back of the house, and when I looked, I saw a dark figure. No, I couldn't see it really as much as I could feel it, and I knew it was the shape of a large snake sliding through the property. When the snake reached the barn, I could feel it looking at me, sneering at me, then with the flick of its tail, the barn erupted into flames.

I was paralyzed, unable to move. I was not sure if it was fear, or just part of the dream, but I was helpless to prevent the creature from wreaking havoc. As the snake slithered through the yard, everything it passed burst into flames. I could hear the malicious laughter as the buildings on the ranch burned to the ground. When it had finally burned all the outbuildings, it slithered closer to me, closer to the main house. Suddenly, I could move, and I turned to look through the windows, and saw Jimmy and

Emma Jean sitting at the dining-room table, oblivious to the evil that was coming toward them.

Just as the snake was about to reach the house, a man stood in front of it. The snake reared back in anger, ready to strike. Before it struck...

I woke up in a pool of sweat.

My granny used to say some of our people had the sight. They'd have dreams or premonitions and that if I ever had one that concerned me, I should tell her. Too bad she wasn't here to talk to. This was my first, and it was very intense. My rational brain immediately began to convince me the dream was just a reaction to all the stuff I'd been through during the last few days.

It was still early, but there would be no more sleep for me, not after that nightmare.

I hoped a shower would wash away the uneasiness left by my dream, but it didn't. Instead, I called the ranch.

"Wow, good to see you got into a better habit while here," she said, when she answered.

I chuckled. "Sorry, Mrs. Emma Jean, I doubt this is a permanent fix."

"Oh?" she asked. "We'll see once you get back here."

"I'm sure you will," I said with just a little dread. "Mrs. Emma Jean, I had a really nasty dream, and it feels like one of granny's premonitions she used to talk about. I thought I should warn y'all so you can keep an eye out."

Emma Jean was quiet for a moment. "I know your people have some of the sight, but that stuff has always worried me, don't want to invite the devil in, you know," she replied.

I knew she was a religious person, but hearing her say that sort of shocked me. "Well, you're probably right, and it's probably nothing."

"No, wait. I didn't mean it like that. It's just I was raised to shun all that stuff. I lived with your grandparents long enough to know there is only goodness in your blood. If you had a premonition, we'd better hear about it."

I sighed, and told her about my dream. "It's probably nothing, Mrs. Emma Jean. There's just been so much going on that I'm having bad dreams."

"Did it feel like just a bad dream?" she asked.

"N-no," I stuttered.

"Did it feel like something important?" she asked.

"Yes, ma'am."

"Then, we'll just take it as a precaution. I'll tell Jimmy to turn on the cameras your grandpa put up when those rustlers started hanging around, and see if Lucille'll let us keep her dogs here for a few nights, just to be safe."

I sort of remembered who Lucille was, but I couldn't quite recall. Maybe a neighbor.

"Okay, but I'm feeling like an idiot now for bringing this up. It's probably just stress."

"Maybe," she said cheerfully. "But, better safe 'an sorry."

I hung up and sat in the chair across from my TV. When I first got my inheritance, I'd thought about buying a little condo or house further out in the suburbs, but I remembered how wrong it felt to spend my grandparents' money on a city house.

After last night's experience, I was beginning to wonder if maybe that was intuition as well. Was something steering me away from the wrong path, or at least away from that path?

Dang, it was easy to go down that rabbit hole. No, it felt wrong, because I knew how much my grandparents loved their West Texas life. They'd have rolled over in their graves if they thought their hard-earned money was going into some square box the size of their living room.

I pulled the ranch's ledgers out and began looking at the last few years' accounts. As I suspected, the cattle industry had slowly declined over the past few years.

I leaned back in my chair. Was I making the wrong decision? It sounded like this guy *really did* want to own the ranch, and he was desperate enough that he'd probably give us top dollar. The problem was, I no longer wanted to sell. I wanted, maybe even *needed*, to make this work. Not even the snake dream had put me off.

With a conviction I only sort of felt, I wrote my resignation letter, then got dressed and headed into the office, resignation letter in hand.

My boss wasn't really all that surprised when I handed him the letter. "You inherited a large estate. I figured you wouldn't be able to handle both this job and that. I'd hoped you'd sell up and stay here, though."

I thanked him. "I'm going to use up my comp time," I said, expecting to have an argument. Instead, he just shrugged.

"We don't have much for you anyway," he said. "Just make sure you clean out your desk and return all the office equipment before you go."

I was shocked that after six years of work, I had so little stuff here that I was able to completely erase myself from the office in less than fifteen minutes. I said goodbye to the three or four people who'd even notice I was gone, and walked out the front door.

As I drove home, I decided I might as well go all in. It wasn't smart to live in West Texas without a truck. My pitiful old sedan had seen better days, and it was time to embrace my new life choices. Throwing caution, and maybe my common sense, to the wind, I drove to the dealership. Mark, a guy that dated my mom for a while, was the only dealer for me. He was a good guy—one of the few men mom dated that I liked. I also knew he wouldn't screw me.

When I walked in, Mark must've recognized me, because he came out of his office, quickly strode over to me, and pulled me into an embrace.

"Fletcher, son, what brings you over to this side of the zoo?" he asked.

"Well, I'm having a life crisis, so being a man, that means I need to get a new car."

Mark laughed loud enough that lots of heads turned his way. "You've always been a smart-ass, that's probably why I liked you," he replied, and pulled me back toward his office.

I remembered coming to his office when I was still in my early teens. Mark hadn't been a dad replacement, more of an older guy who didn't make me feel dumb, or like I was the unwanted child that came with my mom.

During the few years mom and he had dated, we'd spent several days in this office, chatting about the drama of being a teen. He'd been the first person I'd come out to, and he said it'd be hard to live that life in Texas, but he'd always been taught that a man had to be himself, no matter what that looked like to others.

When we sat down, I went into detail about my life, and how it was rapidly changing. "I decided to keep my grandparents' ranch yesterday, and quit my job today. Now, I'm trading in my Honda Accord for a truck. I can't live in the damned desert and drive a stupid Honda through the back roads."

Mark laughed. "No, you'd stick out like a sore thumb. I'd also be very concerned for your safety driving around a foreign-made car."

"I hadn't thought of that, but you're right. I think they'd forgive my sexuality long before they'd forgive my being un-American!"

"So, what are you thinking about?" he asked.

We talked about what I'd be using the truck for, potentially, and eventually settled on three options for me to choose from. However, it was clear he was leaning toward the Ford F-150.

"I'm guessing the one you're bragging about the most is the most expensive one?" I asked, pointing at the truck he showed me.

Mark chuckled. "I make the same, whether it costs the most or the least, but, yeah, it's not cheap."

"How much do I get on the family discount?"

He leaned back. "I don't hand out family discounts to just everyone," he said, teasing.

"Hey, it's not my fault you couldn't close the deal with my mother. I was rooting for you. Heck, that's worth a few thousand off the top right there."

"Let's go take a look, I'll grab the keys, and you can see which one fits you best."

The second I saw the monster, it felt right. They had three colors on the lot, blue, white, and candy-apple red. Mark took me right to the red one. I chuckled, and he turned around to look at me. "What?" he asked.

"Is it just a gift, or do you just know me from when you dated my mother?"

He smiled. "I'm not giving away any more of my secrets, not even to my dating advocate."

I crawled up and into the truck, and just like that I was a five-year-old boy watching the monster trucks with my dad, jumping and crushing cars.

"I'll take it," I said, causing Mark to laugh. "You haven't even taken it for a test drive," he said.

"You and I both know I'm buying this truck. Hell, I bet you already have your assistant running the numbers on my old Honda, but if it makes you happy, I'll take you for a drive, old man."

Mark just shook his head. "You really are too big for your britches, boy." Then, he crawled into the seat next to me, and handed me the keys.

The vehicle purred like a well-satisfied man, and that was exactly what I thought about this truck. It was a hunk of a male that begged to be driven.

I realized, if I'd been straight and personified a truck with a woman, I'd have been nothing less than a sexist shithole, but feeling that rumble under my seat and the smooth ride as we cruised down Interstate ten, it was hard not to think about sex. Maybe that's how they sold so many of these to guys like me.

When we got back to the office, Mark brought the paperwork with him.

"I'm not gonna keep you here all day. Although I'd fire my salespeople if they did what I'm doing, you're as close to a son as I've ever had, so they can just stuff it."

When I walked out of the dealership, I left my Honda behind. I drove away in my brand new truck, with the maximum extended warranty, and a tire package. There was other stuff I didn't even realize you could get with a vehicle, since if I were buying from anyone else, I'd have blown it off and said no to it.

After Mark included everything, I still got the truck for less than the list price. When I signed on the bottom line, I asked the lady who sat across from me, "So how much did he lose on this?"

Her face turned red. "You know I can't tell you that, Mr. Patterson would fire me in a minute."

"Blink if I get close. Five-thousand?"

The woman blinked and looked down at the paperwork. "Well, shit," I said out loud. "I didn't want him to lose money on me. He swore this was what he had in it."

The woman shrugged. "He never loses money, so it's all okay. Besides, he told me before he brought me in that you were his stepson and I needed to treat you with respect."

I smiled. "I'm pretty close to that, for sure."

I'd have to figure out how to pay him back. Maybe I'd have him come out to the ranch. He used to love to hunt. There were several invasive species we had to control on the ranch to ensure the native species weren't pushed out. Grandpa used to hire the job out to some of the state's rangers, but I figured Mark might enjoy it.

My new truck didn't fit into my parking space at my apartment. I knew it wouldn't when I bought it, but it definitely sucked that I had to park in the open parking lot, knowing any idiot could crush their door into my new paint job.

Since I was jumping into this all at once, quitting my job *and,* buying a truck, I might as well go all the way. My apartment lease was up for renewal in two months. So, before going into the apartment, I stopped by the leasing office and dropped in my notice to them as well.

Unlike at work, Tiff, the manager, acted like she was sad to see me go. "We'll miss you," she said.

As I was about to walk out, she stopped me. "Hey, Flex, do you plan to move out earlier than sixty days?" she asked.

"Yeah, probably in the next week or so," I replied. "Why?"

"I need to run this by the owner, but we have a waiting list for apartments your size. If he agrees, would you be interested in surrendering your apartment early?"

"If I could get my deposit back," I said. "Sure."

She smiled and came around the desk to give me a hug. "You've been one of our best tenants, and we *really will* miss you," she said.

I left her office feeling pretty good. Now, all that was left for me to deal with was my mom.

After slipping into my apartment long enough to give myself a moment for my head to stop spinning, I called mom and left a message. My mother never answered her phone. She kept her phone on silent, saying she paid for the phone for her convenience, not for others.

Of course, god help anyone who didn't answer on the first ring when she called, but that was just how things were with my high-maintenance mother.

"Mom, it's your favorite son. I'm coming over, so get dressed. I just got a new truck and I want to take you for a drive."

I knew she'd call back. First, because I'd bought a truck and she'd naturally assume I bought it from Mark. There would be at least an hour-long inquisition about what he looked like, how he was doing, what his financial status was, was he married? I figured I might as well get that out of the way, then I'd take her to dinner and get the rest out of the way.

I knew she was livid that I'd decided not to sell the ranch. Sure, she was playing coy at the moment, but that wasn't going to last long. I was even prepared for it.

As predicted, when I arrived at her little cottage, she came right out dressed to the nines. This was another indication that I was in for a lecture. My mother *never* dressed up, unless she was going to intimidate someone into doing what she wanted.

"Oh, honey, the truck is beautiful." My mom never gave a compliment first, without giving at least two things she found wrong. She once told me it was because that way, the compliment would feel bigger and more authentic.

"Thanks, Mom," I replied, trying not to roll my eyes. I was being played, but I guessed this play was about Mark, not my keeping the ranch.

When she crawled up the side, I could tell she wasn't happy it required her to lose her ladylike finesse to get into. My grandpa used to tell me how my mother would refuse to ride a horse when she was only four, saying it was undignified for a woman to climb up something to take a ride. He would shake his head, and say, "If I hadn't been there and seen it with my own eyes, I'd swear that woman didn't come out of your grandma."

The thought always gagged me, but as an adult, I understood that statement more and more. "Mom, do you need a hand," I asked, knowing that would just piss her off more.

"No, dear, I'm good," she said.

"Is your mouth hurting?" I asked.

"What an odd question," my mom said, putting on as many southern airs as she could. "Why would you ask such a thing?"

"Cause, all those sweet words coming out of your mouth has to be causing you to pucker."

My mom looked at me. I could tell she wanted to keep up the pretense, but she also knew the gig was up. "Okay. What made you sell that cute little Honda and buy this... this... *beast!*" she said, punctuating the word beast.

"Well, because the Honda wasn't practical for West Texas."

My mom looked at me side-eyed. I could feel the internal war waging inside her. I just let it rumble, knowing if I interrupted, it would end in a loud argument that included Mark, the ranch, her sister, and possibly even my dad, who'd died too early leaving her with a burden.

Finally, I could tell the war was subsiding, and she looked at me. "So, where did you buy the truck?"

I almost laughed. She was losing her touch. Usually, she used a lot more tact.

"I bought it from Mark," I confessed.

"Oh, that's nice. Did he give you a good deal?" she asked.

We'd returned to the *cordial mom* stage, which was fine. She had her way of pulling out information, and even though she didn't want to admit it, she needed to do it this way to convince herself she hadn't made a mistake when she'd thrown Mark to the side.

"Yeah, he did. I think I took him for about five grand."

Mom sucked in a breath. "Fletcher Henry, what do you mean you took him for five thousand dollars? We don't do that kind of thing. We are upstanding people. We do *not* take charity, especially from..."

She caught herself and forced herself to calm.

"Mom, he didn't give me a choice. He threw every warranty he could at me, then didn't charge me for them. He's a good man, Mom, a really good man."

She patted her dress, like I'd seen old southern women do all my life when they didn't want to face something, or needed time to get their wits about them.

"I know you were close to him, I'm glad for that," she said. Although I knew for a fact, she considered my ongoing friendship with Mark to be a disrespectful and hurtful betrayal. "A boy is supposed to choose his mother over an ex-boyfriend of hers," she said, when she first heard I was still hanging out with Mark, after they broke up.

There was no arguing with my mother, though. Once she had something in her head, you had two choices, avoid her, or accept the fact that you were going to be wrong, no matter how right you were.

When she regained her composure, she looked at me until I glanced over, then she went for the kill. "You are keeping that property, even though you know how much I hate it there. Why are you doing that to me?"

I looked over at my mom, refusing to take the bait. "I was planning to take you out to our favorite barbeque place tonight, but I'm afraid you'll get barbeque sauce on your nice dress. Would you prefer steak maybe, or do you have a suggestion where we could go?"

My mom turned away, and I could tell she was thinking about pouting. I'd long ago learned how to ignore the pouting, and if she didn't tell me what she wanted, we could end up at McDonald's. I'd pulled that one a couple times when she was being particularly manipulative, not unlike she was being today.

"I think barbeque sounds the best. I'll just use extra napkins."

That seemed to be the icebreaker. She ran her hands over the interior of the truck. "I do so love the smell of a new car. Oh, the interior is beautiful, and you got the extended cab too. It's too big, and no dignified woman would want to climb up into it, but that isn't really gonna be a problem, is it, honey?" She reached over and patted my face. "Speaking of that, are you dating anyone? You know I still want to be a grandmother before I'm too old to enjoy my grandbabies."

I smiled. When I'd told my mother I was gay, she didn't even blink. "That's nice, honey, but I still expect a whole parcel of grandbabies. Now don't you dare keep me from having that."

My mom was an expert at twisting things back to her.

"I'm working on it, but I'm not seeing anyone enough to ask them to marry me yet."

My mother naturally glommed onto the word marry. "Oh, I can't wait until you get married. It'll be a dream wedding, lots of white, and you and your beau can both wear white tuxedos. I've been looking at magazines with gay weddings, and some of them are so beautiful. I hope you decide to get married on the

Gulf, maybe Padre Island. Some of those weddings on the ocean are so beautiful, you could just cry."

She carried on about gay weddings until we pulled up at the barbeque restaurant. "Oh, I haven't had barbeque in too long. You were right to pick this place," she said, and now that she wanted out, she crawled out of the big truck like an expert. I just shook my head. The woman was truly a work of southern art. I thanked the good lord in heaven, I was old enough to live on my own.

Barbeque seemed to be my mom's soft spot, and even when things were nasty between us, we could often work it out over a slab of Jo Bryan's ribs.

"So, I'm not going to fuss at you anymore about moving to hell, but you'll rue the day, son," she said. "Just don't throw that man's number away just yet. You'll probably want to sell to him in the near future. So, baby, just keep your options open."

I had no intention of keeping the man's number, no more than I intended to work with the realtor beast my attorney had referred to me. Still, I smiled at my mom, and nodded, which she took as confirmation that I was going to take her advice.

I let her go on about whatever subject she wanted to spout on about, surprised that she was letting the ranch subject go.

Finally, and certainly not wisely, I asked, "Mom, it isn't like you to let this drop so fast. Why aren't you throwing more of a fit about the ranch?"

"It won't do me any good to argue with you about it, I recognize when you've made your mind up. You get that same set in your jaw that your father used to get. He didn't fight me on much, but I knew when he got that look," she pointed to my face. "I was never going to win."

Mom seldom talked about my father, and hearing her say anything about him almost always threw me into an emotional spiral.

I shook it off, though, deciding to push to find the truth about the property.

"Mom, you have never let my facial expression stop you before. What's really going on?"

She looked down at her plate, then picked up the cloth napkin and began to clean off her fingers.

"The truth is, I'm sort of happy you aren't selling right away. Melissa, down at my hairdresser, overheard your aunt the other day, when she was in for her styling, say she was going to try to buy the property from you. Truth be known, I think that handsome man that came to my house to make you an offer is her latest boyfriend."

Light dawned on me, and I leaned back and smiled. My mother might not want me to keep the property, but she'd want me to keep it from her sister even more. Theirs was a rivalry that spanned the ages.

"Have you heard from that man since yesterday?" I asked.

"No, when he left, I told him I'd give you his number. I'm guessing he's waiting on you to call him."

I thought for a moment. My mom was pretty transparent, and I thought maybe I could kill two birds with one stone. On the one hand, I could get the man to leave me alone, and on the other, I might be able to buy some goodwill with my mother over me keeping the property.

"Mom, I have an idea, but it's pretty devious."

She immediately sat up in her seat. I almost laughed. She did love a good plot.

"If you are sure that man is associated with Aunt Rebecca, I'd encourage you to go to her house tomorrow, and ask her to get a message to her man. We aren't interested."

The wicked smile that crossed my mother's face was all I needed to see. I knew she'd handle the problem for me.

I had to work hard not to shake my head. I was happy I was an only child. I couldn't imagine having a sibling I hated as much as my mother hated her sister, and vice versa. The fact they lived less than two blocks from each other, used the same grocery store and hairdresser always confused me. It had something to do with how much they enjoyed publicly hating each other.

I drove her back home, and before I let her out, I said, "Mom, I know you miss Mark, and I think he probably misses you too. Why don't you give him a call and invite him over for dinner? If for nothing else than just to thank him for helping me purchase the truck without having my ass handed to me."

Mom slapped my arm. "Don't cuss in front of your mother," she said, and crawled out of the truck, without responding to my request.

I got out and came to her side. "I love you, Mama. I'll come by before I head back out west."

She hugged me tight, and pulled me down to her four-foot frame, and planted a kiss on my cheek. You are the light of my life, mijo." She only used the Spanish word for son when she was being affectionate for real. "I love you, no matter what, no matter when, and no matter *who* you decide to be."

My mother was full of it most of the time, but during these brief and seldom occurrences, I knew I was loved. These fleeting moments almost made it worth all the crap I had to deal with in between... Almost.

My day had been intense. I was still amazed how I could go from living in an apartment for six years, being employed at my job for the same amount of time, and owning a car that I drove day in and day out, to it all being over in less than twenty-four hours.

I was hoping I'd have a message from a certain motel owner, but to my great disappointment, I had no messages.

I took Ace for a walk, and then decided to lie down. I was out in seconds.

I was immediately alarmed when I realized I was in the same dream again.

This time the snake was staring at me. The anger radiated from it. I couldn't hear it, but I could feel the words. I hate you, I'll destroy you. I turned away from it and tried to move toward the house, but as soon as my back was turned, I felt a searing hot pain.

I woke up with a start again. This time, I had to rush to the bathroom, where I unloaded my dinner into the toilet.

When I was done, I wet a washcloth in cold water and ran it over my face and neck.

These dreams were intense, worse than anything I'd ever felt before. I didn't usually even have dreams, and if I did, I certainly didn't remember them.

It was still just a quarter past midnight, and too early to be up, but I didn't want to sleep again and take a chance on the nightmare coming back again for a second round.

So, I got up and found the packing boxes I'd saved from my move here.

I began going through my guest bedroom first, separating my belongings between keep and toss. I pulled out a huge old box I kept in the extra closet that I'd forgotten I had. Well, not forgotten as much as ignored. I dumped the box on the floor and began going through the stuff, separating it mostly into the toss pile. I came across an old medicine bag my grandmother had given me when I was having nightmares about losing my dad.

I'd kept the bag hanging over my bed. I wasn't sure if it was just a placebo, or if it worked for real, but once I kept it near my bed, the nightmares had subsided.

When I saw it, I immediately had the feeling of being tossed into a parallel universe. I hadn't seen or thought of that old bag since I'd moved out of my mom's house and into this apartment. The fact that I'd come into the room I rarely went into, and dug through a box I should've just tossed, seemed a little too much of a coincidence.

I carried the little bag out of the room and into the kitchen. I crossed over to the sink to get a glass of water, and noticed I had a message on my phone.

I hope this isn't too weird, but I wanted to say hi before I go to bed. Wish you were in bed with me.

The feeling that went through my heart was pure relief. Mitch still liked me. That was one good thing I had to look forward to as I prepared to move to the middle of nowhere.

I checked the time on the message, and realized it was sent three hours earlier, too late to message back, but I reread the message a couple times just to reinforce the happiness I felt from seeing it.

I hung the medicine bag up on the corner of a picture I had over the bed, prayed it worked and kept the horrible nightmare at bay, and crawled back in bed.

The sky had opened up sometime in the night, and it was rain-ing like only it could in Houston. I went to the kitchen to turn my coffee pot on, when I noticed another message on my phone.

This time when I opened it, I saw my cousin had texted me.

Hey, I have the day off because of the rain, and the kids are in school, which would make it easier to manage a conversation. I can come over if you have time.

I sighed. This was a conversation I was both looking forward to and dreading, but it needed to happen.

I texted him back.

Sure, I'm just making coffee, though. If you come in the next hour, I'll have breakfast done.

"Yes, free breakfast!" was his response.

We hadn't talked in close to five years, but just like that, things seemed back to normal.

I left my door open and climbed into the shower, knowing Effie would come straight in. Well, that was what he used to do anyway. We were best friends before his mom acted like a damned fool, then the attorney had said, "You need to keep anyone who could spy on you at bay, or you could lose the fight and the ranch."

I regretted it, but didn't feel I had much choice. The ranch was worth millions. Effie was the son of my legal enemy, and I had no evidence he wasn't as much against me as she was. That didn't mean I didn't feel like a total asshole for pushing him out of my life.

Sure enough, when I got done with my shower, Effie was sitting on my couch, playing on his phone.

"Hey," he said, when I came out of the bedroom.

"Hey," I replied back, and sat across from him. "So, shall we do this now, or over breakfast?"

Effie just shook his head. "Ain't much to say, except my mom is a bitch who has driven a wedge between me and every person I've ever cared about."

I just nodded, thinking to myself, *So, we're doing this now.*

"I've missed you, Effie, but I didn't feel like I had a choice. The attorney told me I had to stay away from your mother and y'all, or that your mom would probably squeeze something out of me that caused me to lose the lawsuit."

"I know, I figured as much."

"I'm surprised you're this cool about it, actually. I was expecting you to be pissed at me."

Effie looked at me. "Well, I am really, but it's been five fucking years, and I don't want to lose any more time just because of all this. I'd rather bury the hatchet and move on."

"Yeah, like that ever works... they even wrote a damn song about it, bury the hatchet and leave the handle sticking out!"

Effie laughed, but wouldn't look me in the eye. "That's true, I guess."

"Okay, have your say, and I'll have mine, then we'll see if we can work it out. You're pissed, 'cause I kicked you out of my life. I'm pissed, 'cause your mom put me in an impossible position, where I didn't really have any choice."

"I haven't spoken to my mom in almost as long as I haven't spoken to you. When I found out about the lawsuit, I tried to get her to change her mind, but you know how she is. She screamed at me that I was siding with the enemy, that I knew my brothers had more right to that ranch than you did, and so forth and so on. Then, she told me if I was going to side with you, then I should get out and never come back. So, that's what I did."

"Effie, I don't believe it, why didn't you tell me? No, I know you tried, but I ignored your texts." I sighed. "What about your brothers? Are you speaking to them?"

"No, none of them. They all ostracized me over the court case. Mom's convinced them they have more rights to the property than you do. I'm the Judas, or that's what they've all told me."

"Well, shit, I'm sorry, man. If I'd known, I'd have been more open to you."

"I know, but I'd rather have waited, then you wouldn't have to second guess whether I was going to turn on you too. At least, now you know I was never against you."

I stood up, and pulled my cousin into a hug. "I'm so sorry, Effie. I hate that this whole thing happened. You must have felt so abandoned."

A tear slipped down my cousin's face, and I felt more like a piece of warmed-over shit than ever in my life.

I'd known my cousin since before either of us knew how to talk. Effie was older than me, but barely. Our birthdays were just a few weeks apart, and our family often had our birthday parties together, although that was mostly, because my mom and aunt wanted to one-up each other in gifts and party favors, and well, you got the idea. It was more about them than us.

Effie and I once admitted to each other that we didn't mind, because if they were being crazy, we got more gifts and a bigger party.

When Effie's parents got a divorce, his dad moved to Nashville, and married another woman who had three kids of her own. After that, his dad adopted her kids, and all but ostracized Effie and his brothers. I always assumed that was why my cousins were so loyal to their mother. She really was all they had.

Effie spent most of his time at my house growing up. We went to school together even, but he was a grade above me. He tended to be my protector, although I was a full foot taller than he was and ended up being the jock. If anyone ever bullied me, though, even after I started playing soccer full-time, my shorter cousin would go in for the attack, and more often than not, win. Eric nicknamed him the badger, which was such a perfect fit. Most of the kids we hung around with called him that as well.

We sat back down, and this time I joined him on the couch. "So, how are Theresa and the kids?" I asked.

"The kids are good, at least I hope they are. Theresa left us two years ago, and I haven't seen her since. Rumor has it, she's shacked up with some drug dealer in MacGregor. We're not even sure she's still alive."

"Fuck, Effie, how are the kids dealing with that?" I asked.

Effie sighed. "Truth is, she wasn't around much the past few years. Less and less every year, really. She went into rehab right when Mom's shit hit the fan with you, and when she came out, she relapsed right away. She was angry, saying I wanted to change her, or that I wanted to force her to be something she wasn't. By the time she left for good, the kids didn't even seem to notice she was gone."

"So, you're on your own with the kids? Are you still working construction?" I asked.

"When I can, but the weather here has sure put the skids on that. I was moved over to dozer work, and because it seems to rain every damned week, I'm out of work more than in."

"How have you been surviving?" I asked.

"My inheritance money. It's all I've had, and it's almost gone. I'm going to have to find different employment, but it's hard when you're a single parent. At least, with all the construction layoffs, I was home for the kids."

I stood up, crossed to the counter, and grabbed the keys to the truck. "Come on, I'm taking you out for breakfast, and I have a proposal for you. And, before you get all self-righteous, I asked you here to propose this even before I found all this out."

Effie looked at me and refused to budge. "What are you up to, Flex. I may not be talking to my mom and brothers, but I'll not go against them either."

I laughed. "You are as stubborn as a damned burro. Like I'd ask you to go against your family. Shit, do you think I've changed? I'm me, not them!"

"Then what do you want?" he asked.

"Get in the goddamned truck and I'll tell you!"

Effie reluctantly walked out of the front door and looked toward my parking spot for my car.

"It doesn't fit there, I had to park it in the parking lot."

He followed behind me, but his head stayed bowed. I had to wonder what the hell he thought my proposal was going to be. The man looked like he'd been beaten down since I last saw him. I knew part of that belonged to me, but most of it belonged to his fucking asshole of a family. I'd never understand parents who could turn against their children. It never made sense to me. I just thanked the good lord, none of my cousins were gay, because there was no way in hell my Aunt Rebecca would've ever accepted them. Hell, she kicked Effie out, because he didn't bow down to her every desire and demand. I tried not to hate people, but my feelings for that woman were about as close to hate as you could get without committing to it full on.

I traipsed all the way over to the far end of the parking lot, and when I finally got to the truck, I turned to see Effie's eyes were as wide as saucers.

"This is your truck?" he asked.

I nodded and pointed for him to get in.

When he climbed up and looked around at the new vehicle, I could see the battle between admiration and envy on his face. "I need it if I'm going to be working on the ranch full-time."

"What? You're going to keep the ranch and run it by yourself?"

"No, not by myself. I have to have help. Yours, if you'll consider it."

Effie looked at me in shock. "You want me to come help you run the ranch? Like an employee?" he asked.

I shook my head. "No, I want you to help as my partner. I'm not going to give you half the land, or anything like that, but we split the profits fifty-fifty."

Effie leaned back as he buckled up, and stared out the front of the vehicle.

He was quiet as we drove the short distance to the restaurant. I could tell he was thinking over my proposal. It wasn't unusual when things were big, or involved a lot of consideration. Effie always tended to go quiet when he thought stuff out.

I pulled up in front of Cracker Barrell, the one we used to go to all the time, before we stopped talking to one another.

Once we were seated, Effie looked me in the eye, and asked, "Do you really want me to help on the ranch as an equal, or are you just feeling sorry for me? And before you answer, don't you dare lie to me, Flex. You've always been straight up with me, and I don't think I can handle it, if you of all people lie to me, even if you're trying to help."

"My God, Effie," I said, "Calm the fuck down," I whispered the last part, knowing if I cussed too loud in the Cracker Barrell, I would more likely than not be asked to leave.

"I done told you, I contacted you with the thought in mind that you could come help me. That was before I knew your mom had ostracized you, and it was before I learned your wife had cut out on you. So, unless you think I hired some private investigator, or some shit like that, you know as well I do, that I asked you to help me, 'cause you're the only other relative I have that gives a flying fuck about that place."

I didn't try to hide my upset with my cousin. I wanted him to understand, I needed him and wasn't feeling sorry for him.

I leaned back in my chair, letting my frustration flow around me. "I do feel bad for you. I won't pretend I don't, because you're as much a brother to me as my cousin. The fact your mom is behind our relationship mess pisses me off to no end. Now, knowing you've been struggling to raise what are as close to nephews as I'll ever get without their mama, well, that makes me even angrier. That said, though, I need you to know I *need* you. I don't know much about ranching. All I know is what the grandparents taught me back during those summers we spent together on the ranch. When I think back, all I remember is you, Eric, and me, having fun and playing around. I don't remember much about tending cattle, keeping cowhands in line, or repairing fences, although I know we did a hell of a lot of that when we were there."

The server showed up at that point, and I asked for my usual coffee, biscuits and gravy, with a side of scrambled eggs scattered on the biscuit, and the gravy poured over.

Effie ordered his usual as well, and the server disappeared to get our food started. Once she was gone, he looked at me and sighed.

"I want to say yes. I'd give everything to be able to raise my boys on that ranch and away from the hell my wife has put them through here in Houston. They're both still young, but nothing scares me more than the two of them becoming teenagers in a town, where their mom is shacked up with one of the city's most notorious drug dealers."

The server interrupted him by bringing us both a cup of coffee. When she was gone, he continued, "I always wanted to stay on the ranch. I tried to talk my mom into just letting me move in with our grandparents, but she wouldn't hear of it. *'No son of mine is going to become a redneck hillbilly stuck in some backwoods desert, worthless piece of garbage property',*" he mimicked her voice. It would've been comical if there wasn't so much bitterness in his tone as he said it.

"Then, after all that, she goes to war with you to take it from you, and you and I both know why, right? She wants the money, she's always wanted to be *Alexis* from *Dynasty*. In her mind, she was always meant to be, and it was a cruel twist of fate that kept her from it. God, that woman disgusts me, and you know what? That makes my stomach turn too, 'cause a man isn't supposed to feel that way about his mother."

I sat back and crossed my arms, this time not trying to lower my voice. "Damn, cousin, bitter much?" I said.

Effie looked up, shocked, squinting his eyes at me. "The fuck you talking, Flex. You're just as bitter as me."

"That cinches it," I said. "Unless you have some reason against it, you're moving down to the ranch with me. We're gonna bring that place back to what it's supposed to be, and your wife won't have access to the boys there. It's too far away, and I don't see her as being someone to travel out to the middle of nowhere, even if she does come to her senses."

Effie continued to stare at me, until the server brought our food, not committing to or declining my offer.

We both dug into our breakfasts, and the subject changed to what Eric was up to and how my visit went. I even told him about Mitch, which I was fairly surprised at myself for sharing. I'd held onto that information like a kid with coveted candy. So far, I'd only talked to Eric about him, but something about being with Effie again felt right, felt like I had my friend back. No, to be honest, it felt like I had my brother back.

I paid the check, and when we got into the truck, Effie asked, "So, when do you plan to move back?"

"I've already given notice on my apartment, sold my car, and bought this truck. I quit my job yesterday too, so as soon as I get packed, I guess."

"Where would I live?" he asked.

I shrugged. "I haven't worked all that out yet. Jimmy and Emma Jean have taken over the house, and I don't want to kick them out, but they only use the first floor. I'm thinking, we could get one of those modular houses delivered and put up on the old foundation where the workers' housing used to be. I looked while I was up there, and it appears the old hookups for the campers are still there too, so we could probably put an RV or two out if that was needed."

"Sounds like a lot of work, and it's not really ready for habitation yet. I have two little boys, Flex, I can't go down there and put them on the ground."

"I don't expect you to," I countered. "I just need to know if you're interested. We can work out the details afterward."

Effie fell silent again as we drove back toward my apartment. When I pulled into the parking lot, Effie said, "Yeah. I'm interested, but you need to have that attorney of yours write up an agreement saying we are partners. I don't want you to be my boss and able to fire me just 'cause you get mad at me."

I was just about to argue with him, when he put his hand up. "I'm sorry, cuz, but I've been screwed by everyone in my immediate family, first my dad, then my mom and brothers. It isn't that I don't trust you, but I have my boys to think about, I can't just take your word for it."

He climbed out of the truck then turned to look at me. "That's my counteroffer, Flex. Take it, or leave it."

I smiled at him. "I'm more than happy to take it." Then, I pulled my badger of a cousin into a bear hug. "God, we're really gonna do this!"

Effie smiled back at me. "Looks like it!"

8

Mitch

THE DAY FLEX LEFT was one of the worst I'd had since owning the motel. I was late opening the office, having decided to take my time to see Flex off. I didn't usually mind, because my number was on the front door, and if I had any customers show up, they could just ring me.

When I finally got the door open, the widow crew were there to meet me—all seven of them. Luckily, Mrs. Stanfield wasn't with them.

"Apparently, you are tossing poor old women like Mrs. Stanfield to the dogs, because you don't stand for her religious beliefs." This came from Mrs. Templeton, another troublemaker my grandfather told me to watch out for.

"I'm sorry ladies, as I discussed with you before, I can't share personal information about any of the people who stay on the premises."

I wasn't going to argue religion or politics with anyone, and certainly not this lot.

"Well, we're here to give you an ultimatum. Either you allow Mrs. Stanfield to come back and respect her religious beliefs like a real American, or we're all leaving."

I put my pen down and looked at the women who stood before me. I thought through my words as I looked them over. I knew I had to be careful, unless I wanted to add fuel to the fire.

"I've spoken my final word on this matter. I will not discuss any decisions I've made, or plan to make in the future, about anyone who has stayed, or may stay on this property. We, however, reserve the right to deny services to anyone, and that is clearly stated on the entry to the business, as well as on our website, and any other public document we have displayed.

If, for any reason, you are unhappy with our services, you are welcome to leave." I stood up at this point, and added, "And just so we are crystal clear. This business is compliant with a nondiscrimination policy, and if anyone chooses to go against that policy or to harass, or cause harm to anyone based upon someone's color, race, religious beliefs, sex, *or* sexual orientation, those people will be asked to leave, and will be banned from the property forthwith. Is all that clear, ladies?"

I didn't think the women expected me to lay the law down quite so clearly. Mrs. Templeton harrumphed and stomped out the door, the other women following closely behind her. Mrs.

Ruth waited until the women were all out the door, before she turned to me and winked, causing me to smile.

Later in the day, I noticed six campers pull out of my parking lot and into the Events Campground. Not an hour later, I got a visit from Mr. Banks, our town's local attorney, who said I was being served for religious discrimination, and he said I probably needed to find an attorney to represent me.

"Thank you, Mr. Banks," I replied. "Are you representing them?" I asked.

The man was hesitant for a moment. "Yes, sir, I will be their attorney."

"That's what I needed to know," I replied, and walked away from him.

I looked through my grandpa's book, and found the number for an attorney he kept on retainer for this kind of thing. People, especially in the nineties, threatened to sue all the time, and my grandpa finally just hired an attorney to manage the suits.

The attorney my grandpa used was probably long gone and possibly dead, since he seemed to me to be old as dirt when I was still a kid. When I told the secretary who I was, she sent me to a woman attorney who had the old man's last name. I asked her if Mr. Franklyn was still practicing, and she chuckled. "No, my father is no longer able to practice, but I've taken on most of his cases. How can I help you, Mr. Armstrong?"

I broke down the events that started with Mrs. Stanfield and ended this morning with at least six of the seven remaining women leaving the campground. I told her about the visit from the local attorney, Mr. Banks. "I think he was trying to scare me into accepting Mrs. Stanfield back, but I'd rather close the place down than do that," I told her.

"No doubt," the woman said. "So, can you send me a written statement with all this clearly stated, so I have something to go by?" she asked.

"Is your fax number the same?" I asked her, and when she confirmed it, I walked over to my desk, printed the documentation I'd made after speaking to Mr. Banks and then faxed the paperwork to her.

"You should be getting it any second," I said.

"Oh, wow, okay. I didn't expect you to be that... okay, I can hear the fax machine now, hold on," she said, and put me on hold.

When she came back to the phone, she said, "Well, this is pretty thorough. Is this exactly what you said to them?" she asked.

"It is. I was trained by my grandpa to make sure I didn't ever say anything that could be used against the motel in a lawsuit."

"Do you have a nondiscrimination policy on your website?" she asked.

"Yes, ma'am. It's under the tab, 'Nondiscrimination Policy'."

I heard her type on her computer and then the clicks as I assumed she was scanning the website.

"Oh, that's good. You included sexual orientation in the policy."

"Yes, I included that when I took over the motel from my grandfather."

"Are you gay, Mr. Armstrong?" she asked.

"Is that going to come up?" I asked her.

"Definitely," she replied.

"Yes, I am, and I'm out with anyone who asks."

"Good, then they can't pretend you aren't being honest. Let me give Mr. Banks a call. I'll let him know I'm on the case, and if he could send the paperwork to me, it'll help me as I'm preparing for your case. Most of the time, these issues go away pretty quick when these country attorneys find out how much work is going to be involved. Also, even in Texas, it's unlikely they'd win this case, since you have been thorough on your policy of nondiscrimination. One more thing, do you have any witnesses that heard what you said, and will be honest?"

I thought back to Mrs. Ruth, and remembered that only six campers had left. "I think it's possible, but I'll need to go visit one of the tenants who is still here to be sure."

"Perfect, and let me know. Also, Mr. Armstrong, you need to talk to your potential witness sooner than later, I'd like to get a statement from her before things go too far."

"Thanks, Miss..." I hesitated, realizing I hadn't gotten the attorney's first name. "I'm sorry I didn't get your full name."

"Oh, dear," the woman said. "I'm Lisa Franklyn, *lesbian* daughter of your original attorney, Kip Franklyn."

I chuckled when she dropped the lesbian bomb. "Well, this just got more interesting," I said, and she laughed.

"Let me go talk to my resident if she's still here, and see what I can find out."

I hung up and closed the office door, then slipped out the back toward the RV park. Sure enough, Mrs. Ruth's trailer was still hooked up in the little shaded area that everyone who came to the park coveted.

I knocked on Mrs. Ruth's door, and she came out. "Well, hello, Mitch," she said. "I figured you'd come see me today."

"Hi, Mrs. Ruth," I replied, grinning. "So, I wanted to find out if you were part of the whole rigamarole going on."

"I most certainly am not," she said. "You were right to kick that old bat out, and the rest of them got what they deserved too."

"Is that so?" I asked her, not wanting to give too much away in case she was here to trap me.

"Yes, son, not all us old ladies are bigots, you know. My dear son, Christopher, came out way back in the eighties, and has been married to the same sweet man all these years. I don't see him as much as I'd like, since he lives in Boston, and I live here on account of my rheumatism, but I'd go to war with anyone who dared threaten him or my sweet son-in-law."

I smiled. "I just heard from Mr. Banks, the attorney in town, that the ladies are gonna file a lawsuit against me."

Mrs. Ruth narrowed her eyes. "Those bitches wouldn't dare!" she said.

"Apparently, they would."

"Well, I never," the spitfire said.

"Anyway, I contacted my attorney after speaking with Mr. Banks, and she asked if I had anyone who could tell the truth on my side of the discussion."

"Don't say another word. I'm here for you, whatever you need."

"Thanks, Mrs. Ruth," I said, and turned to leave.

I turned back around, and said, "I'm sorry you are losing your friends over this. It just seems so senseless."

"I ain't lost nothing," she said. "Those old biddies were mean as snakes. Hell, most of the time, I felt like I was back in high school having to dodge the mean girls all over again. Them moving over to the nasty Events will end up being a blessing for me! Now, go on, I need to get back to my stories, and you can give my number to that attorney of yours, I'm sure she'll want to get my official statement."

I chuckled as the older woman all but closed the door in my face. She was a card. I guessed, despite the nuisance, in the end, I'd separated the wheat from the chaff.

****

As with any small town, word was out as soon as I was served with the paperwork. I hated that this would divide the little town, but I knew people would take sides. Hell, this was gonna be as much a sporting event as the high school football game.

Over the next week, I had people come by my office just to tell me they supported me, while at the same time, I had kids throwing shit at my sign, and by shit, I literally mean shit.

Unfortunately for the perps, my neighbor was on the friendly side, and turned in a couple of high school students named Lance and Kenny. They ended up being forced by the sheriff to clean, not only the area they hit with the crap, but my entire entry road frontage and fence. After that, there were no more things thrown at my property.

But, that didn't stop the name-calling. I went to the grocery store, and the pastor of the local Baptist Church stood across the street and called me a faggot. I noted he was a total coward, clearly not brave enough to face me on the same side of the street. I almost called him that, but decided to take the route most appropriate for the situation.

"Pastor, you better get your Bible out and turn to Matthew 5 and 22. Whoever insults his brother will be liable to the council; and whoever says, 'You fool!' will be liable to the fire of hell."

The self-righteous ass stuck his nose in the air, and yelled, "You aren't a brother of mine."

I laughed. "For a preacher, you don't know much about scripture, do you?" I asked, then walked into the store. I heard cheering, but I didn't stick around to see who'd chosen my side.

When I came out of the store, the pastor was gone, and only a few people were around. Old Jim Hurst slapped me on the back, and said, "You told him what for." Then, laughing, he walked away.

The pastor had never been that popular. He moved here from somewhere up north and spent most of his time condemning anyone who stepped outside his views of Christianity, which, in most people's opinion, looked more like the Devil's than Christ's.

After the first week, things died down and returned almost to normal. Most insults came from sneers, or things said under people's breath, and to my surprise, none of the businesses in town had turned me away. I figured that would have been the first thing, which, to be honest, if they had, that would have probably done the most to break me. Places to shop were few and far between. As it was, I had the diner and the pizza place for eating out when I just didn't have it in me to cook something, or eat warmed-up frozen dinners from the grocery store. Most of the other businesses were designed to attract tourists who ventured through our little town on the way to the national park.

I managed to text Flex a few times, but I didn't really share my drama with him.

I texted him the night after the lawsuit was started against me...

Hey

Hey yourself

You busy?

Not much... you?

Sorta... wish you were here.

That was what we both said in most of our texts.

Same here...

The conversation snagged at that point like it usually did. I realized just how precarious things were for him deciding to take on his grandparents' ranch. I was afraid if I told him how insane things had gotten here, especially considering he was involved, that it'd make him change his mind. I had no doubt this would blow over, just like most things did in our little town, but I needed to stand up to the bullies, which meant things were gonna be hot for at least a little while.

We had our first court date a couple weeks later. My attorney, Lisa, laughed, saying it was strange for a case to come up so fast, but because we were in a county of less than ten thousand people, things moved quickly.

I didn't know the judge very well. Our county seat was Alpine, and I hardly went there, unless I was picking up supplies for the motel, and when I did that, I was in and out, since I never had anyone to replace me at the desk.

The judge called the courtroom to order, and asked Mr. Banks to address the court first regarding my attorney's motion to dismiss, which she had told me was a long shot, since Texas was known for wanting to protect religious liberties over individual rights.

Mr. Banks went on and on, basically preaching a sermon about how evil homosexuality was, and how children were at risk of being molested by the deviants, basically, reiterating every stereotype about the LGBTQ community we'd all heard before.

Finally, after a long-winded and frankly ridiculous bunch of crap, he pointed to me, and said, "This man forced these women to leave their home, without notification, without warning, because they dared to question him and his disgusting lifestyle."

With that, the old man plastered a smug look on his face as he sat down. Lisa looked at me, and making it look to the judge like she was talking to me, she crossed her eyes and made a face. I had to work hard not to laugh.

She stood up, stuck her hands in her pockets, and said, "What a load of crap!"

The room erupted with laughter. I noticed the judge, although he was slamming the gavel to regain order, had a smile on his face before he was able to hide it as well.

"Mrs. Franklyn, we may not be a big fancy courtroom, like you are used to, but you'll remain respectful nonetheless."

"Well, of course, I will, your honor," she said. "Yet, as a native Texan, it is my duty to call garbage what it is. This man has come into this courtroom and preached a sermon, like the people of this fine county can't worship and believe as *they* see fit. Even if we ignore the free-exercise clause, which says the state shall not accept one religion over another, you have a passel of women who want this court to say that my client, as a business owner, must allow his customers to harass his other customers, because they don't approve of them. Or, in this case, worse, they, his customers, don't approve of them. Can you imagine what kind of chaos would ensue if a business no longer had the right to keep people safe from harassment?"

She went on to talk a lot about how Texas fiercely protected the rights of businesses, and that this was a direct violation of my rights as a business owner.

Her speech was clearly landing on fertile ground, because a few times, I saw the judge nod as she spoke.

"The plaintiffs argue that they were forced off the property by Mr. Armstrong, when in fact, only one of them was asked to leave, and that was after she hit one of the other plaintiffs in the nose, and after she lied about a customer to the motel for the purpose of getting him kicked out, because she believed him to be gay. Also, we have an eyewitness statement that says Mr. Armstrong didn't force the other plaintiffs to leave. Rather, he said they might leave if they weren't okay with his nondiscrimination policy."

After looking around the courtroom, Lisa continued. "Your honor, this isn't about religious freedom, or any other protected rights, it's about these people's..." She pointed to each of them as they sat behind Mr. Banks, "...ability to force Mr. Armstrong to do as *they* see fit, to force him to abide by their belief, which may or may not be religious in nature. Most likely, this case isn't about religion, it's about control and bullying a business owner into cowing to their demands."

She went on and on about rights and evidence, then when she was done, she took a long, deliberate breath before she finished.

"We ask the court to dismiss this case based on frivolous allegations on the part of plaintiff, Mrs. Stanfield, and in regard to the other plaintiffs, they left on their own accord, without being forced, or harassed by Mr. Armstrong, so their damages are negated. Thank you, your honor." My attorney sat down next to me then, back straight, and not taking her eye off the judge.

"Mr. Banks, rebuttal?" the judge asked.

"Yes, your honor. Clearly, this woman..." The old man pointed at Lisa, and snarled, "...is a degenerate herself. She would ask this court to rule that homosexuality is a right, that these nasty child molesters can come into our communities and destroy our morals, and valued..."

"Thank you, Mr. Banks, that'll be quite enough," the judge said.

"But, your honor, I'm not done."

"Yes, you are. You will not turn my courtroom into a mockery, sir. I'll give you one more chance and that's it. Do you have any evidence to counter Mrs. Franklyn's statement?"

The man puffed and knocked around the papers on his desk, clearly trying to figure out what he was going to say.

When he didn't respond, the judge said, "I'll take that as a no." After a brief pause, the judge looked at both attorneys. "I'm ready to make my judgment. Regarding the charge against Mr. Armstrong and the Alamito Motel for discriminating against Mrs. Alia Stanfield by asking her to leave following her aggression plus attempt to get a customer removed because she *thought* he was gay, I find the case frivolous, and therefore, I dismiss it. Regarding the case against Mr. Armstrong, for Plaintiffs, not asked to leave, but who chose to leave on their own accord, I see no recourse for damages. Therefore, I dismiss this case as well for failure to make a claim. Court dismissed." The judge stood up and left.

The room descended into chaos. Several of the women were crying, and Mrs. Stanfield was livid, but this time at Mr. Banks. "That was the worse mess of a court case I've ever seen. Where did you get your law degree, kindergarten?" I heard her say.

She huffed off and left the room, with most of the women trailing behind her.

Two or three hung back, and I knew they were going to ask me to let them move back over to the motel, but I'd be damned if I'd allow it, after all the homophobic mess they'd dragged me through. No, they could stay at the Events, along with the meth addicts and potheads for all I cared.

I put Lisa between myself and them as I walked out the back door of the courtroom, knowing they'd never confront me when she was nearby.

When we had made it outside the courtroom, I asked Lisa, "So, how the hell do I deal with these women now? You know they'll all want to come back now they've lost. If I say no, that'll prompt more ill will than the damned court case did."

"Not a problem, send them to me, and I'll tell them no. That way, it's that evil female attorney, not the sweet little cutie pie that runs the local motel, who denied them."

I gave her my evil look, but it was poorly executed, considering I was fighting myself not to laugh.

"I like you, Lisa Franklyn. Come on, I'll buy you lunch, and you can tell me all about your degenerate lifestyle."

Lisa laughed and put her arm through mine, and we walked a block from the courthouse to a restaurant. The fact that we passed the women who'd sued me and lost was the icing on this delicious cake.

9

Flex

THINGS HAD BEGUN SPINNING after my meeting with my cousin. Luckily, we fell into our old routines from before the Aunt Rebecca mess had hit. We'd both come to the conclusion that she was the problem, that both of us did what we had to do, and that Effie and his boys were the real victims in all of this.

My landlord took my apartment over a full month early, allowing me to focus on moving. We weren't quite ready to head west, though, so I moved into my cousin's extra bedroom. My god, I didn't have a clue how loud two preteen boys could be. I'd called myself Uncle Flex to them when they were very little, and the moment the oldest one, Drake, saw me, he hugged me, and asked, "Where've you been, Uncle Flex? I've missed you."

I hugged the nine-year-old back. "I've been stupid and let my anger keep me away, but now I've told your daddy I'm sorry, so we're friends again."

This seemed to satisfy both boys, although the youngest eyed me warily, like I was some monster who could pounce at any moment. He was just two when I'd pulled away from the family. "He'll get used to you," Effie promised. "Little Luke is not as trusting as his brother, but I warn you, when he warms up to you, he'll talk your ear off."

It took about three weeks before Luke would come near me on his own. As promised, however, once he did, he was on me like a flea on a dog.

I missed Mitch. We texted quite often the first week, then our texts slowly dissipated. I could tell something was going on with him, but my own life was so chaotic, I didn't have a clue how to process it all, and him as well.

By the end of the month, we weren't texting each other at all. I figured that was probably best, considering how much work lay ahead of Effie and me.

My mom caught wind that I'd moved in with Effie, and we both knew that meant shit was about to hit the fan.

Mom and Aunt Rebecca hadn't spoken in years, but they had a very thorough network of spies that kept the other informed, which, of course, all revolved around the beauty parlor.

Southern men knew the power of a ladies' beauty parlor, and the smart ones feared it. One particular governor of a neighboring state recently learned the hard way when his wife divorced him. She turned in a very damaging report regarding a salacious affair between himself and a senior advisor, as well as several allegations of campaign finance and state ethics violations, which she'd learned about through the vast network of women who'd come to her beauty parlor.

As predicted, Rebecca showed up on a Saturday about a week later, and demanded that I move out immediately. I just walked away, taking the boys with me, promising to show them a caterpillar I'd found in the back yard that I thought was about to become a butterfly. I wondered why neither of them seemed upset by their crazy grandmother showing up screaming outside their home, then I remembered the kids hadn't really seen her in years. Even Drake all but ignored the woman. What's more, I didn't notice Rebecca being too overjoyed to see them either.

We could hear the two arguing in the house, and I asked the boys if they saw their grandmother much.

"No, she doesn't like us. She told our daddy to keep us away," Drake said.

"But, you like us, don't you, Uncle Flex?" That came from Luke.

"I love you boys with all my heart and all my soul," I said, just like my grandparents used to say to me. "You know who used to say that to me?" I asked. Both boys shook their heads, no. "Your great-grandmother and great-grandfather. They'd have loved you two so much. I wish you could've known them."

"I met great-grand…" I could tell Drake was trying to figure out what to call him. "Great-grandpa," he finally remembered. "But, I don't remember much about him."

I looked at Luke and smiled. "He looked a lot like your little brother—blond hair, and a sharp chin like he could poke you with it if you weren't acting right."

Luke loved that and began chasing Drake around, trying to poke him with his chin. I was laughing so hard when Effie came out, I was wiping tears off my cheeks.

Effie stood looking at the three of us, and I could tell he was about to go back into the house, when Drake ran over to him and grabbed him into a hug. Luke came up right after that and hugged his dad's legs.

"Was she mean to you again?" Drake asked.

"She was fine, and I saw you two out here, making your uncle laugh like a silly person."

Neither boy let go. I realized then that these two had experienced way too much sadness in way too little time. I prayed that they would find the open desert as freeing as their dad and I had when we were their ages.

Effie sent the kids into the house to get ready for dinner, and he and I sat on the swings he'd built for the boys.

"So, how'd that go?" I asked.

"You know how that went. She demanded that I send you away, and then reminded me she had cosigned on the note with me."

"Shit, she did?" I asked.

"Yeah, it was when Theresa and I were first married. She insisted that we shouldn't live in a rental like vagabonds. At the time, I still trusted her, at least marginally."

"What can she do?" I asked. "Are you up to date on your mortgage?"

"Oh yeah, I don't know what she can do, but I'm stuck with her as long as I own the house."

I looked at him. "Why don't you sell it then? If you hate the ranch and decide to move back, you can buy one without her."

Effie sighed. "It's where the kids have always lived. They've lost their grandmother, uncles, and their mother. It seems this is the only constant thing left in their lives."

I patted my cousin's shoulder. "It's up to you, but if she's holding something over you, it might be better for you and the boys to make a clean break, once and for all."

Effie shrugged and stood up. "It'll all work out in the end. For now, let's take the boys out for pizza. I'm not really in the mood to cook." He got up from his swing and turned around. "Rich uncle's treat!" And walked into the house.

I laughed. I hated to tell him, but this Daddy Warbucks wasn't rich. One year on a ranch that wasn't making money and all the slush fund would be well on its way to being gone. Hell, five years fighting my aunt had all but exhausted my financial inheritance.

I had the cattle seed money, but it wouldn't last long either if we didn't get some revenue coming in.

I followed Effie into the house. "Should I move? I can stay with my mother until we head to the ranch."

"No, there's no need. Mom won't be coming back anytime soon. She had her say. Now that she didn't get her way, she'll try to create chaos with the mortgage, but like you said, it's doubtful she'll get very far. The mortgage is what it is, she's stuck until I sell or pay it off."

"Well, let me know if you change your mind. My mother would like nothing less than to torture me for a few weeks."

Effie laughed, but only because he understood.

After we'd eaten and returned to the house, I decided to turn in early. I was tired of all the changes, and mentally exhausted from the daily review of finances, and business idea sessions with my cousin.

As soon as we had the contract signed, Effie became like a dog with a bone, looking for ways to make the ranch work. So far, cattle had some potential, but minimal. Mostly, the cost of hiring the hands and managing the rest was so high, cattle barely made enough money to make it work.

We both finally agreed, the only real way to pull this off was to keep the herd small and process our own meat. Effie had a friend who was a butcher, who was always looking for specialty meats for the yuppy class in Houston. If we could sell beef that was raised in West Texas, in the open desert, it might fetch a better price.

We were assured by the butcher that there did seem to be a bit of a different flavor to the lean cattle from that part of the world. As long as people liked it, maybe we could go in that direction.

I'd begun talking to Effie about agritourism, but the fact was unless we were selling to tourists who came to Big Bend, we were not going to attract that many people our way. Big Bend National Park was a short-term fix, since most of its visitors came in the winter months.

We could open the RV park, which might work, but doing the numbers showed we'd need to have an average of twenty people staying on-site, or we'd have to put up a lodge or something. If we could keep our costs down, we could see enough in that area to keep us solvent, but not particularly profitable. When you considered how hot the summers were, it was highly unlikely we'd be able to keep the numbers that high.

We considered goats, which, truth be told, could be our best option considering the birth rate compared to cattle, and the fact the Mexican market is pretty good for goats, but then we looked at tariff rates between here and Mexico, and were quickly dissuaded.

We looked at hunting, especially the invasive species, and although it was also a good option, when we talked to Jimmy, he said there were several landowners who'd tried that and regretted it almost immediately. "Those guys don't seem to give a shit about anyone but themselves, and even with game wardens around, they'll shoot up any damn thing that walks in front of them."

Basically, we were out of options. I laid my head down on the pillow and wasn't able to fall asleep. Thoughts of going under seemed to pound back and forth in my mind.

Around two in the morning, I was about to get up to go to the bathroom, when I got a phone call. I picked the phone up, confused who'd be calling me this early. I saw it was the ranch phone.

"Hello!" I answered.

"Hello." Emma Jean was crying. "Oh, Fletcher, someone has burned the barn down, they tried to burn the house too, but the dogs musta scared them away."

Memories of the dream with the snake who slithered through the building, trying to burn them down, came to my mind instantly.

"Mrs. Emma Jean, is the sheriff there?"

"Yeah, he came right away, do you want to talk to him?"

"I do, thank you, Mrs. Emma Jean."

"Hello, this is Sheriff Walters."

"Sheriff, this is Fletcher Henry, I'm Cliff and Ester Madison's grandson. I own the property now. Can you tell me what happened?"

"Well, son, we aren't quite sure," he said. "By the looks of it, someone deliberately set fire to your barn. There's some evidence they also tried to burn the house down, but luckily, the dogs here musta scared them off."

It was frustrating. Emma Jean had given me that much information, but I needed to know who.

"Do you have a clue who it was?"

"No, sir. Jimmy here has a video, but it was too dark to tell. It appears he was male about six feet tall, but that's about all we could tell."

Shit, I thought to myself.

"Can you tell Mrs. Emma Jean and Jimmy I'll be down tomorrow? I need to get some more sleep before I tackle the drive, but I'll be there as soon as I can."

"I'll tell 'em. When you get here, can you plan to stop by the office? We need to get some information from you, so we can get the report filed."

"Thank you, yes, sir. I'll stop by probably the next day if that's okay."

"That'll do just fine," he said, and hung up.

I didn't know what I was thinking, I'm not going to sleep now anyway, might as well get up and go.

I crawled the rest of the way out of bed, and found Effie standing at my door, hand up like he was about to knock.

"I heard the phone ring. Is everything okay?"

"Not really. Someone burned down the old barn at the ranch, and apparently, tried to burn the house down too."

"Fuck me," he said. "You gonna head out now?"

"I ain't gonna sleep, so I might as well," I replied.

"Hey, I don't like the idea of you out on the road this late at night, on such a small amount of sleep. Why don't you wait until morning, and me and the boys will come with you? I know they'll keep you awake."

"Where will everyone sleep?" I asked.

"Not sure. Can we stay with Emma Jean and Jimmy?"

"There's the bedroom we used to sleep in upstairs, but no, besides the master bedroom, there isn't a place for all of us."

"Let's think about it overnight. I'll need to talk to the kids' school before we go, and get any of their homework they'll need while we're away, but I can have us ready to go by nine."

"Sounds like a plan, and Effie?"

He turned to look at me. "Thanks for going with me, I... well... I need to have someone with me on this one."

He smiled back. "We're partners, Flex. That's what partners do!"

I smiled too, although the stress of the situation almost made my head hurt in the process.

I turned back to my bedroom and began packing up for the next day. I figured, if I were gonna drive all that way, I might as well pack up the pickup with as much of my stuff as I could. Besides, Effie's little house didn't seem to have enough room for all my boxes anyway. It was something I should've already done.

****

The drive out was as pleasant as a seven-hour drive with two young kids could be. I'd swear Luke needed to pee more than an old man. I suspected after the sixth stop, he was just messing with me, though. I thought about ignoring him, but Effie warned me if I didn't want a permanent stain on my back seat, I'd best stop when he said he had to.

It was after five in the evening when we got to the house, and Emma Jean met us as we drove up. "Jimmy's out back, trying to make his way around all the burned mess." She shook her head like we'd lost a million dollars.

When the kids crawled out of the back-seat, she exclaimed, "Oh my goodness, look at these little monsters. I bet you're both hungry as an ol' grizzly who's been hibernating all winter." Drake smiled, and Luke looked at the woman in the weary way he tended to when confronted with a stranger.

"You boys go on out there and join Jimmy, and I'll get these two settled. I'll have dinner ready in about thirty minutes."

I smiled as she made her way with the boys into the house. "She's a natural at that, you know."

"She sure kept us in line when we were that age," Effie said, a sad look crossing his face.

"What's up?" I asked.

"Oh, nothing, just think it's a shame my kids don't know this place better'n they do."

"Well, they will now, right?"

Effie looked at me, but I could tell something else was bothering him.

I shook my head. "Come on, let's go see about the barn. I figure you'll spit out what's really got you tore up when you're ready."

Effie looked at me and shrugged. "Ain't no use complaining about what can't be fixed."

I figured he was thinking about Theresa, so I just let it be and walked out toward where the barn once stood.

The first sight of the barn sent my heart into my stomach. It was exactly like I'd seen in the dream. It looked like the sides of the barn had blown apart. Burnt lumber was scattered across the lawn almost all the way up to the house.

Jimmy was pawing around in the rubble, apparently trying to salvage stuff, but I could tell there was little left to salvage.

"Hey, Jimmy," I yelled, hoping to get the older man to leave stuff where it lay.

He looked up and smiled, but it didn't quite make it to his eyes.

"Hey boys, it's good to see you here together again."

"Jimmy, whatcha doin'?" I asked.

"Trying to see what, if anything's, salvageable," he replied.

"It ain't," I said. "I can tell everything's ruined, and if you don't get out of there, you're gonna be in a mess too."

"Now you listen here, I may be old, but I still know how ta get around without some kid telling me what to do."

"True enough, Jimmy, but you're too valuable to us alive, so you can't blame a man for protecting his assets."

"Smooth talker," he said, but he did crawl out of the damned ashes at least.

"Any new leads on who did this?" Effie asked.

"None since the sheriff left. They think it could be a prank, or maybe a tourist come through on the way to the park, nobody really knows."

"Well, we're here now, so we'll do our own snooping around. Emma Jean said she'd have dinner ready in a minute. You wanna go on up so you can get ready? You know she ain't gonna let you sit at the table covered in soot."

Jimmy laughed. "No, she'll make me sit outside on the porch 'til I strip and get a shower. Used to be able to do that up at the workers' cabins, but those are burned down same as the barn."

"Yeah, that's different, they were struck by lightning."

"True, but your grandpa dreamed it just like you did this barn. We needed to be more prepared after you had your premonition. Ain't no use havin' them if we ain't gonna listen," he said.

Effie looked at me strangely. "You dreamed about the fire?"

"Yeah, sort of. It was more of a nightmare, but I remembered Granny telling us if we ever had a vivid dream, it could be a premonition, so I called and told Jimmy and Emma Jean."

Effie looked at me strangely, then we turned back toward the house.

Jimmy went through the back, I was assuming it was so he could strip without an audience, or more likely, so Emma Jean didn't come after him with a broom.

Effie and I sat on the front porch while we waited. "You know the legend about that, um... skill, right?" he said.

"Yeah, sort of, but I barely remember it."

"Granny told us if you ever had a premonition about the ranch to tell her, 'cause our great-great... well, way back there, grandmother put a spell on the place. Whoever is supposed to keep the place safe, its true master will know when it's in danger."

"Oh, Effie, that's a bunch of nonsense, they told us that to keep us quiet."

"You must have believed it, 'cause you called Jimmy and Emma Jean."

"I'd just been woken up by a bad dream, and I regretted calling as soon as I did."

"Except, you dreamed what was gonna happen. Right?"

"I dreamed a stupid snake was slithering around burning down the buildings. If you'd have been facing all that I was, you'd have been having nightmares just like me."

"Except that I didn't. You did."

I looked at him for a long moment. "What's going on, Effie?" I asked.

"What's going on is you were just given proof that you are the heir to the property, and you have the same gift our ancestors passed down to keep the place safe."

I stood up to go. This was getting too weird.

"Have you had any other dreams?" he asked.

"Effie, I'm done with this crap. It was only a dream."

"So, that's a yes then."

I walked away from him and into the kitchen. The boys were just finishing their meal, and Emma Jean sent them out to the front yard. "Now, you boys listen here. There are snakes everywhere. You can play on the porch and along the driveway, but until we do a good cleaning of the yard, it ain't safe for you to be wanderin' off. You promise to stay on the porch, or in the driveway?" she asked them.

Both boys nodded and took off. "If you mind me, I've got pie in the oven." Both boys stopped mid-run and turned slowly.

"What kind?" Drake asked.

The older lady smiled, a twinkle in her eye that I hadn't seen since my own childhood. "There's two different kinds, chocolate, and lemon meringue. You get to choose."

Both boy's eyes lit up like they were on fire. I had to bite my tongue, not to laugh. In two seconds, they were both out the door, and neither kid left the porch, except to play ball in the big driveway.

"I'm gonna have to find some of our old toys for them until I can get back to Houston and get more of their stuff," Effie said.

"You plannin' on staying then?" Jimmy asked.

"I asked him to," I said. "I can't do this alone, and he knows the place as well, if not better, than me."

Jimmy looked at Effie out the corner of his eye. I could feel the distrust flow between them. Effie's mom had done a number on everyone at this table, and as the new owner, it was my job to clear it up.

"Let's get this all out in the open now. Aunt Rebecca has fucked over everyone who's sitting at this table in one way or the other." I put my hand up when Emma Jean started to chastise my cussing. "Mrs. Emma Jean, if there's a time for such language, this is it."

The older woman nodded and remained quiet. "Effie can't help that he's her son, any more than I can help who and what I am. We need each other, and that means we gotta trust each other. I ain't gonna share Effie's private business, but suffice to say, Aunt Rebecca has been out of contact with him as long as we have."

I looked at Eddie before I told him the rest. "Effie, you know your mom sued me, and that's why this place is in the mess it's in. What you don't know is she made Jimmy and Mrs. Emma Jean pay rent on the place, which she didn't have permission to do from the court, and I'm sure they didn't know anything about it. Jimmy and Mrs. Emma Jean have been paying rent, keeping the place up, and spending their own savings to keep the place running in our absence. As far as I'm concerned, they've put enough of themselves into this, with little in return. They have a stake in it as much as we do."

The table remained quiet after I'd spoken.

"Jimmy, Mrs. Emma Jean. Effie and I have been racking our brains trying to figure out how to make this old ranch work again. Even before grandpa died, the cattle business was beginning to fail. Now, five years on and the fences are rotted, our barn's burned down, and we don't have any help besides ourselves. Even if cattle could bring in the money it used to, we'd have a long way to go to get back to the point we were at before grandpa sold out. We've talked to Effie's friend, a specialty butcher in Houston, who'll buy about a hundred head a year, I know that's nowhere near what we used to raise and sell, but it's a start. Also, I figure, Effie and I can fix enough of the pasture between the two of us, to get things back up and running for that number."

Jimmy looked at Emma Jean and sighed. "We've been a talkin', and we're in agreement with all you just said. It's gonna take time to get the ranch back up to the level it used to be, and like you said, it ain't likely to be worth the effort, unless you can find some more of them specialty butchers, you mentioned."

"It's something to consider, but it's one foot in front of the other for now. We need to discuss accommodation also, but dang, I'm about to pass away from hunger. Can we eat before we get into that?"

Emma Jean smiled and got up. "It's like usual, buffet style. Bring your plates over and fill up, while I go get the boys for their dessert."

"No, let them play. They're still wound up tight as a drum after being in the truck all day. They can have dessert later," Effie said.

When we all sat back down, both Effie and I dug in. "Nobody cooks like you, Mrs. Emma Jean," Effie said, his mouth still full.

"I'll still wallop your bottom if you keep talking with your mouth full, but thank you, nonetheless," she said. Despite her threat, her face glowed.

"I've missed cooking for a crowd, and oh, I do love having boys back in the house. Jimmy, don't it seem the old place has cheered up since they got here?"

Jimmy chuckled. "It sure is a lot noisier."

Just as he said that something fell over on the porch, causing the entire table to laugh. Effie started to get up, and Emma Jean waved him down. "You finish your food, I'll check on the boys." And, she was up and out the door before Effie could move.

Effie sighed. "It sure feels good to have another adult in the house besides me."

"Maybe for you. If those poor kids broke something, I feel sorry for them once Mrs. Emma Jean sees it."

Jimmy chuckled. "They can run faster 'an her these days, that's an advantage they have that you didn't when you were young. My Emma Jean was a track star in school, could outrun almost anyone, including me. Y'all thought you could outdo her, but that was a big mistake. Which of you ran off that time and got a paddling all the way back to the house?"

Effie's face turned red, giving him away. Both Jimmy and I laughed at his reaction. "You never were good at hiding your guilt," I said between guffaws.

Emma Jean never did spare the rod. "That's what you think. That woman cried every time she had to get onto you two. You both were the apples of her eye, and when you started bringing that handsome Eric around, well... there weren't much you could do wrong. Having you three boys running around made her light up like a Christmas tree."

"I always had a soft spot in my heart for a scoundrel," Emma Jean said, coming up behind Jimmy and kissing him on the head.

Jimmy chuckled. "Good thing for me!" Then, winked at us both.

"They knocked an old ironing board over that I put out for Jimmy to put in the shed. I'm deathly afraid of those rattlesnakes, that's why I didn't take it out myself. You'd think a woman that's been here most of her life wouldn't be scared of them. I've moved enough of them darn things out of the yard, but now that I'm old and slow, I'm scared to death of being struck by one."

"Seems you're wise to be wary, Mrs. Emma Jean. If they strike you, you'll be in for quite a recovery process," I said. "Speaking of that, do y'all still have antivenom stored in case we have a strike?"

"No, son, what we have is old, and it's too expensive to stock anymore. We carry a radio with us these days, and if someone is struck, we call an ambulance, just like city folks do," Jimmy said, shaking his head. "Was a time, we didn't even have ambulances."

"Lucky for you they do. I'd have buried you in the ground if they hadn't come when you had that heart attack."

Jimmy looked at Emma Jean like she'd just slapped him. She shook her head. "Fletcher is the master of the house, Jimmy, and he said we needed to get it all on the table." She turned to me, and said, "Jimmy had a heart attack three years ago in August. Doctors say he's doing better, but he has to walk every day up to the mailbox and back, and he has medication he takes. His cardiologist up in Alpine made it clear if he didn't take them, he wouldn't be around long."

"Damned quacks, it's a racket. They just use us old folks to keep their ol' pockets full of cash."

"Be that as it may, if these boys are gonna depend on you, then you better do what them quacks say."

I could see a drag-down, blow-out fight coming, so I intervened to reduce it. "Jimmy, we can't do this without you. Neither Effie nor I are prepared to run the ranch on our own—not yet. Even grandpa told me so in a letter he wrote. You do what you gotta do to stick around, okay?"

Jimmy looked over at me and sighed. "I'm fit as a fiddle. Even that ol' quack said so last time I was in. I just got carried away with all that was goin' on back then. Let other people's business get me carried away." He looked at Effie, then over at me, and back down at his plate. "I let things go nowadays. If'n I can't fix it, I don't study on it."

"Maybe you can train us all in that skill," Effie said. "I need y'all to know, my mother has made life hell for me…" He turned toward the porch, and confident the boys couldn't hear him, he continued, "Me and those boys out there. They cried on and off for a year after she kicked us out of her life. When their momma left, neither kid shed a tear, but their grandma, well, she was as much their mom as their real mom ever was. Me, well, she never really cared much for me. Said, I took after the rednecks she came from." He laughed bitterly. "Apparently, my father, at least in her eyes, was high class, and her family was trash. I represented the trash, of course."

He stood up and walked to the window. "Y'all know her differently than I do. Everyone was surprised when she sued for the ranch. I wasn't. My mom was always a snake in the grass. She'd wait on my brothers and say how smart and gifted they were, then she'd say something like, *I guess two out of three ain't bad.*' I ain't looking for sympathy, but I ain't the enemy. I assure you she hates me more than she'll ever hate y'all. Flex, she'd be over here in the length of time it'd take for her to get here if you'd call and invite her over. In her mind, it was a noble fight, she would say things like that 'bout your mother when I was little, *'She fought a noble fight, and I lost this time, but next time I won't.'* If I were to call, she'd block my number. So, I can say I'm sorry for how she treated y'all, and I really am, but don't think I had any power to stop her, or even to influence her, one way or the other."

Emma Jean got up and came over to him. "Honey, we know how your mama treated you. Your grandma lamented it when you was little, and your grandpa and she had more than one argument about it."

"Emma Jean's right about that. Your grandpa threw a dog-devil fit when he saw how she treated you. He even tried to get her to let him keep you here, but she said it would look unseemly," Jimmy said.

"Neither Jimmy nor I blame you for your momma's actions," Emma Jean said, putting her arms around him, and pulling him into a hug.

"Neither do I, Effie," I said. "I didn't know all this, and I wish I had, so I could've maintained our friendship, but now that I do, I'm here for you and those boys."

Effie smiled. "Well, at least we all have a common enemy."

None of the rest of us returned his smile. It wasn't right that someone Emma Jean and Jimmy had raised like their own would turn against them, and it sure as hell was wrong for family to go after me and him, as she'd done. I was beginning to see I came out of the good side of that relationship, though.

I shook my head as I stared at the delicious food that was beginning to go cold. "Y'all know my mom is crazy as a rabid jackrabbit, but she never treated me like that. Hell, she'd have loved it if you'd moved in with us, Effie. She thought the sun rose and set in your ass." I chuckled. "As I was growing up, she'd say things like, *'Well, if you'd work as hard as Eddie, then you'd get better grades,'* or *'If you'd work as hard as Eddie, you'd have money saved by now.'* I swear, when we were kids, she liked you more than me."

Effie chuckled. "Aunt Katherine was my favorite. She did all but raise me, since I spent every night possible over there. I only went home when my mom called and threw a hissy fit. Luckily, that wasn't very often."

I laughed. "You know, between you and Eric, we pretty much had company all the time, and she never did fuss once about it."

Emma Jean shooed Effie to the table saying she didn't work all day so her food could go cold. "Y'all finish up, and I'll check on my pies. All this carrying on, I bet I burned them."

The thought sent fear into all three of us. I couldn't imagine a day when Emma Jean burned her perfect pies. When she pulled them out, they were indeed a little brown on top, but thank goodness, they weren't burned. "Well, they ain't perfect, but you can't pile all this on an old woman and expect her to keep her mind on pies, now, can you?"

"No, Ma'am," Effie and I said in unison, then we both laughed out loud at how quickly we'd switched back to the days of Emma Jean lecturing us on causing her to lose attention. We were the cause of more than one close kitchen catastrophe, but like the pies, she always pulled it off, even though we paid the price for whatever we'd done to distract her.

As we finished our dinner and the pies rested next to the sink, the boys came back in and Emma Jean sent them both to the bathroom to get cleaned up. She sat them at the counter in the kitchen, and when each boy had a piece of pie, she came back in and sat down with us.

"So…" I said, getting everyone's attention again, "…my thought is, Effie can take our grandparent's bedroom, and the boys can stay in ours. I'll sleep out here on the couch, and tomorrow, I'll run to Marfa. I saw an ad while I was in Alpine saying someone out there had an old Airstream for sale. Jimmy, do you think the wiring and plumbing where the campers used to sit are still any good?" I asked.

Jimmy shook his head. "I doubt it, they were wired into the old bunkhouse. I figure the plumbing is still okay, though. That all runs into the same septic tank anyway."

"Well, you were a licensed plumber and electrician. Do you think with Effie's and my help we can get it all rewired?"

"Maybe, but all the wiring tools we used to have were lost in the fire. I'm afraid we're at square one on everything here."

"Um, well, maybe not," Effie said. "I got my classes done a couple years back for electrical when the dozer work was going to shit, sorry Mrs. Emma Jean… to crap, but I didn't get my license yet, because well... it cost too much at the time, but I did bring my tools with me. Maybe tomorrow when you're in Marfa, you can pick up the wiring. Jimmy and I can stay here and mess around with the area and see what's what."

"That's perfect," I said, feeling optimistic for the first time in a while. "Mrs. Emma Jean, do you and Jimmy want to stay in the house full-time? If so, Effie and I will see if we can figure out how to get him and the boys set up somewhere on the property."

"No, son, these stairs are too much for me. I'll keep the kitchen goin', but if you're gonna move anyone, it'll need to be us."

I nodded. "I'll talk to some folks tomorrow in Marfa or Alpine about the best option for us short-term. For now, I think we have a plan, at least if y'all agree."

Everyone nodded. I knew I was asking a lot of everyone there. I couldn't imagine how hard it would be for Emma Jean and Jimmy to go from silence to two boys, Effie *and* me running around and getting into everything. I'd do what I could to fix that as fast as possible, but unfortunately, if this was going to work, it had to be what it was.

1O

Mitch

S MALL TOWNS WERE ODD places. I'd never really lived in a huge city. El Paso was the closest I got, but it still seemed strange how things worked around here. I'd always kept my sexuality on the down-low, although I knew early on that everyone knew and gossiped about it.

When this whole religious discrimination thing blew up, I knew I had to stand up, or I'd lose integrity quickly. It was like watching chickens in a chicken pen. If one hen cowered, the entire flock attacked her. So, I stood up to the bullies.

As predicted, several of my attackers asked to return, and I sent them to Lisa, just as she suggested. I later heard all of them had moved away from Alamito and into a backwoods RV lot just outside of Marfa. I chuckled when I heard since Marfa had burst onto the art scene, more than a few gay folks had settled down there.

The pastor of the local church, of course, couldn't let it go, and rumors spread that he was preaching against me in particular. Of course, the town desperately wanted me to sue him for slander, always hungry for another layer of drama, but I knew better than to poke an injured rattlesnake, and ignored him instead.

In the end, his hateful preaching gained him a new convert in Mr. Banks, whose practice pretty much fell to nonexistent after my case. However, over five families left his church and joined the Episcopalians, which was the only other church in town.

I'd neglected Flex. I figured he probably didn't want to see me again, because neither one of us had texted in over a month. I felt bad about that. If this case cost me anything, it was the possibility of dating a guy I really liked.

As fate would have it, after the court case, I got multiple referrals for long-term campers from folks in town. I filled the seven spots the widows had left within a few days. Best part was, the going rate for an RV spot was almost double what my grandpa had charged them. Where the RV lots had barely been bringing in enough to cover the cost of utilities, now for the first time since I'd taken over from my grandpa, we had a good chance of making a profit.

Mrs. Ruth began hanging out at my home more often, and the two of us became quite close. "Why didn't you come by more when the other ladies were here?" I asked.

"Well, it's like I told you before, it was a lot like being back in high school, if I were to spend too much time with you, then they'd accuse me of being a suck-up, and then they'd make my life miserable. So, now that they're gone, and I've got you to myself, it doesn't matter how much I suck up!"

I laughed. "Mrs. Ruth, you are full of spit and vinegar."

"Well, best you know that up-front. Now that we're friends, you can stop calling me Mrs. I'm Ruth Ellington, and you can just call me Ruth."

I smiled. "I'll do that. Want more tea?" I asked, and she handed her glass over.

Almost every night, Ruth would come by to watch the sunset with me, except for Thursday nights. That was when her favorite program, as she called it, was on. I'd never become a fan of reality TV, and truth be known, I seldom watched TV anyway. I did miss gaming, but since I'd taken over the motel, I'd even stopped doing that. No matter how much I like my new friend Ruth Ellington, I doubted she'd ever be a good opponent at those kinds of games.

Ruth headed back to her camper after the sun was mostly down. "You really should start taking photos of those," she said. "They're the prettiest sunsets I've ever seen."

"I'm no photographer," I confessed. "I reckon I'll just have to sit here and enjoy them in real life."

She laughed. "You reckon, huh?"

Ruth was from the Northeast, and although it was rare, she would occasionally tease me for my southern sayings.

I cleaned up after she left and decided I'd just go to bed early. I lay staring at the ceiling. I couldn't help but think of Flex. Was he back at the ranch yet? I'd let life get between us, and I shouldered the blame for letting things drop. Yeah, he could've texted too, it took two to tango, but still. I knew how much I liked him, and if I'd just kept up with things, I could've possibly had a chance.

I rolled over, willing myself to put him out of my mind. It took what felt like hours, but I finally drifted off sometime in the wee hours of the morning.

My wake-up call came way too early. One of the guests rang me around five in the morning.

"There's a pipe that just burst in the bathroom and water is spewing everywhere," the woman all but screamed into the phone.

I threw on some clothes and rushed over to the room. Sure enough, it appeared someone had leaned too heavily on one of the handles in the shower. I ran behind the room and shut off the water, then threw the towels onto the floor to soak it up. Luckily the rooms were all built of concrete, so there'd be no permanent damage.

"I'm afraid you and your husband will have to pack up and move to one of the adjoining rooms," I told them. I knew they were the reason the plumbing had broken, but I figured they were in the throes of passion when they did it, and right now, I would love to have had some of that in my life. I wasn't doing anything to discourage lovemaking in anyone's life, if I could help it.

By the time I got back to the office, I was both frustrated and tired. I had a full house this weekend, though, so no rest for the wicked. I went over to Ruth's trailer and knocked on her door. When she came out, she was still wearing her nightgown, and had rollers in her hair.

"Wow, you're a sight in the mornings," I said, laughing.

"Hey, don't pick on me, this is what it takes to stay beautiful."

"I have a request. I need to run into Alpine to pick up supplies to fix a plumbing issue. Could I persuade you to take a shift in my office? It isn't too hard. I just need someone to meet guests when they come in, and to make sure Lucia gets the rooms clean before you let guests in."

Ruth thought for a moment. "Are you offering me a job, young man?" she asked.

"Well, a temporary one, at least."

"Then I accept. I'll be down there in about thirty minutes, and you can show me the ropes."

I sighed in relief. I had three guests expected to show up late morning, and Lucia, my housekeeper, although good at what she did, was notorious for skipping things. I'd already had a few bad reviews, because I hadn't come in behind her to check her work.

I rushed back to the office to make a checklist for how to check guests in. I'd made Lucia a list, but the woman didn't seem to be able to read. I printed that out for Ruth as well, so she'd have something to check against to make sure the rooms were up to par.

When Lucia came in, we looked over the mess, and she got to work cleaning it up.

I came down to find Ruth sitting in the office waiting. I showed her the checklists and asked her to come in behind Lucia and check off each area, making sure they were clean. If not, she'd need to get Lucia to clean those areas again, before the guests found creepy stuff in their room.

Ruth laughed. "I used to work in a men's dorm. I know how to force someone to clean, even if they don't want to."

"Perfect," I said. "You're hired. Hey, do you need anything while I'm in Alpine?"

Ruth thought for a moment. "Well, I do love those *Mrs. Smith apple pies,* and I haven't had one in ages. I keep trying to get Illa Mae to carry them at the grocery store in town, but she says I'm the only person who'll buy them."

"I'll get you a case if it'll repay you for saving my neck," I said, in all sincerity.

"No need for a case, one'll be just fine. A woman of my years has to watch her figure like a hawk," she said.

I left the office, confident the building would still be standing when I got back, and headed toward Alpine's hardware store.

I got there early, and as such, was able to get help right away. Alpine had grown quite a bit since I was a kid, and since the hardware store was still the favorite one in town, they tended to get busy.

Unfortunately, they didn't have the part I needed, so I'd have to go over to the other store and pray they did. I was already thinking about how I'd retrofit a different part when I walked in and saw Flex at the counter.

He turned around, and when he saw me, a huge grin crossed his face. "Howdy stranger," he said, then looked back at the cashier to take his change.

When I saw him, my heart did that fluttery thing where it felt like it skipped a beat or two. As he walked over to me, I managed to get myself together just in time for him to ask, "So, what brings you to the big city of Alpine?"

I smiled and shook my head. "Had a bit of a gusher in one of the rooms this morning. I'm full this weekend, so I've got to get it fixed before then. What brings you here? I thought you'd still be in Houston."

He shook his head. "I was until some jackass burned my barn down. I had to rush back here to, hopefully, discourage any more burnings."

"Man, that sounds awful. Is everyone okay?" I asked.

"Well, no injuries, but I am sort of in a quandary. I have too many people living in a house that's way too small for all of us," he said with a sigh.

"You can always stay at the motel," I said, and winked at him.

He chuckled. "Oh, man, would I like that, but you're a thirty-minute drive from the ranch, and I need to be there to keep an eye on the place."

"I understand. What do you plan to do?"

"Well, I'm headed over to Marfa in a few moments to check out an old Airstream that's for sale. I'm hoping the thing is in good enough shape to house me until other accommodation can be built."

I shook my head. "No, that Airstream belongs to a shyster. I checked it out a few months ago for the RV park behind the motel. It's an Airstream, but one axel is broken, the tires need to be replaced, and the entire inside of the thing looks like it needs to be gutted and refurbed. For what he's asking, you'll be way in the hole before you drive it off his property."

Flex sighed. "Well, there goes that idea. I saw one advertised in Pecos, but I don't really have time to drive up there today."

"I have one you can use if you'd like. It needs refurbishing before I can rent it, and I won't have time to do that until summer when my busy season is over. You're welcome to it until then."

Flex's face lit up. "Can we go look at it now? I need to get something figured out sooner than later."

"Sure, just let me get my parts. Oh, I also promised one of my residents a *Mrs. Smith* pie from the grocery store, do you have time to wait?"

"Sure, I'll call over to the ranch to see if I need to pick up any groceries while I'm there."

We left the hardware store after I found the part I needed. Flex laughed when I did a little happy dance in the middle of the store. I wouldn't have to do a stupid patch job after all.

We stopped by the grocery, and since Flex ended up having to pick up a lot of stuff for whoever he'd called, I ended up shopping myself. I tended to try to get what I needed from our local grocer mostly because of advice my grandfather had given me when I was a teenager, *"You use your local businesses, or they'll leave."* I couldn't imagine having to drive all the way to Alpine just to buy groceries. So, I patronized Illa Mae's for most of my food needs.

It'd been long enough since I was in a regular grocery store and I couldn't help but stare at the selection. I lived on frozen pizza, and Illa Mae kept three varieties, all of which I could get sick of pretty quick. The store here in Alpine had a huge variety. I ended up filling my cart with those alone. Flex laughed at me, calling me a typical bachelor. "Hey, a man's gotta do what a man's gotta do."

"Especially when said man refuses to learn to cook."

I laughed, knowing he had my number.

I was so excited about the pizza I almost forgot the pie and had to run back to get it. I grabbed two in case I needed to bribe Ruth into helping me again.

"Hey, it's getting late. I've got a half hour's drive, and by the time I get back, lunch will be over and all the food will be put away. I think I'm gonna grab a bite to eat. Join me?"

"Wow, like a real date?" I asked.

He laughed. "Well, something like that."

The weather was cool enough today that I wasn't afraid my pizzas and Ruth's pie would thaw too quickly. So, I thought, *Why not?*

"Give me a minute to see how my replacement is doing, I may need to rush back."

Ruth picked up immediately. "Alamito Motel, this is Ruth speaking. How may I help you?"

"Wow, you sound like you've been there all your life."

"Could've been if you'd have asked," she said with her clipped New England accent.

"So, is everything okay?" I asked.

"Just dandy, Lucia finished cleaning all the rooms, and they are spick-and-span. All three of your guests have arrived and at the same time no less. They are all now hanging out on the patio happy as clams. They got checked in and said they loved the rooms, so you're good to go."

"Okay," I said, waiting for the but. When it didn't come, I said, "Well, I ran into a friend who asked me to grab lunch with him. Do you think you can hold the fort down for a little while longer?"

"Oh, sure, honey. I got my soaps on and the place is back to its sleepy self. Do you have any other guests coming tonight?"

"No, no one else is expected until tomorrow."

"Perfect, honey, but I've gotta go. Alice is up to no good again, her granddaughter Hope... oh, you don't care. I'll call you if I need anything." Then, she hung up on me.

I laughed out loud. "Sorry," I said to Flex, who was looking at me oddly. "I had one of my residents take the reins from me today, so I could rush into town to pick this part up. I just got dumped for *Day in the Life,* or I think it's *Days of Our Lives.* Which of those soaps is still going?"

Flex shrugged, putting Ace back in the truck and leaving the air running, he locked the doors. "My mom used to watch that one, but I have no idea. For me, watching them was always like watching grass grow."

"I feel about the same, well, Ruth sure loves it."

"I think it might just be a generational thing."

"Maybe, but long story short is I have time to get lunch with you, so first date, here we go!"

We went to the little café and ordered, then leaned back, chatting about nothing in particular. Occasionally, when Flex smiled, the same flutter that'd happened earlier hit my chest again. This time, I guessed it was anticipation. Would he let me touch him again?

After the server left, I decided it was best to dive straight in. "So, I'm sorry I haven't been in contact. Things went to shit right after you left."

Flex laughed bitterly. "Clearly, it did for me too. I had an insane real estate agent. Which, if you ever need to sell, avoid that woman like the plague," Flex said, shaking his head. "Then, I had some strange man harass the crap out of me to buy the place, reconciled with my long-lost cousin and rushed here to deal with a barn burning. What's been going on with you?"

"You remember the battle-ax that came after you when you first arrived?"

He nodded.

"Well, she and her friends came after me with a lawsuit for, get this, religious discrimination. They were saying, because I wouldn't let them pick on you and lie to get me to kick you out, I was discriminating against them."

"Man, you can't be serious."

"Oh, yeah, it made it all the way to court, but it didn't last long. We were in court within a month, and the judge kicked it out for being the lame lawsuit it was."

A tall man looked around the booth, and said, "Hey, I'm sorry I overheard you talking about that lawsuit. That was you?"

I moaned inside. I shouldn't have brought this up in public.

"Yes, sir, it was," I replied in a professional tone, hoping it would stave off any homophobic attacks.

"Well, I'm Lander Diez with the *Texas Cowboy*. We're a magazine that caters to the gay community out of El Paso. We heard some women came after you for religious liberty violations. We were hoping to speak to you, especially since you are the opposite of the typical lawsuits," he looked at Flex, then back at me. "Most of the time, its businesses refusing services to gay people, we thought it'd be nice to interview you."

"I'm not sure. I'm just happy the drama's over," I said, and the man smiled. "Well, here's my card. Think it over. My magazine is written for LGBTQ audiences. Well, mostly the G part. It'd be a good story, especially since you won."

I thanked him, and he turned back around.

Flex looked at me in shock. "You went through all that just because that old woman thought I was in a relationship with Eric?"

"Pretty much," I said, and dug into the breakfast sandwich the server literally dropped off in front of me.

"Damn, well, I'm glad it worked out for you. Do they still live on your property?" he asked.

"Thank the good lord in heaven, no, they're all camped out up close to Marfa. Well, except for one of them. She didn't follow the flock and stayed back. She's the one who's manning the desk while I'm gone."

"Well, ain't that something," he said. "I guess things happen fast around here. The lawsuit with my aunt lasted well over five years."

"Thank God mine didn't last that long," I said, and took another bite of the sandwich.

Flex had barely touched his. I thought to myself, that a person who took time with his food didn't have as many issues to deal with as a motel owner who had no staff.

When he took a bite, he looked at it and frowned. "Well, this ain't very good, is it?"

I shrugged. "I thought it was fine."

Flex shook his head. "This from the guy that just bought out all the frozen pizzas in Alpine."

"Hey, you picking on me?"

Flex laughed. "I'm trying," he said.

He finished up his fries, but didn't touch the sandwich again. "If you ain't gonna eat that, I'll take it with me back to the motel. I can eat it tonight."

"I have a better idea. You let the waitress throw that in the trash where it belongs and come to the ranch and eat with us tonight. Our housekeeper's cooking can make any man melt in his seat."

"I don't know, I need to get the plumbing fixed before tomorrow. I don't think I can make it work tonight."

"Hold on." Flex pulled his phone out, dialed a number, and turned the speaker on.

"Hi, Mrs. Emma Jean, do you have room for one more person to join us tonight?"

"Of course," the vaguely familiar voice said. "How many?"

"Just one," he said, smiling. "Hey, can you see if Effie can join me in Alamito? I'm working a deal on a motor home."

The woman said she was going to ask Eddie, and a few seconds later I heard her say it was good.

"Cool, have him meet us at the motel in Alamito."

When he hung up, he was smiling like the Cheshire cat.

"So, that's solved. Effie can help you get your plumbing problem fixed, and you'll be free to come hang with us. Wait 'til you eat Emma Jean's home-made burritos. Dear lord, you'll think you've died and gone to heaven."

I chuckled. "Are you always this demanding?"

His eyes darkened, and he grinned wickedly. "I'd have thought you'd know that by now."

The blood left my brain and rushed to my groin. I'd forgotten how this man made me feel, and the social hour we'd been having had allowed me to forget.

I swallowed hard, and said, "Um, I remember plenty."

"That's good, I like it when a man knows what I like."

The man who'd wanted to interview me stood up to leave and winked at me, before he walked up to the cashier. He'd clearly heard our conversation, and from the look of him, it'd had a similar effect on him.

"I think you just gave that old man a woody," I teased.

Flex glanced at the man. "He ain't that old." Then, he looked back at me. "If you toss me to the side, he might be an option."

I kicked him under the table. "If you're that easy..."

He grabbed my hand and looked me in the eye. "I'm a guy, so easy is a given, but for right now, I'm only interested in one guy, and that's the one sitting across from me."

"Smooth talker," I said, and rolled my eyes. "You're dangerous, Fletcher. I'm gonna keep my eye on you."

I grabbed the bill our waitress had dropped off a few minutes earlier, and walked up behind the newspaper guy, to wait my turn to pay.

When he noticed me behind him, he smiled. "Seriously, consider the interview. If nothing else, it could increase the traffic to your motel. I'm here doing a piece on Big Bend National Park. Lots of gay men are beginning to travel here from all over, wanting to take advantage of the hiking and nature. It'd be fun to show how one of the local West Texas businesses is friendly and family-owned."

"I'll think about it," I told him, and he winked at me again, before he left.

Flex had come up behind me and tried to get me to let him pay his share. "Nope, if this was a date, I should pay, like the gentleman I am."

"Well, I'm a gentleman too, and if I remember right, I invited you."

"True, but I've got this one. Next time it's on you. Besides, you're treating me tonight, remember?"

He nodded and smiled. "No comparison, though, seriously!"

We walked back to his truck that still sat in the grocery store parking lot. He drove me back to mine that I'd left at the hardware store, and while we were transferring my groceries, he asked, "Why don't you give the interview?"

"I don't want to create any more waves. I'm on thin ice as it is with my little community."

"So, you think the folks in Alamito are all avid readers of *Texas Cowboy*, gay magazine?"

I chuckled. "No, in fact, I'd never even heard of it."

"Well, if it's free advertising and the people in Alamito aren't likely to ever hear about it, why not go for it. Wouldn't it be nice to have more *family* staying at your place? Everyone these days seems to be marketing to us. You know, with all our disposable incomes and all."

I laughed. "You sound like you're working for him. I'm seriously thinking about it, but I wanna weigh all my options, and any potential fallout before I do."

"Sounds good. Shall I follow you back to Alamito?" he asked.

"Sure," I said, as I climbed out of his truck, and headed toward mine.

11

Flex

S EDUCTION, THAT WAS WHAT was on my mind. I wasn't going to pretend like I wanted anything else. Mitch Armstrong was one of the most beautiful men I'd ever laid eyes on. All I had to do was think about him, and all I could do for the next thirty minutes was think about pure, hot, and delicious sex.

It hadn't escaped my attention that men usually came and went in my life, pun intended. I loved men, don't get me wrong. There was no sexual ambiguity to me. I liked and wanted sex, and when things weren't stressful, I tended to go find it. Hookups, well, that was what tended to be the norm for me. I wasn't quite a Grindr hook-up, I did like to know a man's name before I screwed him, but I wasn't far from that.

What was different about Mitch was we'd done the hook-up thing, and the next morning I'd wanted to hook up again. I wanted to hook up the next night. Now, all I could think about was when I could get my hands on his sexy body again.

Was I neglecting my work at the ranch? I was. Was it stupid to pull my cousin off the ranch, so I could get my new obsession to come visit my family, my new life and obligations? Yes, it was totally stupid. I had absolutely no business getting involved with anyone, especially when my entire life was hanging in the balance, but fuck if I wasn't going to ignore good sense and chase this man with everything I had in me.

My mind must've been full of him, because it seemed like only moments passed between Alpine and Alamito. If I had to drive more than fifteen minutes while in Houston, I thought I was going a long way. Here, an hour was just a typical run to the grocery store. Sometimes the distance could get the best of me, but thinking of the man in front of me, or more importantly, getting him under me again, was enough to make the distance fly by.

When we got back to the motel, I pulled up beside him in the parking lot.

There was a little white-haired lady bustling about the place, scrubbing under everything. The entire office smelled like glass cleaner.

"Ruth, you didn't have to do all this," Mitch said.

"Oh, don't you worry, I love to clean. Not like you don't keep the place spick-and-span, but well, sometimes a place needs a woman's touch."

Mitch chuckled. "Ruth, you are a piece of work."

She turned to look at him, probably trying to decide how to take his comment, and seeing it was in good nature, she said, "I've decided to come to work for you full-time. As long as I can catch my soaps, you can get on with all the work you need to do."

Mitch almost choked. "Um, Ruth, honey, I don't have..."

"Before you finish that statement, I haven't asked for money. I like having something to do, you need help, and I could use some free rent. As long as I work here, you forgive my monthly payment. Does that work for you?" she asked.

"Well, um. Let me think on it," Mitch said, and the woman smiled.

"You think more than any man I've ever met. I basically just offered my services to you for free. You think on it. Meanwhile, you had an RV pull in about half an hour ago. I put them in Mrs. Latham's old spot, not knowing where you'd want to put them. I tried calling, but didn't get through, figured you were out of range on your way back here. They didn't hook up 'cause I said I didn't know where to put them 'til you got back. You might wanna go on up and deal with that."

Then, the woman locked eyes with me. "Now, what have we got here?" she said, full-out flirting.

"He plays for my team, Ruth," Mitch said, and caused the woman to belt out laughing.

"All the really cute ones do," she said, and winked at me. "Well, I suspect this is who you *ran into*?"

"Hush, nosey," he said, and went over and gave the old woman a peck on the cheek. "Enjoy that 'cause it's all you're gonna get. That one you're flirting with is all mine, at least, for the moment."

The woman he called Ruth cackled and smiled at me. "When he's done with you, come on over to see me, you hear?" she said, and disappeared into a back room.

When we were outside, I whispered, "That was scary."

Mitched laughed. "I think she's harmless, but you might want to wear a chastity belt from now on when you come for a visit, just to be sure."

I laughed, but only to be courteous. If I knew where to get a chastity belt, I'd probably take him up on his advice.

"I'm gonna take care of my new guests first, then I'll show you the camper. Do you mind hanging out a bit?" he asked.

When I shook my head, Mitch pointed toward a large camper that sat gleaming in the far corner. I thought, if this needed refurbishing, I sure didn't understand why.

I wandered around the RV and was surprised to see it was indeed in excellent shape. Even the tires looked relatively new. I tried the door, and to my surprise, it opened. I knew it was a small town, but most people wouldn't leave an RV like this one open.

The moment I opened the door, however, I understood, one, why it would never be stolen, and two, why it needed a refurb. The place stank like a mixture of dog shit, ruined and rotting meat and cigarette smoke.

I pulled my shirt over my face and went in. The layout was beautiful. The floors were hardwood around a kitchen island. There was a beautiful living room in the back, and it even had a fireplace that sat under a flat-screen TV.

Unfortunately, the smell was so bad I had to leave before I started gagging.

Mitch came up, and when he saw my face he started laughing. "I told you it needed refurbishing, but at least it won't fall apart on you as you try to drive it to your property."

"My god, did someone die in there?" I asked.

"Well, not in there, but the old man that owned it died shortly after buying it. It sat for about six months on his property before his sons went out to check on it. By the time they did, everything in the refrigerator had rotted. He'd evidently been sick for several months before he was taken to the hospital, and didn't always make it to the restroom, according to his daughter-in-law, and he was also a chain smoker. So, it needs a lot of work."

"Damn, that's the understatement of the season."

Mitch laughed again. "Don't feel like you need to take it on my account. I already took the refrigerator out and gave it to a couple who did some sort of magic with it, but I couldn't get the stench out of the floors or the carpet after that long being closed up. You'll want to strip out the carpet and the laminate, and I'm afraid the furniture is probably toast too. It'll all probably need to be discarded before you move in. The good news is, once you get upstairs, the stink is much more manageable.

I covered my face again and went back in and up the stairs. As promised, the bedroom in the upper part of the RV was luxurious with a king-size bed, another flat-screen TV, and plenty of storage.

"It's really a beautiful RV, isn't it? Too bad it stinks so bad," I said.

"Too bad for you, maybe, but I got it for a tenth of what it's worth. I'll put about five grand back into it, and I'll have a luxury suite for my guests when I need overflow."

"Yeah, well, maybe. Do you think you can get rid of the smell?"

"Oh, yeah, I used to help clean homes when people died in them. If we can clean that up, this is a cinch."

"What, you cleaned houses where there were dead people?" I asked, surprised.

"Well, they weren't there when we were, but yeah, the construction company I worked for also hired out for that kind of thing. I made a ton of money doing that."

"Yeah, but..." I just shuddered.

Mitch laughed again. "I can help you pull the flooring and furniture out, and we can toss that into the dumpster. After that, I'm afraid you'll be on your own."

I nodded unconvinced. "Let me have my cousin take a look and see if he can help me. He knows this stuff a lot better than me, and I'll be making him help me clean it up!"

Mitch laughed. "Okay, princess. Just let me know."

I followed him back to the office, and after he relieved Ruth and sent her back to her trailer, I came over and gently pushed him back against the wall of his office and kissed him. "I'll show you, princess," I said then kissed him again, making this one much deeper and more intimate.

He moaned in my mouth, and I would've taken it even further if I hadn't heard my damned cousin calling out from the main office.

"Shit," I said, and pulled away. "Cockblocked by my own kin."

Mitch just stared at me, then swallowed hard. "I want a do-over later. I'll even call you princess again if it puts you back in this mood."

"Hello?" my cousin said again.

"Yeah, wait a damned minute, Effie, God!" I cried out, then saw Mitch blanch. "Oh, sorry," I said. "I forget not everyone is used to us."

Mitch smiled. "Well, might as well go on out. I'm gonna wait here a moment."

I looked down, and when I noticed the hard-on tenting the man's pants, I smiled what must have looked purely evil. "No need to promise, I'm definitely coming back for that!"

"Jesus, man," I heard from the other room, "Do you want me to leave and come back later?"

I kissed Mitch's forehead and pushed away from him, and although I was sure I had my own tent, I waltzed right out to where my cousin was standing. At least, he would see what he'd got in the way of.

Effie smiled like the Cheshire cat when he saw me, and his smile broadened even more, when a red-faced Mitch came out a few moments later.

"Well, I'll be! Already flirting with the locals," he said. "Hi, I'm Eddie Crawford. I'm this one's cousin."

Mitch smiled. "Well, good looks run in y'all's family, I see. I'm Mitch Armstrong, owner of this here establishment."

I wasn't sure why the two men had reverted to backwoods Texas drawl, but, whatever.

"Effie," I said, wanting to change the subject, especially after Mitch had said he was good looking. "Mitch has a Fifth Wheel that is about as nasty smelling as I've ever been in, but it'd be perfect for me while we're figuring things out on the ranch. Do you think you can take a look to see if you can help me get it in shape enough for me to live in it until he needs it back?" I asked.

Effie smiled and nodded. "Sure thing, cuz. Y'all want me to go on out there now and leave you two alone?"

"No, I'd rather you'd been an hour later, but that opportunity has passed." I looked at Mitch and smiled again. "At least for now."

Mitch shook his head. "Is he always this way?" he asked Effie.

"No, actually, I've never seen him like this."

"Really," Mitch said, and a smile crossed his face. "That's valuable information."

I squinted at the two men who'd just shaken hands. "Okay, enough of all that, come on, let me show you the RV."

Both Mitch and Effie laughed as I walked out the door. I could see I'd need to keep these two apart, Effie was gonna really screw with my sexy, tough-guy routine, and I wanted to keep that up at least until I convinced Mitch I was cool enough not to toss out with the next day's trash.

Effie did a once over of the Fifth Wheel and shrugged. "Yeah, she stinks, but it ain't nothing really to fix once you get all the flooring out. I saw some furniture in the shed this morning that ain't beautiful, but it'd work until you bring it back here. In fact, I'm sure it'd fit right in that space."

"In that case, if you've got a mask, Mitch, I'll begin stripping the carpet and flooring out now, while Effie over there fixes your pipes."

I looked up after saying that. "On second thought," I said.

Both Mitch and Effie were laughing at me.

"Come on, Eddie, or is it Effie? I'll show you the room."

Effie laughed. "The rest of the world calls me Eddie or Ed, but my cousin can't pronounce that, so he calls me Effie."

"I can pronounce it fine, but since I've been calling you that since I was one? It's how I know you."

"Whatever, dude," my cousin said, following Mitch toward the buildings. All of a sudden, jealousy flowed through me. Did Mitch really think my cousin was handsome? Wait, no problem, right. Effie was straight.

"Hey, cuz, remember hands off!" I said, trying to sound light-hearted.

Effie shot me the bird, and Mitch gave me a scowl which alerted me, I'd maybe gone a bit far. Damn, but jealousy was something that ran deep in my genes. *Thanks, mom,* I thought.

Mitch had forgotten to tell me where he kept face masks, so I just took that as my punishment for having acted like a jealous ass in front of a guy I'd just reconnected with.

I went in and almost gagged, but I forced myself to stick with it. I found a screwdriver and undid the furniture, and one by one pulled the big pieces out. I was surprised how heavy the two recliners were. But, I was able to get them out single-handed.

The couch, however, was a hide-a-bed. It was both too heavy and too bulky for me to get out on my own, at least without damaging the rest of the RV. I pulled the carpet up on the side where the recliners were and managed to pull it, so I could lay the couch back and get it out from underneath.

By the time Mitch came back, I'd managed to get all the carpet in the living area and around the kitchen pulled up.

He studied me for a moment. "You know I don't do jealous men, right?"

I stopped and put my hands on my top of the island. "Yeah, sorry about that. I'm not sure what got into me."

He looked like he wanted to say something else, but he just shrugged. I noticed then that he'd changed into some old clothes, and as he came in, he grabbed the edge of the smelly carpet and pulled, lifting it out the door.

Just having the carpet out immediately made the place smell better.

"Wow, that's better!" I exclaimed.

"Figured it would be," he said, then looked back into the living room. "Need help with the sofa?" he asked.

We pulled the furniture out and then the laminate flooring, all of which helped.

When we walked back inside, there was still a slight whiff of the stench, but it was significantly less.

"I've got a chemical treatment I can put in here overnight after I bleach the bathroom subfloor and clean down the cabinets and countertops, then there shouldn't be any smell left."

"What do you want to replace the flooring with?" I asked.

"I thought I'd just replace the entire thing with laminate hardwood. Some of them are really nice, and if they get broken or scratched, you can just pop it up and replace it."

"I saw a flooring place in Alpine. I'll pay to have the flooring replaced if you'll go with me tomorrow and show me what you like."

Mitch looked at me. "No, that'll be way too expensive, but I'll tell you what, if you and your cousin will help, I can carve out a little time to help. I'll find out when I can get the flooring delivered, and see if Ruth can cover the front desk again."

I nodded. "I'm sorry this is so complicated," I told him. "I know you didn't want to have to worry about this until your busy season was over."

"Trust me, I have ten more rooms to renovate, not to mention all the crap that comes at me like the plumbing issue your cousin is working on at the moment. If I can get this thing done, and all I have to do is let you stay in it for a while, I'll come out way ahead."

I smiled at him. "So, you're basically saying you're using me for my brute strength."

The guy burst out laughing. "Yeah, that's what I'm doing."

I went over and wrapped my arms around him. "I could get used to being used for my body."

"You play dirty," he said, and pushed me away. I gave him big points for not looking around to see who'd seen us.

We hauled all the debris over to the dumpster and cleaned up around the camper before going back in.

I got a broom from a nearby camper and swept up the dirt and debris left on the floor. "If you've got bleach and the other cleaners, I'll wipe everything down. Then all you'll have to do is put your chemical treatment down."

He laughed. "It's a machine that blows the treatment out. It smells like bubble gum, but you won't want to be in here while it's running. I can't promise it isn't toxic, but when it's done, the place will smell brand new."

"I'll lean on your expertise," I replied, glad the guy knew what he was doing!

While I cleaned all the surfaces in the RV, he went back to check on Effie. As I was finishing the bathroom, the two of them came back together, carrying some strange looking machine, and a bottle that I assumed contained the chemical solution.

They took the machine inside the RV, and I watched as Mitch plugged it in and then added the solution to it from the bottle.

As soon as he turned it on, a mist came out that did indeed smell a lot like bubble gum. We walked out together, and Mitch locked the camper this time, saying he didn't want to take a chance on someone wandering in.

"Effie, if you wanna head back, I'll follow behind you," I said, hoping he'd get the hint.

Obviously, he did, because he smiled as he was looking at the ground. When he'd regained his composure, he looked up. "That's a good plan, I need to get back before the boys drive Emma Jean and Jimmy insane. I'll grab the boys, and we'll take Ace for a walk when we get home."

"Hey, why didn't you bring them with you? I thought you would."

"They wanted to stay back with Jimmy and Emma Jean. I insisted, but Emma Jean intervened and said she needed more time with them, since she'd been without seeing them so long. I can't imagine she meant it," he said, and chuckled.

"I'm on the same page. I don't feel like I know them well either, and that sucks. Five years is a long time to be apart from a six- and nine-year-old."

"Don't worry, it won't take long before that feeling passes. You'll be begging me to get them out of your hair."

We watched as Effie climbed into the old truck and drove away.

"I need to get a shower before we go," Mitch said, then winked at me. "Wanna join me?"

"Oh, damn, I really do!"

I stripped as soon as we were inside Mitch's house, and the moment I was in his bedroom, I was stripping him as well. Of course, we didn't get to the shower. As soon as I had his clothes off him, I pushed him back onto his bed and straddled him, dry humping our naked cocks together, while I kissed him. I'd been so horny for this man, I couldn't see straight. Well, I couldn't do much of anything straight. I wanted him so bad, even my balls hurt for him.

He pushed me off, saying I smelled like old trailer and pulled me into the bathroom, where he turned on the water. We kissed while waiting for the water to heat up.

When the water was ready, we both stepped into the shower, and Mitch began to wash me, paying special attention to my cock and balls.

After rinsing me, he knelt down and took me into his mouth.

"Fuck, your mouth feels so good," I said, as the man did amazing things to me with his tongue.

I leaned back against the tiles, letting the water roll over me, and blocking it from splashing Mitch in the face.

I grabbed his head as he started taking me faster and faster. "Damn, shit... Mitch, I'm gonna come..." I bellowed, and the man just took me harder and faster.

I spewed into his mouth and cried out as I did.

Out of breath, I leaned over him, then helped him to his feet. "My turn," I said, causing him to laugh out loud.

I filled my hand with soap and began lathering his body, washing his ass, cock and balls, while I watched him enjoy the process.

After rinsing him off, I knelt down and bent him over, letting my tongue move over his tight hole, like I'd done when we first met.

I loved the taste of him. Even after being freshly washed, Mitch had a unique aroma and taste, which drove me insane.

I reached up and soaped my hand again as I turned him toward me. I used the soap to lube my fingers as I breached his hole. He arched back against the tiles as I took his cock into my mouth.

"Fuck, Flex... Fuck, yeah!" he exclaimed, as I finger fucked him and sucked at the same time.

I felt his prostate and decided I'd have a little fun.

I began to massage his prostate, and was immediately rewarded for my efforts when Mitch threw his head back, moaning loudly.

He began to fuck my mouth then, pumping harder and harder. I knew he was close, so I pushed my finger into his prostate. Mitch buried his crotch deep into my face, and shuddered as he came in my mouth.

"Aaa, fuck... damn, that's..."

I'd have chuckled if my mouth wasn't full of Mitch's cock and enough cum to drown me.

I swallowed, as Mitch slumped against the shower tiles.

I licked his head each time post-orgasmic cum appeared, and when he was finally done, I stood up in front of him.

"You're so beautiful, Mitch Armstrong. I love watching you come."

He leaned into me, then kissed me hard before pulling back, and falling into my embrace.

There was something sensual about holding this satiated man as the water poured over us. I reached for more soap and finished washing him off as he did the same to me.

We stepped out of the shower and dressed. Unfortunately, I had to pull my old clothes back on.

Time was getting away from us, and if we didn't get back to the ranch, Emma Jean was gonna have my hide, and probably poor Mitch's, just through guilt by association. I pulled the sexy man up to me, my front to his back, and kissed him gently on his neck and shoulders.

"Mmm, that feels so good," he said. "Why don't you come back with me tonight. You can use the excuse that you're gonna help me get the Fifth Wheel ready to pull out tomorrow morning."

"Can you get away? I thought you had a full house."

"I do, but if we get up early, I can ask Ruth to watch the front desk again until I get back."

"So, you're gonna take her up on her offer of being a full-time employee?"

"Totally, dude. She only pays me half of what I could get anyway. I'm making out like a bandit here. Now that her *friends* are gone, and I'm actually bringing in a little money from the RV lot, I might even be able to afford to pay her, at least a little."

I smiled. "She wasn't gonna take no for an answer anyway. I sort of think she wanted the work."

Mitch shrugged. "Lord knows I need the help. *'Don't kick a gift horse in the mouth,'* my grandfather used to say. I plan to pamper this one!"

Mitch rode with me out to the ranch, and, we arrived before Emma Jean was done cooking the evening meal. Jimmy and

Effie were out where the RVs used to be, and Effie's two boys were running around beside them.

We walked out to where they were, and Jimmy looked up, saw Mitch, and smiled. "Well, if it ain't Mitch Armstrong. What brings you out to these parts?"

Mitch reached out and grabbed Jimmy's hand. "I just got lucky, I guess. I heard some fortunate man had a wife who could cook so good it'd make a man cry."

"That's true enough, but now don't you be getting any funny ideas, young man. That filly in there is all mine."

Mitch laughed. "I wouldn't dare, sir."

"So, you know each other?" I asked.

Mitch elbowed me. "Well, it'd be stranger if we didn't, considering how few people actually live in these parts. Remember, I told you my grandfather used to farm me out for hard labor? Jimmy and old man Madison used to hire me to help round up the cattle when it was time to send them to market."

"Wow, small world. I don't remember ever seeing you here, though," I said, racking my brain to remember someone my age out working on the ranch.

Jimmy laughed. "Didn't need help when you three were here. It's when you went home, we called on young Mitch there."

"Too bad we didn't meet sooner," I said, half to myself.

"Well, probably weren't the right time. Anyway, welcome back to the ranch, Mitch. Why don't you go on in there and say hi to Emma Jean. She'll be pleased as punch about you bein' who our boy brought out to meet us."

Mitch laughed and did as Jimmy asked. I turned to go with him, when Jimmy asked me to hang back a bit.

I turned, concerned about what he was gonna tell me.

Jimmy sighed. "I hate to be the bearer of bad news, but I ran a snake down the sewer, and it's collapsed. This whole place has gotta be reworked before you can move out here.

"Well, shit. Just as we get one thing solved, the whole thing caves back in. Remind me not to do any mining!" I said.

Jimmy just laughed. "Don't get your panties in a wad just yet," he said. "I remembered we used to have a single RV spot next to the house attached to the house's electrical and sewer, for when I needed to stay overnight. I checked that out, and we're in luck. The electrical still works, the sewer is a bit sketchy, but when I ran the snake, it only pulled up some roots that probably hang down between the drain and the septic. We'll need to dig that out and make sure it's connected properly, but that ain't nothing compared to what we'd have to do out here."

"That's at least a silver lining. I'm sure Effie told you Mitch is letting me borrow his camper. That'll solve our current housing situation until we can figure something else out."

Jimmy and Effie both nodded.

"I noticed Mitch rode with you, he planning on spending the night?"

I almost choked. "Um no. I'm gonna take Mitch back and stay at the motel tonight. We'll drive the camper back tomorrow morning before he has guests showing up."

Jimmy nodded, then looked me in the eye. "You know it's really good he's found you boys to be friends with. He had one hell of a childhood. His mama was no good and his granddad, well, he was a hard nut to crack. Everythin' I've seen says he's a good man despite that. Wouldn't do for someone to scratch up his heart now."

Jimmy turned away from us and started walking up toward the house.

I waited until he was out of earshot and turned to Effie. "I think I just got a warning."

Effie just nodded. "You had to know folks out here would take care of their own. He ain't wrong, you know."

"Don't you start, we are two grown men doing what grown men do. I can tell you he ain't no damsel in distress needing to be rescued. He's strong and handsome, and well... he don't need defending."

Effie laughed at me. "Defensive much?" he asked, and ran away when I lunged for him.

"You always were too slow to catch me," he yelled behind him, as he ran toward the house.

"You'll rethink that when I catch you, beaver face!"

"You mean Badger, don't you?" he laughed.

"I meant what I said."

Drake and Luke were running around us, laughing and teasing each other too. The four of us ran back toward the house, Ace barking at all of us as we went.

When we all barreled in, Emma Jean gave us one look, and all four of us stopped in our tracks. "Shoes off, I just mopped the floor and don't want y'all draggin' in lord knows what."

We did as we were told and came in to help set the table. Mitch was stirring what appeared to be lemonade in a large glass pitcher. Apparently, the two of them had added an additional leaf to the table before we'd come in, because it was longer, which was good. Otherwise, we'd have had to squeeze together to get a seventh person around the table.

"This family grows anymore," I said. "...and we're gonna have to pull the old harvest table back out and start eatin' on the porch."

"Hey, I remember that," Effie said. "Where is that old thing?"

"Luckily, we pulled it out of the barn to keep the birds from crapping on it and put it in the shed next to where the hands used to sleep. That building is pretty new and critter-proof... well, more critter-proof than the ol' barn was at least," Jimmy said, as he put salsa and sour cream on the table.

When we sat down, Emma Jean said it was about time to get back to proper ways, now that we were here permanently. She grabbed Jimmy's hand and little Luke's, because she'd put him next to her. We all joined hands, and she said grace.

It'd been so long since I'd had someone pray over a meal, it felt awkward. Did people still do this? Evidently, they did, and what could it hurt? I wasn't religious in any way, but I did appreciate tradition, and for as long as I could remember, when we'd eat around the table, even when there were twenty hands seated around the huge harvest table, Emma Jean would say grace.

When she was done, she jumped up and headed toward the kitchen, calling behind her, "Y'all come on in, and I'll serve you. This meal is too messy to do it buffet style.

We sent the kids in front, so Effie could keep an eye on them, and make sure they didn't spill the food. I'd been to hundreds of Mexican restaurants, and Emma Jean's burritos were at the top of the list. She put beans and Spanish rice on our plates, then slipped our choice of one, two, or even three burritos onto our plates. Mitch and I both asked for three. After stripping the nasty carpet out of the trailer, I was starving, and well, the thing I'd already noticed about Mitch was he was a human vacuum cleaner when it came to food.

When we sat down, I asked Emma Jean if she'd eaten at the diner in Alpine. "The food is horrible. Mitch and I had their breakfast sandwich, and it tasted like soybean with a bunch of A.1. Sauce on it."

Mitch just laughed. "Your boy here is just too high falutin' for Lidia's diner."

"High falutin', I tell you that food tasted like warmed up..." I looked up to see the boys were wide-eyed, and quickly replaced my cuss word with crap.

"He ain't lyin', Mitch," Jimmy came to my defense. "I ate there when they first reopened, and the food was like eatin' cardboard. Not only that, but they want insane prices for the pleasure of eating their crap."

I laughed. "See," I said, looking at Mitch, and pointing at Jimmy.

"Well, I think it's interesting while we were here working, you and Mitch were in Alpine getting your nails done," Effie chimed in.

"Now wait a minute," I said in defense. "I didn't plan on running into Mitch, but when I did, and he offered to help out with the trailer, I thought I owed him breakfast."

"Hey, don't pull me into the middle of this. I was just minding my own business, and you came around trying to figure out how to get out of work. Ain't my fault you talked me into playing along. I promise, Eddie, I was an innocent bystander."

Effie looked at Mitch, then at me. "Nope, I don't trust either one of you. You've both got guilty written all over your faces."

"Now, now, don't be arguing over my wife's hard work. We'll settle this tomorrow. Mitch, Flex said you was coming back out with the Fifth Wheel, bring an extra shovel. Heck, bring three if you got 'em. The barn was where we stored ours. We'll have a competition to see which of you three boys works the hardest."

Jimmy had always been the king of getting ranch hands to get hard work done, while thinking they were competing. Everyone knew what he was up to, but having a little fun while doing manual labor was always the easiest way to do it.

"Well, I don't know about Mitch," Effie felt Mitch's biceps, causing me to give him the evil eye, which I could tell he enjoyed way too damned much. "But, I can kick scrawny Flex's bootie in half the time."

"Psst, you've been saying that lie since you were an infant, but you couldn't dig a hole in sand."

"Hey, we wanna dig holes too," Luke said, causing Jimmy's face to light up.

"Well, a course you do, and I know for a fact, I've got two shovels in the shed out back that'll fit you two boys right perfect."

"Now, I don't know about you, dear husband," Emma Jean said. "But, my money is resting on this one right here," she reached over and tested Luke's bicep. He quickly pulled up his sleeve and made a muscle to show her.

"What about me, Mrs. Emma Jean?" Drake said, showing his muscle too.

"I don't know, Luke, your brother's got three years on you. You think you can outdo him?"

Luke looked sad. "No, he's a lot bigger."

"Seems like Luke needs a three-minute head start, one minute for each year. Don't you agree, Drake, nobody wants to cheat and win that way, right?"

Drake didn't think anything of the sort, and you could tell he was managing an internal fight between disappointing Emma Jean, and the opportunity to whip his younger brother in a competition. After a moment, though, he nodded. "It needs to be a fair fight. That way, when I beat him, ain't nobody can say I didn't do it fair and square."

Jimmy rolled with laughter, as did the rest of us. Luke just stuck his tongue out at Drake, but smiled too. The brothers were typical and reminded me of Effie and myself. The two loved each other completely, but they still wanted to outdo the other, if at all possible.

By some miracle, there was still pie left over from the night before, and Emma Jean brought those out for dessert. I was personally stuffed, but I'd never pass up a piece of Emma Jean's chocolate meringue pie. Somehow, I forced the pie down, but it left me feeling lethargic.

We all went out and sat on the front porch.

"I forgot how bright the stars are here," I commented.

"Ain't no light to get in the way," Effie said.

"Was that a telescope cover you had set up at the motel?" Effie asked Mitch.

"Yeah, it belongs to a guy that stays here during the winter. He took the actual telescope with him, but it's worth going to see when he's here. You get to see the stars really close up, which is amazing. Some nights you can even see the rings of Saturn."

"Whoa," both boys said at once. God, I really had missed them.

Jimmy pulled his old guitar out and began playing. There was so much I'd forgotten, having missed all my adult years on the ranch. Jimmy turned to Mitch. "You still remember the words to *Danny Boy* you sang at the talent show at Illa Mae's last year?"

"Well, course I do, why?" he asked.

"Cause I'm about to play it, and you sing it better'n I've ever heard before."

Mitch chuckled. "Well, get to playing it then."

If I hadn't been infatuated with Mitch before, I certainly was now. His beautiful tenor voice rang out crystal clear across the night. Jimmy played and sang along after *Danny Boy*, singing the old songs I remembered from when my dad and I would sit elbow to shoulder, watching old westerns on Saturday afternoons.

It was a special treat when Emma Jean would join in with her crystal-clear alto voice, and harmonize with them. When Jimmy put the guitar down, Emma Jean was leaning her head against his shoulder. He put his arm around her, and the older couple snuggled close together. Love that spanned the ages, that was what I craved, but I'd always wondered, could a gay man have that with another guy? That was a question I didn't have an answer for, but I couldn't help but look over at Mitch as I wondered.

When Mitch yawned, I excused us from the group. "Tomorrow we'll come early, and we'll need to get the Fifth Wheel out here before Mitch has to get back. Besides, I have to kick y'alls butt too."

"Psst," Effie grunted. "Hardly."

The peace that'd settled over us after dinner had calmed us all down, and I pulled Mitch up from where he sat and wrapped my arm around his shoulder as I pulled him toward the truck.

"Night boys," Emma Jean said.

"Night everyone," Mitch and I said together.

Ace sleepily followed us out to the truck, and Mitch picked him up and held him on the way back.

We held hands all the way. It still shocked me that we could drive the whole way to the motel from the ranch and not pass one car. How was it possible in this day and age to live in a part of the world where no one else was out and about.

As we neared the motel, I began to feel the excitement of having this gorgeous man with me tonight, again. I really was flying on cloud nine.

After Mitch tucked the old dog bed into the corner of the bedroom, we stripped and climbed into his bed together.

"This feels nice," Mitch said, as he snuggled into my chest.

"Mm-hmm... I agree," I said drowsily.

"I've always liked Jimmy and Emma Jean, but I'd never enjoyed them more than I did tonight. You guys are lucky you have them," Mitch said.

"Yeah, I'm a lucky guy."

I reached down and let my hand rub over his half-hard cock. "Very lucky," I said, as I moved down under the covers and took his cock into my mouth.

Our lovemaking took on a different feel. Instead of the drive, I just savored him, moving over him and feeling his pleasure and happy moans as I sucked.

"I can't get over how good you taste," I said, as I pulled off him, and the sexy tired smile that crossed his face did something funny to my heart.

I lifted back up to him and ran my hand down his handsome face.

When I kissed him, all the emotion I'd felt a moment ago poured out of me and into that kiss.

Mitch moaned like he had when I was sucking him, causing both my heart and my cock to swell.

I lay back, and Mitch climbed on top of me this time. He opened the condom and rolled it over my cock, then lubed me and himself.

We made love as he rode my cock, slowly writhing with pleasure. Any other time this sort of slow sexual dance would drive me crazy, but it was exactly what we both needed and wanted. Somehow the slowness made it that much more erotic.

Mitch shifted and looked me in the eyes as he rode me. I thrust into him, each of us getting into a rhythm, neither of us taking our eyes off the other.

When he came, his ass tightened on my cock, sending pleasurable tingles throughout my body.

My own release came quickly after, and I once again emptied myself into the condom while still inside him.

I shuddered when I thought about what it would feel like to release inside him without a condom. Would we ever be serious enough to bareback?

I immediately checked my thinking. I was sure my heart was already getting too attached to this man. When you talked fucking without a condom, that was another level of partnership. That was a real relationship. I was pretty sure I wasn't ready to go down that road. Even if my heart was happy to take that leap, my brain sure as hell wasn't!

12

Mitch

W E SNUGGLED THROUGHOUT THE night, not something I usually wanted or liked, but my smaller frame seemed to fit perfectly up against his taller one. I'd wake up and feel his broad shoulders and hard pecs pushed up against me, and fall back asleep in blissful peace.

I woke up before him, slowly pulled away, and slipped into the kitchen to start the coffee.

Ace had gone to his bed that I'd left out for him. It was almost like he'd been sleeping here for years. I let him outside to do his business, then looked at the clock, and decided I could give Flex another hour's sleep before I had to kick him out of bed, so we had enough time to hitch the trailer and get it to the ranch. We also had to plan enough time to follow through with Jimmy's competition, which I planned to win, and get back in time to make sure all my work got done.

I clicked onto my computer while I was waiting for the coffee to brew, and made my purchases for the RV flooring. When the coffee was done, I took my mug out back to the swing to watch the sunrise. Ace followed me, then snuggled up next to me when I sat down.

I'd always been a finicky sleeper. My mom and grandfather both told me I took after her, so I had decided this was our spot, hers and mine. Even as a young kid, I'd come out here and watch the sunrise, imagining she was sitting beside me.

I sat on the swing and stared east, as I petted the now-sleeping dog next to me. I thought about how much I enjoyed hanging with Flex and his family. Sure, things were massively different out there since I'd worked with his grandpa all those years ago, but I thought for the better. The place felt content.

A few moments later, I heard movement, and was surprised when Flex came out of the house with his own cup of coffee, and joined me and Ace on the swing.

I snuggled into his side. "I was gonna let you sleep another hour."

"It got very lonely in that bed without you," he said.

"Want me to come back and join you?" I asked.

"I really do, but this feels too damned good to mess it up."

I smiled and kissed his stubbled cheek. "It feels good to me too," I said, and we both settled in to watch the sunrise.

The warm rays of the sun contrasted with the cool breeze and made me feel content all over.

Flex was great for snuggling into, all hard muscles mixed perfectly with nice long arms that seemed to wrap me up perfectly.

I must have dozed off, because the next thing I remembered was Flex kissing me gently on the temple, and me waking up with the sun fully blazing over the morning horizon.

"Wow, I fell asleep. That never happens."

Flex chuckled. "It's okay. The sunrise was pretty, but I'm sure the rest was better. I'm guessing you're gonna want to get going, though. It's getting pretty late."

I looked at my watch and sighed. "You're right. Gotta reheat my coffee, though, it's stone-cold now."

"I'll do that while you get dressed. I'm ready to go when you are."

"All I need is coffee, and I'm good."

Flex watched me with wonder as I backed the old pickup up to the Fifth Wheel, released the jacks and pulled it out.

"How'd you learn to do that so fast?"

"We've moved a lot of RVs over the years. My grandfather opened this part of the park before I was born. In fact, I was hooking up RVs and moving them around the campground before I had a license to drive on the main road."

Flex shook his head and followed me back to the office to lock up and make sure I had my wallet.

"I'm guessing you know your way to the ranch."

"Yep, been there many times. You go ahead, and I'll come in behind you. You and Jimmy can direct me into the spot you want this when I get there."

He agreed and disappeared down the road.

I made it to the ranch. Jimmy was standing on the far side of the house. He motioned for me to pull up to that area, and when I pulled through the yard, parallel to where he stood, he came to my window.

"You just need to back her into this spot right here. If you can put the front of the camper so it's hidden from the front porch, It'll save me all kinds of grief from the misses. She hates these things and says they're an eyesore."

"I can tuck it into the side where she won't see it from the porch, no problem," I said.

As soon as I had it disconnected, I jumped out and showed Flex where the connections were. Jimmy helped me connect them. I went to the pickup and pulled out three shovels. "Okay, now let's see who the champion of the ranch is."

Jimmy cackled. "Whoo-hoo, I'm sure these two butt-dragging city slickers were hoping you'd forget."

"Not on your life, Mr. Jimmy. A challenge is a challenge, after all. Let's get to it, though, 'cause some of us have work to do. I grinned over at where Eddie was sipping his coffee in what looked like a sleep-deprived stupor, and Flex, who was leaning up against the porch railing.

"Where are the little ones?" I asked.

"Emma Jean let 'em sleep in," Jimmy said. "Although, I told her it wasn't nice to get the boys' hopes up that this was how their lives would be. Ranch life starts before the chickens get up, and modern times ain't gonna change that."

I laughed and tossed Flex one of the shovels. Eddie had yet to come down off the porch.

"Effie, you forfeiting your rights to this challenge? I don't blame you really, since we all know I'm the best digger of the two of us."

Eddie growled from the porch, and stood up. "I'm gonna show you up, then I'm gonna kick your butt, cousin."

"What's crawled up your butt this morning," Flex asked.

"My estranged mother called. Hadn't talked to the woman in five years, and now I've seen her and talked to her twice in the last month."

"What'd she want?" Flex asked.

"For me to talk you into selling. She was the opposite to what she was like in Houston, now she's sweet and *'Oh, how I love you and my grandbabies. You are so important to me.'* Blah, blah, blah. It's enough to give a man ulcers."

"You know you can just silence her calls," Flex said.

"I know, but she never calls, so I thought it was important."

"Sorry, cousin," he said. "But, not sorry enough to let you win."

"Psst, like I need you to let me win!"

The hole we were supposed to be competing against each other to dig was where the septic and the RV connection supposedly met. As it was, there really wasn't room for three of us, so I sat back and watched the cousins go at it. Surprisingly, Eddie seemed to be the one throwing the most dirt, but it wasn't in the good humor of friendly competition. It was clear the man was working out his frustrations on the dig.

Finally, Flex even stepped back and let his cousin work it out. When he hit the area where the PVC pipe connected to the septic, he climbed out of the three-foot hole, tossed the shovel down and left.

Flex looked like he was going to follow, and Jimmy put his hand on his shoulder to hold him back. "No, that boy needs some time to himself. You can go find him after we finish fixing this old pipe."

I stayed around to see if they might need my help, but fixing PVC was one of the easiest plumbing jobs. It was only a matter of minutes before it was done.

I helped Jimmy and Flex out of the hole, and said my good-byes just as I heard the sound of two boys coming our way.

When the boys arrived, I said, "Looks like the reinforcements have arrived, so I'll be leaving."

I nodded to Jimmy and smiled at Flex, who I could tell was still concerned about his cousin.

"Go on out there and find him. He's likely to punch you, but that'll probably help him more than anything else."

"Yeah, thanks, that's just what we all need, a fistfight between us."

"Welcome to West Texas," I said, and walked toward my truck.

"Hey, wait up. When can we get together again?" he asked.

"Don't know. When you gonna be back in town?"

"Probably tomorrow, since I need to find flooring for this RV."

"Oh, sorry, never mind that. I already ordered some, and it'll be delivered to the motel by Monday. You'll just have to make do until then, I'm afraid."

"When did you do that?" he asked, surprised.

"While you were sleeping in this morning." I chuckled at the shock on his face.

"If Ruth'll fill in for me, I'll bring it over when it comes, and help you lay it. It's the same stuff I used in my renovated motel rooms, so I'm getting good at putting it in. Hardest part is cutting around all the corners, and the RV has a lot of those."

"So, probably won't see you until Monday then?" he asked, and his face went all pouty, like a little boy who wasn't getting his way.

I turned around and pulled him into a hug. "I think it's probably good for you to miss me. Absence makes the heart grow fonder and all that, you know?"

"Whatever, if I can get away, I might just show up at your door. A man has needs, you know."

"I may or may not let you in, just so you are aware," I teased.

"You want it as much as me, dude. Don't think I don't know that!" he said, and skipped backward toward the house.

I climbed into my truck, hoping desperately that he'd decide to come by. Monday seemed like a long way away.

****

When I got to the office, Lucia was waiting for me. One of the guests had stopped up the toilet, and I had to go plunge it. Ruth came in about an hour later, and said the new RVer banged music until eleven in the morning. When she went over and said if they didn't settle down, she was gonna call the sheriff, they complied, but not before she'd been called various names in the process.

Thankfully, when I walked back to talk to them, they were already packing up to leave, which made them one less problem for me to deal with.

That afternoon, one guest after another checked in. Luckily, because they'd all booked ahead, all I had to do was hand out the room keys. I had several RVs come in, which almost put me at capacity. I hadn't had this much RV traffic in ages. Usually, RV people went to Alpine of Marfa. Maybe this was a positive shift in the energy flow, now that the grouchy old women were gone.

By closing time, I was pretty much wiped out. I locked the front door and walked back into the office and noticed the house phone, which no one ever used anymore, showed a message. I pushed the play button, and the reporter's voice from *Texas Cowboy* came on the line.

"Mr. Armstrong, this is Lander Diez with the *Texas Cowboy*. My editor asked me to contact you again and ask for that interview. We have several subscribers who are avid hikers, bikers, and outdoor enthusiasts, and again, knowing there is a family-friendly institution for them to utilize would be quite a boon for this group. We are publishing our Big Bend National and state park segments next month. We'd very much like for you to contribute to this piece."

I deleted the message, but pulled the card out of my billfold. *What could it hurt? It isn't like I'm ever going to be closeted again.* If people had a hard time with my sexuality, they were gonna avoid me whether I did the interview or not.

I picked up the office phone and called the number. To my surprise, Lander answered after the first ring.

"Hello, Mr. Lander?" I asked.

"Yes, who is this?"

"This is Mitch Armstrong at the Alamito Motel. I've thought about your request, and I'm willing to do the interview, but with some specific requirements, which I'll need you to agree to before I give you the interview."

As I described how I wanted him to paint the community in the positive light it deserved, showing there were a few bad seeds, but the rest were just good downhome folk, I heard him sigh. I knew I was asking for a lot. The press seemed to love a scandal, well, so did my community for that matter, but that wasn't what I was about. I wouldn't be having my words twisted around to make people in Alamito look bad just so he could sell some more magazines or ads or whatever they sold.

Lander was quiet for a moment, then said. "I'll have to speak about specifics, but I don't have to mention names, I suppose."

"I'm fine with that. Also, and this is non-negotiable, you're gonna have to make sure you're clear in your article that we don't play favoritism, and we don't ostracize folks neither. When a guest checks into my motel, they are all treated with the same level of respect as everyone else. I hope you're right and this helps increase my clientele, but I don't want any of my customers to think they won't be getting good service just because they *aren't* gay."

I could tell Lander was smiling, when he said, "That's all perfect. Can I come by Monday for the interview?"

"I'll be helping on a nearby ranch, but if you don't mind meeting me there, you're welcome. I'll need to call the owner, of course, just to make sure he doesn't mind."

"You can text me when you get permission," he said, and we made our salutations and disconnected.

Well, it's Flex's encouragement that's led to my acceptance of all this, after all, I thought to myself. If I'm lucky, he'll get dragged into this damned article as well.

The thought of a bunch of drag queens parading across the ranch property *Priscilla, Queen of the Desert*-style warmed my heart.

I started to text Flex, but realized their phones didn't work out there. I picked the office phone up again, flipped through my grandfather's old Rolodex to find Cliff Madison, and made the call. People didn't tend to change numbers much around here. If I was lucky, Jimmy and Emma Jean had kept this one.

One of the boys answered. "Henry... Crawford Ranch, Drake speaking."

I had to force myself not to chuckle. I couldn't imagine what folks would say about the boy putting both his dad's and Flex's name in front of the ranch's.

"Hey Drake, this is Mitch. Is Flex available?" I asked.

"No, only ones here is me and Luke. Mrs. Emma Jean went back to the cellar to get something, but she said she'd be right back."

"That's fine. Would you have Flex or Mrs. Emma Jean give me a call back, please? You got a pen so you can write down my number?"

The boy said he did, so I gave him my mobile number since I was gonna lock the office down as soon as I got off the phone.

By the time I got to my kitchen, where I was about to pour myself a shot of whiskey, I got a call. Sure enough, it was the ranch number.

"Hello?" I answered, assuming it was probably Emma Jean, but not wanting to say anything until I knew for sure.

"Howdy, Mitch," she said. "Drake said you called."

"I did. Can you give a message to Flex for me? I have a guy that wants to interview me for a magazine article about all the mess I got into last month." I knew for a fact, no one within a five-hundred-mile radius wouldn't know exactly what mess I was talking about, and sure enough, Emma Jean didn't ask. "I'm supposed to do that on Monday, but I already told Flex I'd come out there and help him with the Fifth Wheel. Can you ask Flex if he'd mind?"

"Why, honey, I'll ask, but I already know he won't. Want me to have him call you?"

"Only if Monday's not convenient."

The older woman laughed. "Boy, you know he's looking for every excuse to talk to you. I'll tell him, though, and he'll do what he does."

"Thanks, ma'am," I said and hung up.

I shot back my whiskey, kicked my shoes off and fell asleep on the couch, watching some ridiculous garbage that came on when I flipped a couple channels. Of course, the only reason it caught my attention was because the reality TV show had several muscled-up men doing various things without their shirts on.

I was woken up sometime later, when my phone rang. "Hello," I said, still half asleep.

"You already in bed, old man?" I heard Flex's teasing voice ask.

"Somebody wore me out last night. Gotta catch up on my beauty sleep," I said, yawning into the phone.

Flex laughed. "Emma Jean said you'd taken the interview with that Sexy Cowboy magazine."

"*Texas Cowboy*," I corrected. "But yeah. Do you mind if I have him meet me out there?" I asked.

"Not at all. Should I have Emma Jean set him a seat for dinner?"

"I'll ask and let you know," I said.

"That'll work," Flex said, and the line fell quiet.

"I almost drove over there tonight when Emma Jean told me you'd called. I wish I was holding you right now."

I moaned slightly, thinking how good it'd feel to have his big strong arms around me.

"Don't tease me, Flex. I'm too tired."

"Aah, poor baby, I didn't mean to tease."

"You're forgiven," I said, feeling just a little pouty.

"Want me to come tomorrow?"

"Yeah, but with all the guest rooms full, and most of the RV spots, I'm guessing I'll just be chasing my tail. You'd just have to sit and watch me run around like a lunatic."

"What's Sunday looking like?" he asked.

"It'll look like me washing sheets and cleaning rooms. Lucia takes Sundays off, so I'm on clean-up duty. You can come help me swab toilets," I chuckled.

"Yeah, I'll pass, but you could come out and spend the night Sunday."

"I could, but then I'd have to drive back and pick up the flooring delivery then drive back to your place."

"Dang, I hate it when you're practical."

"I know, me too. I guess we could talk dirty to each other until Monday."

Just at that moment, I heard the boys in the background, and chuckled.

"Yeah, thinking that won't work right now either. Maybe after I figure out how to get a line put in the RV, or at least get some mobile coverage to work out here."

"Oh well, I guess I'll just have to be thinking of you while I jack off," I said. "Like when you put your hand on my cock and slowly jack me off like you did yesterday, or when you slid your cock into my ass while we were in bed together, you know sort of like that."

I literally heard the man gulp, then in a squeaky voice responded to something one of the boys asked him.

"Um, Mitch. I gotta go, okay?" He squeaked again, causing me to laugh out loud.

When he heard me laugh, he said, "Go ahead, laugh, I'll punish you later, mark my word."

This time the joke was on me. I could imagine exactly what that punishment might look like, and I wanted him to show me right now.

"Okay," I said. This time it was my turn to squeak. His laughter was a low rumble that vibrated down to my groin. "Remind me never to tease you when it's two days until I see you again."

He laughed again, and we disconnected the call.

Was it okay to be falling for a guy after just meeting him? I knew a lot of men who fell in and out of love, but I wasn't one of them. What concerned me about Flex was I was almost sure if I let myself fall for him I'd be at his mercy. I was a one-man kind of guy. My people were like ravens. Once we found our one, we tended never to have another. I couldn't pretend that it didn't scare me that this guy could be my one. If he was and he grew tired of playing rancher and went back to his city life, it could be the end of love for me.

13

Flex

MONDAY FINALLY CAME AROUND, and by then I felt like I was about to explode. Luckily, I had plenty to keep me busy. I'd gone back to Alpine to buy a mattress for the RV, because, finished or not, I'd prefer to sleep in there than in the overcrowded house. Not only that, I was sure Emma Jean hadn't gotten too used to having Ace sleeping in the house with us.

Although Effie remained moody, he and I were able to survey the pasture, and through some divine act of God, the repairs needed on the first tier of fencing were minor. We finished them enough that Jimmy was fairly convinced they'd hold cattle, and recommended we let him call the Mills' right away, before they thinned the herd for winter. "You'll probably get a better deal this time of year anyway, but you'll need to play it cool, like you two are just getting back into it as a weekend hobby or something. If he thinks you are gonna wanna go big, he'll likely want to stick it to you."

"Can you tell grandpa's stock from his?" I asked.

Jimmy laughed. "Boy, Mills' stock and your grandpa's stock were the top two herds in this part of the country. The fact your grandpa's stock always took top prize in competitions makes me think they bred their cows to every bull we owned. There're probably no differences in the stock at this point, but I 'preciate you thinking that way. You'll have to spend some time building yer herd back up to what it was when your grandpa had it. I'll go out there and see what he has rounded up, and decide if you want to even consider any he has for sale. Pick the best now, and you'll have fewer headaches in the future."

I nodded in agreement, and let Jimmy take the lead. I was still too green to do any negotiating, and Jimmy knew Grandpa's stock as well as, if not better than Grandpa had. He'd spent his entire adult life managing it after all.

On Saturday night, Effie announced he'd need to go back to Houston to gather the boys' things so he could enroll them in school. I could tell there was more to it than that, but he didn't elaborate. I'd known my cousin long enough to know when he got into this kind of state, it didn't do any good to push him. If history was any indication, he'd spill what was bothering him sooner or later anyway.

"The boys can stay here," Emma Jean said. "I doubt they'll enjoy that long trip back to Houston, and I have about a hundred chores lined up for them to do."

The boys whined, but I could tell they were relieved they might be able to avoid the long drive to Houston and back.

"I don't know," Effie said. "I don't wanna put that on you, Mrs. Emma Jean."

"I'm here too," I said. "I'll keep an eye on them while we're out working."

"I haven't seen a snake around here since the barn burned," Jimmy said. "Seems that drove them further back, so ain't no major concern there, and I could use a couple strong boys to help me around here too."

Effie just shook his head, but I could see the relief in his face as well. "Why don't you fly back," I offered. "That way you can drive your truck back when you're ready. I have a few extra airline miles on my account that I could give you, and then you could be back sooner that way too."

Effie eyed me, knowing I was offering to pay his ticket, but he seemed too exhausted to argue.

"Y'all are being kind and trying to help, which I appreciate, but you know we ain't no charity case," he said.

"No, son, you ain't," Jimmy said. "But, we ain't offering you no charity, we're offering you support, just like any family would."

I could tell it hit him in the emotions, because he straightened up and looked around at us.

"Well, if that's the case, I accept your support. I'll only be gone a few days, especially if I don't have to drive a rental car all the way to Houston. My guess is I can be back here by Wednesday." He looked over at me. "You think you and Mitch can do the RV without me, or should I hold off until Tuesday?"

"No, he's a pro, and I figure if he thinks he can get it done in a day, he'll be able to. I'd rather you go get your business done and get back here. If Jimmy gets a deal worked out with the Mills', we may have cattle here by the end of next week."

Both Jimmy and Effie nodded. "That's sort of excitin'," Effie said. "Something to look forward to getting back for. I know it's silly, but the place don't seem right without some cows milling around. Maybe we can also talk about getting that barn replaced and getting some hogs in here too. I've got a hankering for a good ol' barbeque and not a hog in sight to butcher for it."

"Oh my," Emma Jean replied. "That does sound good, doesn't it. And the best part, if we got the hogs back in place, we could keep them danged snakes at bay. I'm glad the fire drove them off, but we all know it's just a matter of time before they come back. I'd prefer it if we didn't have to rush a six or nine-year-old off to the hospital anytime soon."

Effie nodded his approval to that. "Here, here," he said.

"Okay, it's settled. I'll get onto Grandpa's antique computer and see if I can get a flight out booked tomorrow for Houston.

If not, I may need to drive into town and use my phone. Boys," Effie looked at his sons. "You two think you can behave and mind the adults here until I get back?"

Both boys nodded, but little Luke's eyes begin to fill. "Good," I said out loud. "Because, I know for a fact, I wanna go into town Monday night and treat Mitch to an ice cream. Can't have a party with just two people, so since y'all are gonna be responsible young men, I figure I'll want the two of you to come with me. Maybe Mrs. Emma Jean and Jimmy too. What do you two think?"

Luke's eyes dried up, and both he and Drake jumped up and hugged me, while they were yelling, "Yay!"

I wasn't sure that'd work, considering how computer games and phones had taken over the world of playing in the dirt and getting excited over ice cream. Luckily, it seemed to do the trick on these two.

Effie smiled, and for the first time in a long while the smile seemed genuine. *Good,* I thought. *This is progress, at least.*

His flight left the next day at eleven thirty in the morning. I gave him Grandpa's credit card to pay for his ticket. That way, he'd see it was on the ranch's account. Fair's, fair after all, and the guy had uprooted his family's lives to move out here, so the least we could do would be to foot the costs for him. I was glad he didn't catch on to the fact I didn't use any miles, since I really didn't have any.

All was good until Sunday night. I hadn't unpacked anything since we arrived at the farm, sticking it all inside the storage shed that Jimmy said was the most critter tight.

I hadn't put my granny's medicine bag next to the bed in the RV.

The dream came on me suddenly the moment I closed my eyes.

I was lying on the ground bleeding, not sure why other than the memory of the last dream where I felt the searing pain after I turned my back on the snake.

A man stood beside me. He looked like me, but older, sadder.

"Love is your strongest weapon," he said, and disappeared.

I could hear something as it slithered toward me. I was frozen in place, like what a mouse must feel like as it lies paralyzed, before it's devoured by its venomous predator.

I was shocked, because instead of terror, a feeling of calm came over me. Like it was okay. This was my time, and I was almost glad it was over.

My chest throbbed with pain, and I could feel blood dripping from it and down my back.

The snake slithered toward me until I saw it rise up, preparing for the final strike.

Just before it did, a blinding light struck as if from the heavens, almost like lightning.

Next thing I knew, I was awake in my bed. No fast breathing or fear this time, just acceptance that the dream had showed me my death, and that something more powerful had stopped it before it could complete its deed.

I crawled out of bed, feeling nauseous, and ended up vomiting into the toilet.

I contemplated who the man was. What or who he represented in the dream. Was it myself as an older man, warning me to keep my loved ones close?

The sun had risen, and I knew Emma Jean and Jimmy would be up and there'd be coffee in the kitchen. I cleaned myself up and pulled on some clothes, took Ace for a short walk, then he and I went to tell them about my dream. Maybe they could make sense of it, help me understand what it meant, because what I knew now, beyond a shadow of a doubt, was these were no ordinary dreams, these were premonitions, and if there was any possible way, we needed to use them to protect us from whatever was attacking us, and prevent it from being my demise.

Neither Emma Jean nor Jimmy reacted to the dream for the longest time, then Emma Jean shook her head. "Your granny was the one who could work through these dreams when your grandpa would have them, she being Rarámuri Indian from northern Mexico herself, but the dream don't need a medicine woman to figure it out. Your life is in danger, and likely from the same person who burned the barn down."

"What should we do?" I asked. "It's not like I can call the sheriff and tell him I had a vision where some snake was trying to kill me."

Jimmy smiled. "Well, I'm sure he's probly heard crazier things in these parts, but yer right, we ain't likely gonna get help from the law without some evidence."

"I wish we'd sent the kids with their dad. It makes me nervous that all of us are in danger, not just me."

"I've heard your grandparents talk enough to know if anyone else was in danger, you'd have seen that in your dream as well. No need worrying about them, and sure not getting their daddy tore up about something that he can't help with."

"I'm not sure who can help. What good does a premonition do, when you don't know how to fix it?"

"It's just something to prepare you, sometimes things can be done, like getting the dogs or putting up the cameras that help. If you hadn't told us about your first dream, it's possible he'd have been successful burning down the house."

"Or she," I said, under my breath.

Both Emma Jean and Jimmy looked sidelong over toward me.

"Do you really think she's capable of that?" Emma Jean finally asked.

"I don't put anything past her, but no, not really. She isn't a get your hands dirty kind of person."

"Do you think your cousins, Eddie's brothers, would?"

"Possibly, but they're more like her than Effie. It doesn't feel right that it's one of them, but that don't mean they aren't involved."

Jimmy sighed and looked up with a smile. "Look who finally drug their lazy butts outta the bed," he said, causing Emma Jean and me to turn around and look toward the stairs.

Luke and Drake looked at us with concern. "Is our daddy okay?" they asked.

"I think so," Emma Jean said, getting up and shooing the boys to the table. "Why do you ask?"

"Cause you are all so serious. Adults are only serious when people are sick or not coming back," Drake said.

"Oh, honey," Emma Jean said. "That's not always the case. Sometimes, adults are serious 'cause they're trying to work through a difficult problem."

"Like when you're doing math?" Luke asked.

"Exactly like when you're doing math," Emma Jean replied. "Your Uncle Flex, Mr. Jimmy and I are working through some tough problems, and the answer ain't real easy to see, so that's what made us look serious."

Luke seemed to accept the answer well enough and went into the kitchen, while his brother remained rooted, unconvinced.

I went over to him and knelt down. "I know what it's like when adults don't tell you straight, but I'm not gonna be that way, okay? If there was something wrong with your daddy, I'd be the first to tell you. Why don't you go over to the house phone and give him a call."

Drake shook his head. "No, it's too early. He's probably still asleep, and I don't wanna wake him up yet. Maybe we can call him later."

I nodded. "Just let us know if or when you do."

The air cleared rapidly after that as the boys played in the living room, while Emma Jean cooked breakfast. I was given bacon duty, and Jimmy ran out to avoid doing any cooking, which made Emma Jean chuckle. "He'd face down a raging bull, or a six-foot rattlesnake, but try to get him to help in the kitchen and he cowers like a mouse."

The mouse reference sent a cold chill down my back, and Emma Jean noticed and put her hand on my shoulder. "We'll figure it out. Try not to worry too much."

We finished breakfast, and I left Emma Jean and the boys to clean the kitchen. I'd decided to do another quick sweep of the RV, so it was ready to lay the laminate when Mitch arrived.

I finished up and sat on the stoop of the RV, pondering my dream and what could be done to resolve it. I could avoid staying at the ranch, I guessed, but would that put everyone else at risk? This was my home, it *belonged* to me, it was my birthright. Besides, if I had fought like the devil to keep it from my aunt and cousins, why would I let the boogieman chase me away?

After a bit, Emma Jean came out of the house, carrying an old family picture album. "Your dream made me think of something, so I went and dug through your family's old albums. One of your way-back ancestors, well, she was the sister of your ancestor, got married to a man that your grandpa always said looked an awful lot like you. It's strange 'cause you ain't directly related to him, so it'd been something your grandparents pondered 'bout off and on, but here's the picture. Is that who you saw in your dream?"

I stared at the picture, and although it was grainy, I could make out the features. The man was clearly older than me when the picture was taken, and bulkier as well. The caption underneath read, *First Lawman, Alamito, Texas 1887.*

I nodded and looked over at Emma Jean. "What does this mean?" I asked.

She shrugged. "Hard to say. It perplexed your grandparents. You know things tend to come around again and again, but I'll say this, if he's the one looking out for you, I like your odds, since he was a lawman and all."

"He's probably the *only* lawman looking after us at the moment."

"Well, honey, if it keeps you safe, then that's all we need."

By the time Mitch arrived, I was resolved to just put it from my mind. I snuggled into his neck the moment we were in the RV alone together.

"Mmm, I missed you... Wanna forget the flooring, and roll around on my new mattress instead?"

Mitch hummed with my nuzzle, but reluctantly pushed me away. "Yes, but I only have today to help. Let's get this done, then I'll reward you later."

I got hard at the thought of what that would look like, and Mitch chuckled, and squirmed away when I began to grind into him, talking about bootie rewards.

He and I got the flooring down in record time. Mitch was all business, but I was able to get him to kiss me from time to time, or I'd come up behind him and nuzzle his sexy neck, causing him to chuckle and fuss at the same time.

He'd brought his sawhorses, cutting tools and other stuff necessary for the project, and after he showed me what to do, I worked the living room, while he did the bedroom. There were a lot more notches to make up there, and he said he felt better with me working where I didn't have to do as much of that, at least until I got the swing of it. By the time we met at the stairs, it was only a little before noon. Emma Jean rang her famous lunch bell, a sound I hadn't heard since childhood, and we decided to finish the stairs after we ate.

Before we went into the house, I caught the sexy man in my arms and kissed him long and hard, thanking him. After we pulled back, he asked, "What was that for?"

"It's for coming out and helping me... but it's also 'cause you're so freaking sexy. It's hard for me to keep my hands to myself."

Mitch smiled. "Well, you won't have to for much longer. I like having your hands on me... when I'm not trying to get a floor down on a short timeline."

Emma Jean had made tuna fish, ham and cheese, and cheese and pimento sandwiches, and we all dug in like she'd served a gourmet meal. You forgot how hungry you could get when you were putting in a day of labor in the Texas heat.

Lander Diez showed up right after lunch and interviewed Mitch, while I helped Emma Jean clean up. He ate up a lot of our day, because he wanted to see the ranch. Finally, Jimmy agreed to take him up to the volcano and some of the other sights on the property.

After Jimmy left with Lander, we were able to finish the stairs in less than an hour. Mitch had also brought the base molding with him, which we were able to install around the newly laid floor. With some quick touch up on paint, the entire project was done.

"Now, all you need is furniture, and you're ready to go," Mitch stated.

"Well, that and a refrigerator."

"Yeah, I was gonna order a new one, but if you're willing to settle, I could bring over one I have in storage. I sold a camper a couple years back that had a new refrigerator in it, but the family that bought it wanted a residential fridge. I'd be happy to go grab it."

"Let's go together. I also need to run to Alpine and get some better sheets and a comforter for the bed. I swear the sheets Emma Jean gave me are older than the Mexican Revolution. They're so threadbare you can almost see through them."

Emma Jean radioed Jimmy, and he said he was gonna take Lander to see the river. When I asked her if Lander needed us again before we left, she yelled back that Jimmy said we could just go, Lander was fine.

"We should've known an old windbag and a reporter would get along this well," Mitch said, laughing.

We took Mitch's truck, after I convinced him he needed to come back for fried chicken. He said he didn't want to be responsible for putting the first scratches onto the bed of my new truck. We were back at the ranch in more than enough time to get the refrigerator installed and framed, even though we stopped at Alpine grocery again and got supplies for Emma Jean, and some snacky foods for me to keep in my refrigerator.

Of course, I had to take Ace with me. When Mitch asked me why, I told him we were all fairly terrified of the coyotes that played in our yard. "Ace is the perfect size for a snack," I told him.

During dinner, we laughed at an epic battle that'd broken out between the boys. They'd been disappointed about missing the hole digging competition, so Jimmy had given them shovels and timed them. Luke ended up winning, because a tarantula had crawled out of Drake's hole, sending him very quickly back to the front porch.

"It wasn't fair. I bet Luke even put it in the hole to scare me."

"Nuh uh," he said defensively. "I won 'cause you're a scaredy-cat!"

When Emma Jean sent the boys out to the porch with a piece of angel food cake she'd talked me into picking up from the store, Jimmy told us about how Drake had screamed and jumped about a foot high, before taking off toward the porch. His recounting of the tale had us laughing so hard, we were all wiping tears.

Ace scratched at the door, and Emma Jean, still chuckling, opened the door to let him out with the boys, instructing them to keep him close so the coyotes didn't get him.

"Tarantulas are scary things if you don't know much about them," I said.

Jimmy hmphed. "I give it three days before Luke has one as a pet in his room."

"Not in this house, he won't," Emma Jean said, causing us all to break out into laughter again.

"How did things go with you and Lander?" I asked.

"He likes the ranch, says we should consider turning it into a gay outdoorsy retreat, or something like that. Said, there was a huge population of younger gay men, and even open-minded fellas, who'd pay good money to be able to hike and bike around the property without the restrictions the national park puts on them."

"Well, that's worth a thought," I replied. "Not sure how that would bring in the money we need, and more likely it'd be a problem with our neighbors, but it could work if it was sold as an outdoorsy LGBTQ-friendly experience, especially if straight allies were included."

We were talking about the possible ways to do it. Mitch was getting into the idea, and suggested we even have an all-male weekend and an all-female weekend, to make sure we were equitable to our potential clients. In the back of my mind, I filed the thought away until I could do the numbers and talk to the local authorities and insurance company, and all that, so I could draw up a cost analysis for the idea.

Effie called right after dinner to talk to the boys, and Luke animatedly told his dad about the adventure, while Drake sat across from him pouting.

While the boys were on the phone, I went over to Jimmy and asked where my grandpa's Winchester twenty-two rifle was. "After last night, I'd feel more comfortable if I had a loaded gun hanging on my wall."

"It'll help you fit in better out here too," Jimmy teased.

I smiled, but I was serious. If the dream were to be believed, and I did believe it after how real it'd felt, I needed a little protection, even though a twenty-two wasn't gonna give me much, it was at least something. I just had to make sure I hung it up high and kept the RV locked so the boys didn't go in.

Jimmy took me to my grandpa's bedroom, and up a set of stairs into the attic, while Mitch hung back and helped Emma Jean clean up the dinner dishes.

Jimmy used a combination to unlock a large gun safe that'd sat up there since I was a kid. He read off the combination as he went, then told me he'd write it down if I wanted him to, in case I wanted something a little more substantial.

When he opened the safe, I saw several revolvers, pistols, and various rifles. I reached in and pulled out a particularly old one that looked like it was from the time of the Civil War. "That'd be your great-great-great-great-grandpa's muzzleloader."

"They never sold it?" I asked.

Jimmy just laughed. "Like yer family would part with something with that much sentimental value. He reached around me and took out one antique gun after another. I'mma guessin' every gun your ancestors have ever owned since moving to West Texas is stored in here. I wouldn't go advertising it, but I know for a fact some of them guns are worth their weight in gold."

"The ones I'm most concerned about at the moment are a certain couple of young'uns that are probably wrestling with each other after the youngest ratted the eldest out about a certain tarantula."

"That could be grounds for murder," Jimmy said, and laughed.

"Let's keep all these locked up for now. At some point, I'd like to display some of them, especially since they've been passed down through the ages."

"Your grandpa installed this gun safe up here after you and Eddie came to stay. Your mama and aunt didn't show any interest in coming up here in the least, but the two of you seemed to be obsessed with this attic."

I laughed. "I remember. We told each other the place was haunted. Old man Brooks who used to work here told us about a cabin he lived in when he was a kid in Tennessee. According to his story, there had been a set of human teeth in the attic. We came up here almost every day that summer looking for teeth."

Jimmy smiled. "Old man Brooks, haven't thought of that name in years. He retired back in Tennessee about fifteen years ago. His son had to come out here and practically drag his old bones back to live with him. Now that I think about it, he was probably younger than me at the time."

I chuckled. "Lucky you don't have some pig-headed son dragging you across the country to live somewhere else."

"Could you imagine how stubborn Emma Jean's kid would've been?" he laughed.

"Why didn't y'all have kids," I asked, before thinking about how that subject could've been hurtful.

"Oh, Emma Jean had an injury when she was little. Got ran over by a tractor after she fell off. Doctor said she wouldn't be able to have kids, then we moved out here, and well, y'all sort of became ours. It ain't like we didn't have you every summer and during the holidays."

I smiled. "So, you got away with having honorary grandchildren, without the misery of ever having to raise your own."

Jimmy winked at me and put his finger aside his nose. "You catch on quick, son," he said.

We locked up the antique collection after I got the ammunition I needed for the rifle.

"I remember shooting this thing when I wasn't much bigger than Drake."

"Yep, wanted you to learn how to keep yourself safe around guns. Your mama never touched 'em, but you couldn't be out here on the farm and not be around them. So, somebody had to teach you."

"One of us probably needs to talk to Effie about that," I said. "The boys need to have a healthy respect for guns, especially knowing any hands we hire will more likely than not be packing. One can't live in West Texas and not be around them!"

"That's the God's truth," he agreed, and we walked down the stairs.

"How long since this gun's been shot?" I asked.

"About a week before you came," he said. "I use it for rabbit hunting. I cleaned it and greased it up then, so it's good to go."

"Perfect," I said. "When you need it, I'll have it hanging over the RV door. That way, it's always handy."

Emma Jean was tucking the boys into bed by the time we came down from the attic. I could hear her telling them one of her old tales she used to tell us. Luke, always one with a hundred questions, was asking something about why the ogre wanted to eat people, when Emma Jean shushed him, saying, "You gotta listen to the whole story before you start asking questions. Most of the time, the answers will come later."

We continued down into the living room, where Mitch was sitting across from the TV, Ace curled up next to him, watching what appeared to be one of the musical talent shows. Although I couldn't tell which one offhand.

He smiled when he saw us, and I could tell he was just as droopy as the kids were. "Come on, let's head out to the Fifth Wheel. I wanna show you my new bed."

Jimmy choked next to me, and I slapped the old man on the back. "Easy there, old-timer, you're likely to swallow your tongue."

"Pretty sure I just did," he said, but he winked at Mitch at the same time.

"Thanks for letting me borrow your Fifth Wheel and helping me put it together," I said. "I wouldn't have thought it'd look this good and smell so…"

"Not bad?" Mitch finished for me.

"Yeah, not bad," I chuckled. "I feel like I'm staying in a brand new one, except I don't have any furniture yet."

"Oh, I was going to tell you, I noticed the furniture has already lost its putrid smell. If I run it through one of the chemical treatments, I think the smell will be gone for good."

"Um, did the old man poop on the chairs?" I asked, unsure that I trusted his furniture after Mitch told me he'd not made it to the bathroom all the time.

Mitch laughed. "No, that was only in the bedroom. The last month or so got bad, but only when he was asleep, the furniture is mostly unused."

"Well, I'll want to use a bottle of bleach cleaner on each of them nonetheless," I replied, making Mitch chuckle again. "It's probably what's going back in when you're done with it, so either way, people are going to use it."

"Yeah, but it's easier when you don't know the seat you're sitting on might be covered with old man poo."

Mitch laughed out loud. "You *are* a princess. Who'd have known?"

I punched him playfully, pulled him into an embrace, then walked toward the door. Ace was jumping around at our feet, excited to go out, but also because we were holding each other.

Once we were out of earshot, I said, "That reminds me, I have some punishment I need to dish out."

The smile faded from Mitch's face and was instantly replaced with something much more feral.

We both heard the noise at the same time, and I sat up in bed. I looked at the clock, and saw it was half past ten. Mitch and I had just dozed off.

I nodded and whispered, "Sounds like someone is outside the camper snooping around. It's probably the kids, I'll go out and scare them," I said. "Little brats were tossing a rubber ball at me from their bedroom window the first night the camper was here. I'm guessing they're trying to scare you, knowing you're out here with me."

Mitch laughed. "Well, don't scare them too much, or they'll not sleep the rest of the night."

I slipped my pants on, being careful not to make too much noise and give away the fact we were onto them.

I'd pulled a pair of slippers out of my packing boxes when the RV had arrived to avoid getting splinters in my feet walking around on the subfloor. I slipped them on and slowly unlatched the door working hard to minimize the noise.

I didn't close the door all the way, afraid the noise of the latch would give me away, and slipped toward where I heard rustling. It was close to the big cottonwood that grew about five hundred feet from the house.

In the moonlight, I could see a figure, it was tall enough that it had to be Drake. I couldn't help but wonder where Luke was, surely Drake wouldn't attempt this on his own.

When I got closer, I acted like I was holding a gun. "Hold 'em up!"

When the man turned around, I could immediately tell it wasn't Drake. Even though I'd startled the guy, he wasn't giving any ground. Instead, he looked at my hand. Luckily, it was dark enough that it wasn't clear if I had a gun or not.

We both stared at each other, not sure what we intended to do, when the man said, "You need to leave here. We're going to make you leave. Ain't nobody here wants the likes of you living in our neighborhood, molesting our children, and spreading your perverted ways."

"Only person who needs to leave is you, we have cameras up all over, and your face is already recorded. Best you leave now while you can. I'm sure the sheriff will want to have words with you."

I could see the man had a gun, and I could also tell he was considering using it. I didn't move for fear I'd give away that my gun was, in fact, my finger.

"If you don't leave, we're gonna kill you and all the people you care about."

Just then a car drove down the back road, and although we were far enough away, the curve in the road was enough for the lights to flash on me, just enough to show that I, in fact, didn't have a gun.

I turned to run toward the house when I heard the shot and felt the searing pain flood my body.

The memory of the snake filled me. I tried to get up, but a boot kicked me in my side, turning me onto my back. It was too dark to see the man's face, too dark to know who my killer was, but just like when the snake in my dream had drawn back to strike, I found a level of peace. Death would not end my life. I could accept it for what it was.

I saw the pistol being drawn back and heard the shell fall into the chamber as the man said, "If a man lies with a man as with a woman, both of them have committed an abomination; they shall surely be put to death; their blood is upon them."

The shot sounded across the yard. I was confused, the sound of gunfire was different, and it didn't hit me. It wasn't the sound of the pistol, but the sound of my grandfather's rifle.

I looked up and saw that the shot had hit the man and he'd fallen back. Relief, along with the pain, flowed through me and was enough to cause me to pass out. I saw Mitch running toward the figure, but the man had gotten up and was gone. Mitch came back and squatted next to me, just as Ace reached me, standing guard and barking at the retreating figure.

Jimmy came out next and called back to Emma Jean to keep the kids in the house. "Flex's been shot. Call an ambulance, then the sheriff."

I could feel the life flowing out of me, not unlike it had in the dream.

Mitch handed Jimmy the rifle and told him to keep watch, in case the guy came back, then he leaned over me, checking my pulse, then pushing the hair off my head.

"You're the lightning strike, you're the one who saved me, you... you saved me."

Mitch's face was too dark to read, and I knew I wasn't making sense, but my body was beginning to feel chilled. The shakes came soon after, which made it impossible to clarify what I meant. The last thing I remembered was light flashing across that beautiful face, the face I'd fallen in love with.

I tried to tell him before I was gone, that I'd loved him, but all my strength had left me, then his face disappeared, and the only thing I could see was the light—a bright white light—and with it, peace. I'd lived, and I'd been loved. I had family, my cousin Effie, his two sons, Drake and Luke, even my mom and Mark, her boyfriend, who was a friend if not a stepdad.

Then I thought of the beautiful Mitch. The sweet moment when we'd held each other during the sunrise. The moments when we'd slept in each other's arms. Him reminiscing about the old gay men in Alamito, and when he teased me over being a princess. I hadn't really known it, not until that moment, but I was in love with Mitch Armstrong, and that filled me with wonder. Somehow, someway, I'd managed to love another before I died. That thought by itself made dying okay. I'd managed to find and fall in love with a man who met my every need, fulfilled my every wish. Death would not end this life...

The man from the dream was back, sadness on his face once again. He reached for me and pulled me up. "Who are you?" I asked.

He just smiled. "Someone who's known love and the loss of it."

"Like me," I said.

He shook his head. "No, you still have a chance. It wasn't stolen from you, not yet, but the evil will keep trying. Your loved ones, those are its enemy, and love is your weapon. Don't be afraid of it. Use it as a shield to protect what is yours."

14

Mitch

I HEARD THE GUNSHOT and knew immediately this wasn't the kids pulling a practical joke. I knew Flex had loaded the rifle and placed it next to the door. I grew up here, and my grandfather was steadfast in his belief that a man needed to teach his kids to shoot a gun, especially if he were gonna live in these parts.

We kept a rifle under the desk the entire time my grandfather ran the place. It was gone when I moved back to take over the motel, and I hadn't really thought about it since, but fortunately, for Flex at least, I knew how to shoot.

I saw the man standing over Flex, and I saw him cock the pistol to shoot while Flex lay at his feet. I didn't hesitate, I lifted the rifle and fired. I saw it hit him in the shoulder, and I saw him drop the gun.

I ran toward him, adrenaline rushing through me. The twenty-two would have to be reloaded, but I could use the butt of the rifle to bash the man in the face if I had to. Luckily, I didn't have to.

Jimmy arrived right after that, and I handed him the rifle to keep watch. I knelt down to examine Flex, saving him was all I could think about.

I opened Flex's shirt and saw the gaping exit wound on his right chest. "Fuck," I said to myself. "Fuck, fuck, fuck!" It was making a sucking sound, and I could tell his breathing was rapidly becoming difficult.

I immediately remembered my high school days when the state park's rangers had set up a camp for boy scouts who wanted to learn first aid.

I saw that the bullet had gone through his lung, and Flex would die if I didn't do something. I ripped off my shirt, tearing it in half and put it over the wound in his back and the rest over the hole in his chest. I hadn't stopped the bleeding and the remains of my shirt were turning red with blood, but I kept the pressure over both spots.

Flex was gasping for air, and I thought I heard him say something about lightning before he drifted into unconsciousness. I sat and held him for what seemed like hours before the deputies arrived. The initial adrenalin was beginning to subside, and I was starting to fear we were gonna be too late.

"I've just found him. God, why would you take him just after I found him?" I heard myself asking, almost pleading for a miracle that would help him make it.

He was still breathing erratically, but at least he was breathing. The deputy said the medics were a few minutes away, and a medevac helicopter should be here soon. I told the deputy what'd happened, and he did a quick search of the area to make sure we were safe.

When the ambulance arrived, the medics quickly assessed the situation, and put a breathing tube in his throat to help him breathe. The helicopter arrived shortly afterward and within minutes he was airborne toward El Paso.

I left Emma Jean and Jimmy at the house. They wanted to go too, but they had the boys. "I'll call as soon as I know anything," I told them.

It took me four hours to get to the hospital in El Paso. By the time I got there, Flex was already in surgery. I paced the hospital lobby, unsure what to do or say. It was too late to call Ruth, but I knew I wasn't going to be back at the motel anytime soon. Luckily, she was efficient enough to handle things for me. Maybe someone was looking out for us after all, it was just too much of a coincidence that she'd agreed to help just before this crisis hit.

Around two in the morning, the doctor came out asking for the family of Fletcher Henry. I stood up and went over to where he stood. "Are you Fletcher's family?" he asked.

"I'm his boyfriend," I said, knowing it was a stretch.

The doctor thought for a moment. "I really can't share much with you unless you're related. If you can have his relatives contact us, we can give them more information."

"Can you tell me if it looks like he's out of danger?"

"We will monitor him closely, but at the moment it looks good. It's fortunate that he's young and strong."

I looked relieved, and the doctor came over and put his hand on my shoulder. "Hang in there. I know this is hard, but he's going to need everyone before this is over.

I looked up, relieved the doctor was taking me seriously as someone who cared about Flex. "Thanks, doctor, I'll let his family know. When can I see him?"

"Not for a while. He'll stay in recovery, then they'll move him to the ICU. Why don't you go on home and you can phone us in the morning? We'll have more information then."

I didn't really want to leave him alone, but there wasn't much I could do in the waiting room. I went back to sit down after the doctor left and called Jimmy and Emma Jean.

"Is he okay," a worried Emma Jean asked, the moment she answered.

"Not out of the woods, if the cryptic message I got from his doctor was any indication. They can't tell me much 'cause I'm not family, but they could probably tell his cousin. It's too far to go home tonight, so I'm going to get a motel room. If someone could call me when they have answers, I'd appreciate it."

"I'll call Eddie," she said. "I haven't told his mother. Lord knows she'd just make things worse, but Eddie'll know how to handle things."

I nodded, then realized she couldn't see me. "Well, either way, let me know. I'll come back by the hospital tomorrow morning to see if I can see him. I'll let you know if I do."

The nurse at the ER window was able to direct me to a small motel nearby.

The motel wasn't much to look at, and the rooms were smaller than at mine, which was amazing since our rooms were tiny.

The full bed pretty much filled the room, but it was clean and recently renovated. I tucked myself into the bed, set my alarm early enough, so I could call Ruth and get her to open for me and still get my shower, before heading to the hospital.

I had dream after dream, all nightmares, and all about missing the shot or worse. In one dream, I missed and shot Flex. The last nightmare left me covered in a cold sweat, and I decided enough was enough. I'd rather be busy, than lying here waiting to see what my brain would conjure up next.

When I left the motel, it was still too early to call Ruth, so I found a diner that was open, and attempted to drown myself with coffee.

I got back to the hospital, and when I was finally able to track Flex down, I was immediately blocked by a nurse, who said she couldn't give me any information because I wasn't family, and then told me visiting hours were not until after 10 a.m. The woman wouldn't budge.

By then, it was late enough that I could call Ruth. She answered right away, and when I told her what had happened, she agreed she could handle everything.

"Ruth, call me when you get the office open, and I'll talk you through any problems you have."

When she agreed, I hung up and found a semi-comfortable spot to hang out until visiting hours.

I didn't have to wait long before I saw Flex's cousin Eddie come into the waiting room, along with a middle-aged woman I assumed was Flex's mom.

When I came over, Eddie grabbed me into a hug. "Man, thank you for saving him!"

The woman heard Eddie say that and came over and hugged me as well. "I'm Flex's mother, Katherine. So, it's you I have to thank for saving my boy's life?" she asked.

"Well, it was mostly luck, but I'm the one who took the shot at the bad guy."

She nodded. "Then I'm eternally in your debt, Mr..."

I smiled despite the fatigue that was beginning to settle in. "I'm Mitch Armstrong."

"Mr. Armstrong, thank you," she said, then turned. I assumed she was looking for someone who could give her information about Flex.

"The nurses' station is behind that door. They won't give me any information, because I'm not family."

"Well, you are now," his mother said, and dragged me along with them through the grey metal doors.

Flex was hooked up to all sorts of machines with wires coming out of him, not unlike you'd expect to see in some television medical drama.

His mother gasped as we walked into his room. The nurse came in shortly after, fortunately a different one than the one who'd blocked my entrance earlier, who told me no one was allowed until visiting hours.

This nurse explained in detail Flex's condition, telling us although he wasn't out of the woods, he was doing okay, considering the severity of his injury. He'd been lucky that the bullet hadn't hit his aorta, or it was much less likely he would've survived. The surgeon was able to stop the internal bleeding quickly after he arrived. The primary concern at the moment was his lung, which had been punctured—a fact I'd been aware of at the scene.

"When do you think he'll wake up?" his mother asked.

"Not for a while," she said. "We've got him heavily sedated, but he'll dip in and out of consciousness as time goes on."

"I want to stay with him," his mother said, and the nurse nodded. It amazed me how different things were between family and just being a guy's boyfriend. But the reality was we were in

Texas, and the woman who handled me was more of what I'd expect from nurses who probably weren't gay friendly.

Now that his family was here, I decided to take my leave. I needed to be at the motel, but both Flex's mother and cousin Eddie agreed to keep me up to date on his recovery.

"I'll be back in a couple days," I assured them. "I'll pick up anything you need. Just text me a list of things to bring back." I also told them about the little motel down the street that would be a good, inexpensive retreat for the two of them, so they didn't get too tired.

I drove back to Alamito, despite not having any sleep. The adrenalin from the night before still coursed through my veins. As I expected, tears flowed most of the way back. I wasn't one to feel sorry for myself, but, *fuck*... I'd finally met someone who seemed so perfect in so many ways. It would always shake me to my core, having a man's life in my hands, but this was a man I'd already begun to feel more for than I'd ever felt for anyone else.

When I got back, Ruth demanded I go to sleep for a few hours. "I'll come get you if you're needed," she promised

To my surprise, I was able to get a few hours rest, before I got up and closed the office down. Ruth proved to be a quick study on the computer and even improved how Lucia was doing the cleaning. The two women seemed to click, and Ruth was able to show Lucia how to follow the checklist in a way I was never able to.

After I closed down the office, I let Ruth know I was running down to the ranch to check on things there. I also wanted to let Emma Jean and Jimmy know where things stood with Flex.

When I got there, the place was strangely quiet, and I immediately grew nervous. My greatest fear was the gunman had returned. When I knocked, Emma Jean came to the door. Although she looked exhausted, she was smiling, and when she took me into the room, I could see they had a movie going, and Jimmy was seated next to the boys watching *Incredible Me. Good choice,* I thought, although I was sure the older one would've preferred something a little more graphic.

I went over and rubbed the heads of both boys, and even pretended like I was gonna do the same to Jimmy, when he pointed a finger and me and said I'd better reconsider if I liked my fingers in one piece. I walked away with the boys and Jimmy laughing.

We walked to the kitchen, and without asking, Emma Jean began fixing me a plate.

"So, are the boys doing okay?" I asked.

"No, not really. They had nightmares all night. After I traipsed upstairs twice, I ended up putting blankets on the floor in the living room, and Luke slept there while Drake slept on the couch."

I shook my head. It was a lot for two boys that age to experience.

Emma Jean sighed. "Oh, I think it's got a lot to do with losing their mom too. Little Luke cried out for her several times last night."

I felt sick inside. "I can't imagine what those boys are going through. How about you and Jimmy? You hangin' in there?"

"Oh, as well as two old folks like us can," she said. "We love having the boys, so that's no problem, but we are worried about our Flex."

"When I left, things looked good. His mom and Eddie showed up, and they're gonna take shifts staying with him. I'm gonna go up on Wednesday and Thursday to relieve them for a few shifts, then I have to be back here for the weekend. Let me know if you want me to come help with the boys some. I could take them out tomorrow morning, for breakfast or something if you'd like me to."

"Well, it might do them some good, are you staying the night in the camper?" she asked.

"I hadn't planned to, but if I'm gonna take kid duty tomorrow morning, that makes the most sense. I still have a set of clothes I brought with me, so yeah, that'll work."

I settled in next to the boys, and we watched the second show. Both began to doze. We settled them back on their makeshift beds, and I went out to the camper.

Jimmy followed me in and shut the door. "I wanna make sure the kids couldn't hear me, but I thought I should give you an update from the sheriff. Them rangers are conducting a parkwide search of the national park, and the state rangers are searching both the state park and wildlife reserves. Everyone is on high alert, since he shot to kill our guy. Sheriff said they did a full sweep of the local towns and haven't turned up much other than the family of Alamito's Baptist Church's pastor saying he left Monday and hadn't returned. They're checking in on him to see where he might'a gone. It's unlikely he was involved, but they're considering all persons of interest at the moment."

"Is there anyone else that could've been involved?" I asked.

"Well, there was a fella who came by here a while back wanting to buy the place, right after Flex decided not to sell. I told the sheriff about it, but so far, they've come to a dead-end there.

They also have the pistol that was left here. They're tracing the ownership now, but I haven't heard anything about that yet."

I sighed. "I know that minister. He and I've had some run-ins recently. I'll use y'alls phone tomorrow morning to call over to the sheriff and let him know."

Jimmy looked concerned. "You should probably stay in the house if that's the case. I don't really want you out here alone."

"I doubt he'll come back to the scene of the crime," I said. "Besides, I shot the son of a bitch once, I'm pretty sure I could do a better job if given a second chance."

Jimmy just shook his head. "Son, it's better you be safe than a hero. I'm gonna grab the radio from the house, and if you hear anythin', or get nervous, you give me a call before you do anything foolish, you promise?"

"Yeah, I promise," I reluctantly agreed. I wasn't a violent man, and up until now, I was sure I'd never find myself in an old western-style shooting. But when I saw that shadowy figure standing over Flex, I had no doubt I could've killed him. Even now, I wanted to protect this little group of people, and would gladly give my life to do so. That was a feeling I'd never had before, and I wasn't entirely sure I was happy about feeling this strong for others, or not.

Jimmy returned with the radio, and I tucked in. I really thought I was gonna have a restless night, especially since I'd taken such a long nap earlier, but bless the stars, I fell asleep soon after lying down. Of course, part of that was because the bed smelled like Flex. A mix of his soap and the natural masculine smell of him. I was glad sleep overtook me before the wailing did, because lying here remembering how much I enjoyed holding him in my arms, how complete I felt with him, could easily cause me to lose my shit, again.

I woke up early the next morning. I could tell the sun was just about to come up. I got my shower, changed into the clean clothes I found where I'd left them Monday, and walked over to the house.

The place was buzzing with movement. Emma Jean and Jimmy were early risers too. Emma Jean was in the kitchen cooking up breakfast, which was good, 'cause her cooking beat any restaurant around.

"Jimmy, I wondered if you'd mind walking the ranch with me this morning." I looked at the boys and winked. "I wanted to see the place again, since it's been so long since I was here. Could you show me around?" I was hoping he'd figure out I wanted to do a sweep of the place, in case there was some sign of the guy who'd attacked Flex, without giving too much of our plans away to the boys.

Jimmy smiled. "Well, that's a good plan," he said. "We'll head out right after breakfast."

"Boys, when we get back, I need to run into Alpine to pick some stuff up. Reckon you'd like to go with me, so we can give Mrs. Emma Jean a break from having too many men around the place?"

"Ain't nothing like that to get a woman riled up," Jimmy said, and Emma Jean came over and agreed.

"True, ain't nothing worse than having a bunch of men underfoot all the time," she said, and winked at Drake and Luke.

The boys were subdued, which I could tell concerned the adults. When Drake shrugged, Emma Jean admonished him. "You need to give a man a straight answer when he asks you something, Drake. That's the way we do things out in these parts. It's part of you being someone others can respect."

Drake thought for a moment. "Yes, sir, I'd like to go."

"What about you, Luke," I asked.

"Yes, sir," he said, but he was still very shy in his response. "Can we take Ace with us?" Luke asked.

"I don't see why not. You just got to give him a long walk before we get in the truck. I don't want any yellow stains on my seats."

When Emma Jean walked away, I whispered, "I hear there's a new woman working down at the Eastside Restaurant. If you can keep a secret, we might go try her strawberry rhubarb pie. Folks been sayin' it's the best in town. If we all approve, I think we should bring a whole pie back for Mrs. Emma Jean for taking such good care of us these last few days."

The boy's eyes lit up at that. I wasn't sure if it was because they could do something for Mrs. Emma Jean, or because they liked the idea of getting pie. Either way, it was good to see them happy about going into town.

Jimmy and I took out across the ranch after breakfast, both of us armed in case we ran into trouble. The guy had dropped his pistol that night, but that didn't mean he didn't have another one, or worse, something more powerful like a semi-automatic. Lord knew those had become popular out here lately.

There was no way to cover the entire ranch in the time we had, but we could cover the trails that led onto the property, the only way the guy could've gone if he were on foot.

There was no evidence, however, that he'd come any further onto the property after he'd been shot. Later we found out the sheriff had already traced the blood back to the road where it disappeared, meaning the asshole had probably driven away. Jimmy and I both agreed, we needed to keep an eye on the property, though, just in case someone tried to come back in.

The boys were out playing when we got back to the house, and I took the opportunity to call the sheriff and tell him about my encounters with the pastor who'd gone missing. I told him, "It was very possible the son of a bitch had been after me. He's had several parishioners leave his church since the incident. Shooting me out on the ranch would've been a good way to look like it was the other folks out here they were after."

The sheriff was noncommittal about the information. He said he'd look into it, which was the way every law enforcement officer tended to deal with someone who called in with information.

The boys and I had fun, which surprised me. I hadn't spent much time with kids in the past. I had to have the booster seat put into my truck for Luke, and Drake automatically sat in the back with him, telling me he wasn't tall enough to sit up front yet.

We got to town, and I ran over to the grocery store first to get Ruth another pie. As I saw it, I owed her a hundred for all the help she'd given me lately. As things were going, I'd owe her all my profits this month as well. Her rent wasn't anywhere near enough to cover all the time she'd spent at the office in my absence this week. Despite the cost, I was so happy I had her help. If all this had happened a couple weeks before, I'd have had to shut the entire office down and turn guests away. I was sure not gonna let these people down while Flex was in such bad shape.

When we got to Eastside Café, the boys were beyond excited. I made them walk Ace around most of the town to pee and sniff. It took longer than I'd anticipated, but we tucked him into the front seat and left the vehicle running while we were away.

I laughed when, before we were seated, they asked for a piece of the strawberry rhubarb pie. "We're here to test it out," Luke told the woman at the front. "If it's good, we're gonna take a whole pie home to Mrs. Emma Jean."

The woman chuckled. "Oh, it's good. I know 'cause it's my grandmama's recipe I used to make it," she said.

I blushed. No matter how bad it was, I was gonna buy a pie today. No way I could get out of it now.

Luckily, the pie was delicious. In fact, the rumors hadn't done it justice. I wasn't a massive fan of rhubarb, but this pie was particularly good.

The boys and I voted, and we all three said we needed to take one home. The woman smiled like she'd won the lottery with the boy's praise.

On the way back, Drake had a load of questions about Flex. "Is he gonna be okay? I know Mrs. Emma Jean and Jimmy told us yeah, but they think we are too young to hear the truth. We saw him that night, and he looked really bad."

I nodded, deciding to tell the boys the truth. "He's in bad shape, but when I left the hospital, the nurses told me he was going to be okay."

I thought for a moment, and decided to dig in a little deeper. "Let me tell you what the doctor said to me right after Flex's surgery. He said that Flex's recovery was going to be really hard on him. He would need the people who love him to be there to help. You two boys know that he was talking about you, right?" I asked and the two boys nodded soberly. "Flex is going to be okay, but he's gonna be in a lot of pain. It hurts to get shot!"

Luke looked at me with wonder. "You ever been shot?" he asked.

I laughed. "No, not many people have, but that sure isn't something I want to have happen to me. I like all the parts inside my body to be left alone."

"Me too," Drake said. "Don't worry, Mr. Mitch. We'll take good care of him. My daddy will too. He's Flex's best friend."

"Is that so?" I asked

"Yep, they've been friends since Flex was a little boy. That's why he calls him Effie instead of Eddie. My dad told us about some of the things they used to do when they were our age."

Luke smiled. "They got lots of whoopings," he said.

"I bet they did. Your dad and Flex are good guys, though. You two are lucky to have them taking care of you."

Drake looked sad at that. "My grandma, she is bad. She made Flex leave when I was little. I don't remember him, except my dad told us stories all the time. Now she wants to make him go away again."

I didn't really know what to say. Flex hadn't told me much about all that, so I didn't want to comment, but I could tell they were both waiting to hear what I had to say.

I waited a few minutes, gathering my thoughts. "Well, I don't know your daddy hardly at all, and I've only known Flex for a short time, but I did know your great-grandparents. I used to work out here on the ranch, and I only heard good things about them both. Even the men who worked out here said they were smart and hard workers, even though they liked to be ornery and played tricks on the guys sometimes. If I were gonna bet on them, I'd say they know how to do the right thing. Maybe you two just need to trust them about all this."

That seemed to mollify them, because the next questions were about all the stuff they used to get in trouble for. I tried to remember the stories I'd heard, and told them the most appropriate ones, especially the ones where they got in trouble for doing the wrong thing. Morals needed to be maintained when two young boys were concerned.

I dropped the boys and the dog off at the ranch and picked up a set of clothes Emma Jean had put together for Flex when he got better and needed something to travel home in. She also found his wallet and personal stuff in the bedroom of the trailer that she said I should take with me when I drove back to the hospital.

I really wanted to go back immediately, but I'd been away from the motel too long and was going to be gone Wednesday afternoon through Friday morning as well. I needed to make sure Ruth was settled before I took off.

The motel seemed to be functioning fine. There were more guests than usual for this time of year, which surprised me. Ruth had done a perfect job checking everyone in. I went through a couple of the empty rooms Lucia had cleaned this morning just to double-check, and to my surprise, those were perfect as well. *Kudos to Ruth and Lucia!*

I spent the rest of the day working in my gardens. With meeting Flex and all the trial crap, I'd begun to neglect them more than I liked to admit, even to myself. Several of the cactus gardens had grown some Johnson grass, and I knew if I didn't deal with that soon, it would be impossible to get rid of the danged rhizomes.

I was in the zone when Ruth came out and sat on the fence beside where I was working. "So, how's that handsome cowboy of yours doing?"

I jumped, not realizing she'd shown up. "Well," I cleared my throat, willing my heart to settle down. "He's hurt real bad and lucky to be alive."

"People are saying the preacher man that you had words with is behind it all."

"Can't prove that," I said. "Unless you know something I don't."

She shook her head. "Just saying what I'm hearing through the grapevines."

I looked up at her and sat up on my knees. "It's strange he disappeared just as all this was going down, but it doesn't make sense why he'd want to shoot Flex."

"Could be mistaken identity," she said.

"Can't argue with that. Still seems like a stretch for a man to go to all that trouble. He might be from up north, but he'd have to know people on a ranch would all be armed. And why would he hate me that much? I know the whole court thing hurt him, but it's just a matter of time before he attracts the haters back. That's just how things roll in Texas, and West Texas especially.

"Oh, people don't always think, Mitch. I don't know if he's your shooter or not, but if he is, I'm guessing it was because he thought he was doing the right thing. Some of the worst criminals in our history thought they were the good guys."

I shrugged and got back to pulling out Johnson grass, and moving the sand around to ensure I got all the little rhizomes out.

Ruth stood to go, but before she did, she said, "I know you understand, but you've got to be careful until they find that man. A snake is always the most dangerous after it's been injured."

The thought of the snake reminded me of the dream Emma Jean told me Flex had the night before. A chill moved down my spine, as Ruth had hit closer to what this monster was than she'd realized. She was right, though. I would need to watch my back. I finished weeding the cactus bed, and headed back into the house to clean up. That was the first night since I could remember that I locked all the doors on the property. I couldn't imagine someone who was a person of interest showing up there in the middle of the night, but if he did, I sure wasn't going to make it easy for him to walk in and kill me.

15

Flex

I FLOATED IN AND out of consciousness. During my times of semi-consciousness, I was able to tell there was something in my throat, so I couldn't talk, and I couldn't move my arms as if they were tied down. If it hadn't been for the man who'd come to me in my dreams, I'd have thought I was dead. I couldn't make heads nor tails of where I was, or what was going on.

At one point, I saw my mom through blurry eyes, but then I was gone again, and the next time I saw Effie, but that couldn't be real. I was far away from them.

When I finally began to come to, it was Mitch I saw sitting in the chair next to me. He had a book laid on his chest and he was sleeping. I could feel his hand holding mine.

I managed to briefly squeeze his hand. He looked at me and then jumped up.

"You're awake," he said. "Let me get the nurse." And then, he was gone.

I dozed off, and when I opened my eyes again I tried to speak, but the tube was still in my throat, and the pain in my chest was like someone was twisting my heart while it was inside my body.

"Shh," my mom said. I looked around, but Mitch had gone. She was the only one in the room.

I tried to mouth, "What happened?" But that's all I could get out before the pain almost knocked me out again.

"You were shot," she said. "I told you that place is cursed." She shook her head and composed herself. "You were shot, honey, and you're in the hospital."

I looked around for Mitch, but couldn't see him anywhere.

"Yeah, honey, he's here." Intuitively, she knew who I was looking for. "He's the one who saved you," she said quietly, then collecting herself, she asked, "Do you want me to go get him?"

I nodded, but even that hurt, so I quickly stopped. Luckily, she'd gotten the message and left the room. A few minutes later, I wasn't sure how long, I opened my eyes again and Mitch was standing there.

I felt the tear trickle down my cheek. He was such a sight to see. I couldn't describe how wonderful it was to lay eyes on him, especially after thinking I was going to die and wouldn't get to see him again.

Mitch wiped the tear from my cheek, and smiled. "You're quite the tough customer," he said. "Ain't many people I know who could get shot in the lung and come back to fight another day."

What he said explained why I had a machine breathing for me, and my chest hurt so much. Despite that, I needed to say it. "Thank you," I tried mouthing, but the pain immediately whipped me for the effort.

"You don't need to thank me," he said, somehow understanding me. "You would've done the same if our roles were reversed."

I just looked at him. I wished I didn't feel like a zombie, or I'd reach up and touch his face. I desperately wanted to feel the stubble that grew there, feel his lips on mine, feel his body pressed up against mine again, but I couldn't say those things. At least not yet.

I fell asleep with Mitch staring at me, but it couldn't be helped. The fact that I'd seen him again made it worth it to wake up and deal with the intense pain.

I was in and out of consciousness due to the sedatives and pain meds, but as they decreased the meds I was able to stay awake longer, and eventually the breathing tube was removed. Once the tube was out, they also untied my arms so I could move them. It felt good to be able to talk again, and to give Mitch a big hug, even though it hurt to do so.

The next day they moved me out of the ICU, but I still had a tube in my chest draining blood and helping my lung stay inflated. It hurt when I moved, but it was tolerable. At least I could have a conversation. A couple days later, they took out the chest tube, and I was able to get out of the bed and walk at least a little ways down the hall. It felt so good to be free again, and my mom and Effie kept me occupied with stories and memories of our childhood. Mitch stayed off and on, and when he was here, he rarely left my side.

When they finally let me go home, Mitch wanted me to stay with him, and Emma Jean and Jimmy wanted me to take their room. Finally, I put my foot down and said it'd be the Fifth Wheel, or nothing. Once settled, I thanked the RV gods for putting the bathroom on the same level as the bed. If I'd had to climb up and down the stairs, I was sure I'd have never made it on my own. Well, by on my own, I meant in my own bed. Nobody let me stay alone.

A week after I got home, the sheriff came by to talk to me about the incident. He confirmed that they did find blood at the scene, meaning Mitch had indeed hit the guy when he'd fired. The pistol he used to shoot me was also found and there were fingerprints, but so far, neither DNA nor the fingerprints had brought up a match. They were waiting for the federal database findings.

"Since your ranch is right outside the park, the rangers are helping us in case the guy ends up trying the same thing with the folks there, and it's possible he's hiding somewhere in the park."

The sheriff asked who I thought was behind all this, but I was embarrassed to say my aunt, because Effie was in the room.

Effie figured me out though and said, "I've already told them about Mom, and she's a person of interest, but she wasn't anywhere near this area. That's been confirmed by multiple people, not just my stupid brothers."

Effie was in the clear as well. He'd rushed back when he heard I'd been shot. The police questioned him immediately, and they were able to confirm he was in the city talking to his wife. She'd asked for a divorce. That was what had upset him so much before he'd left. His mother had called her and instigated a bunch of mess. It must've riled her enough that she'd contacted him. In any event, Effie's wife confirmed she was with him the night of the shooting.

Finally, when I asked the sheriff about the pastor, we were told his family were no longer being cooperative, since it was suspicious that the pastor had issues with Mitch, and had disappeared at the same time this all began.

Besides that, we were told they'd keep us informed as they received new information.

After the sheriff left, I lay in my bed, too tired to be up, but too sick of being in bed to sleep. It still hurt to move much, so I'd tucked pillows around me to secure my body, and keep it still enough to make me comfortable.

I was staring at the ceiling, when Mitch came in to check on me. "Are you doing okay?" he asked.

"Well, no, not really," I whispered, in my new scratchy, shot-lung voice. "I was hoping they'd have more leads by now."

Mitch shrugged. "I think they're doing what they can, but nothing really makes sense, except that the pastor was coming after me. Even that's insane."

I tried to sigh, but the pain caused me to see stars. "Damn," I wheezed. "I can't wait 'til this heals enough that it doesn't hurt every time I take a deep breath."

Mitch laid his hand on my shoulder. "It's healing well, they say, but I can't imagine how frustrating it is."

"I shouldn't be complaining. I thought I'd died, you know."

I hadn't really talked to any of them about that night, or what had happened to me, and I wasn't sure why I felt compelled to now.

Mitch kept his hand on my shoulder as he looked out the far window.

"I dreamed about it, you know," I said, then waited for his reaction.

"Yeah, Emma Jean and Jimmy filled me in on all that. You really are a West Texan if you're having visions," Mitch said.

"I never believed in any of that nonsense. Well, until it stopped being nonsense. Did they also tell you they found a picture of a man who looks like me? It was from a long time ago and he married one of my ancestors' sister."

Mitch nodded. "I've seen the picture."

"What do you think?" I asked.

Mitch sighed. "Well, he isn't your ancestor, Flex, he's mine."

I sat up when he said that, the pain forcing me back down on the bed.

When I caught my breath, I asked, "What did you say?"

"Well, after seeing the picture, I went back to Alamito and rummaged through some old boxes I had up in the attic. As it turns out, your lawman is one of my ancestors. His son eventually became a federal judge in El Paso. The guy you saw didn't live long. He retired from service in Fort Davis. He and his brothers who'd served with him there moved here. He was deputized after he killed an outlaw who'd killed his wife's or soon to be wife's brother. There was some rumor he was killed because of *lewd acts with another man.*"

"You mean he was killed 'cause he was gay?"

"Seems that way, and the man in the picture killed the murderer."

"You don't think they might've been lovers do you?" I asked.

"No record of that, but the record shows he married the sister shortly after. Things were different back then. In some ways I don't think people thought much about homosexuality, especially out on the frontier like this was. In other ways, I think it wouldn't have been uncommon for a gay man or woman to be killed for acting on their sexuality."

"It's kind of strange someone would've gone after the murderer, though, unless he was trying to defend his wife or fiancée's family honor."

Mitch chuckled. "That's unlikely, since my grandmotherly ancestor was a woman of ill repute."

"A what?" I asked.

"She was a prostitute, who worked at the saloon here," he answered, then laughed out loud when my eyes grew big.

"Well, that's weird as hell," I replied. "Who killed him?"

"Ah, that's where it gets interesting. The man he killed had two brothers. The three were notorious outlaws who were shooting up the west, not unlike Jesse James, but in the desert states like Texas, New Mexico and California."

"So, they shot him?"

"Yeah, that's a bit murky. They did, but he must've gotten them too, 'cause the lawman was given a sizeable reward. It went posthumously to his wife and infant son. The reward was significant, and it set my ancestor up for most of his life, including sending him to Baylor University for his law degree. He started out working for the mines as an attorney, but eventually became a local judge, then a Federal Judge in El Paso."

"That's interesting," I told him. "But, it doesn't really have much to do with all this."

Mitch blushed. "Sorry, got carried away. I knew I was descended from a judge, but, Flex, I didn't know we were kin."

"Oh," I said, and chuckled through the pain. "How exactly are we kin?"

"It seems the prostitute, my ancestor, was from this ranch. She didn't inherit it, of course, but she was the sister of the one who did."

"Well, it's a good damned thing it's way back there. What are we, twentieth cousins?"

"It's way down the line, but if we're gonna go with the whole vision theory, it does make a little sense. If we assume my ancestor was in love with a man, and we're both related to him, maybe this is him trying to protect us, so we don't end up dead like they did?"

"Do you believe that?" I asked.

Mitch stood up and paced. "I sure as hell don't want to. It's a bit too woo-woo for me, but what else can it be?" he asked.

"I don't think we really have to worry about all that," I said. "I think if we're being looked after by the ghost of one of our ancestors, well, we need to accept that as a good thing, and if it's all just a coincidence, think of all the stories we can tell our kids one day."

Mitch looked at me, askance. "Our kids?"

"Yeah, you do want kids, don't you?" I asked.

"Um. I-I don't know. Why are you asking about kids?"

"Well, 'cause my mom will be impossible if I don't at least think about it."

"Why are you talking about it with me?" he asked.

I looked at him for several seconds, before I responded, "Do you know who I thought of as the life drained out of me?"

"Me?" he asked.

I nodded, even though it still hurt to do so. "I thought I was gonna die, but at least I was dying knowing I'd been loved by Mom, my cousin Effie, and you. I was going to die and at least I had felt what it was like to be in love with a man."

"Isn't it too early to talk like this?"

I nodded again. "It's absolutely too early to talk about this kind of stuff, but I feel what I feel, Mitch. Now that you've told me about your ancestor, it feels like destiny too."

Mitch stood up and I grabbed his arm, although the pull hurt like a son of a bitch!

He quickly sat back down when he saw I'd hurt myself. When I caught my breath I said, "Listen..." I put my hand on him, willing the pain to cease, so I could return to the conversation.

"Shh," he said, and was about to leave. "We can talk later."

"No," I forced out the word. When I felt the pain ease, I said, "You are so important to me, and I know that's uncomfortable, but I watched my life slip away. I was gone, Mitch. I even saw the damned white light. That don't mean I'm asking you to marry me. I'm not even asking you to spend the rest of your life with me, but I am thanking you for giving me this."

I couldn't help the tear that rolled out of my eye. After having lost everything, I didn't even care that it did. Managing pretenses was the least important thing to me now. I'd rather be upfront and let the chips fall how they might.

Mitch sighed again and put his hand on mine. "Baby," he said, the emotions clearly visible on his face. "I feel the same. I fell for you pretty much the first time we made love. I can't explain why it's different with you, but it has been since day one, but it's too fast, and too soon. We've both been sent down an emotional roller coaster. You being shot and me having shot someone for shooting you. I'm here and I'm gonna keep being here, but let's allow things to move at their own pace, okay? I want the chance to fall in love with you properly, like we both deserve."

"Help me up," I said.

"What?" he asked, perplexed.

"Help me up!" I said again.

He did and when I had my knees over the side of the bed I had him pull me up, so I was standing. "Fuck, if I hadn't overextended myself with the damned sheriff, I'd have been able to do this myself. Fuck..."

When I was on my feet, I said, "Very gently, I want you to come here and let me hold you. Even if it's just for a second, I need you in my arms."

Tears fell from Mitch's eyes as he complied.

We held each other for a few moments. "Fuck, I need to sit back down. This sucks so much. I have no words."

Mitch chuckled. "I can imagine, but damn, Flex I needed that too."

"You know what I'm going to do the second I feel well enough to do it?" I asked.

Mitch shook his head. I leaned over and whispered, "I'm going to make love to you the way a hero deserves to be made love to!"

When he gulped, I said with more conviction, "God help me, I'm going to fuck you so hard you can't sit for a week. I can't stop thinking about being inside you, feeling you move under me. I'm so horny for you, and I can't do a fucking thing about it!"

Mitch laughed a squeaky laugh. "You just made me as miserable as you."

"Good," I said. "Misery loves company. Now, can you come lie next to me so we can cuddle at least some?"

He smiled. "I thought you'd never ask."

16

Mitch

FLEX HURT TO MOVE, much less have sex, but damn... If he ever talked to me like that again, I was going to have him, even if it did hurt. After that little speech, all I could think of was holding and loving him. If he hadn't been shot, I'd be really pissed at him about now.

I laughed at myself. It wasn't just him that had it bad. I cared about him too. I wasn't sure I'd have called it love yet. That seemed too soon. I felt attached, concerned, and totally attracted, but love? That was tough, and seriously, we'd only known each other for a few weeks if you boiled down the time we'd spent together.

I fell asleep next to him, which was a miracle, since his dog had all but stationed himself on the bed next to him since he'd gotten home from the hospital. Luckily, Ace let me have this time. I was woken up by Eddie, who was taking the shift to be with him next. As I drove home, I pondered what Flex had said. Like him, there'd never been another man I wanted to be with as much as I did him. When we were together, it was like electricity—sparks and flame that quickly turned to ecstasy, and then into comfort and tranquility.

If any other man I'd dated had ever come on this strong this early, I'd have been out the door, no looking back. I couldn't quite put my finger on why it was different with him. I guess, possibly, because he'd been shot and all the stuff that went down, but I didn't know if that was really the reason. I thought if he'd said everything before he was shot, I'd have made fun of him and told him to cool his jets, but I'd have probably still wanted to stick it out to see where things ended up.

Tourist season was really kicking up as the temperatures began to slide back down to the eighties. I guessed it was just serendip-itous that it came on the heels of Flex's declaration of love. I was forced to spend less and less time on the ranch, and since he didn't have a phone in the camper, I tended to have to send messages through whoever answered the house phone when I called.

I tried to stay with him at least once a week, but the intensity of our relationship was certainly slowing down. Things became awkward when he began feeling well enough for sex. We tried a couple times, but it still hurt him too much, so we cuddled instead.

Two months after Flex got out of the hospital, he was getting around a lot better, even though his chest still ached a lot. I missed the newness of our relationship, the feeling of anticipation when he'd call or come by. I tried to talk him into coming over to spend the night with me on the three-month anniversary of his shooting, and he declined. He'd begun showing signs of depression, and not only I, but his other family members noticed it as well.

So, we all got together one night to talk it out. "What do you think, guys? Is it me?" I asked, after Flex went back to the RV for the night.

"No," Emma Jean said. "It's the aftershock. He's just tryin' to figure out how he fits in the world after coming so close to dying."

I nodded and agreed that she must be right. I'd planned to spend the night, but it didn't seem right somehow. No matter how I looked at it, I thought I was the thing hindering his improvement. It just sucked that all this happened when we were still so new.

When I went to tell him I was leaving, Flex was staring at the television. "Flex, I'm going back home," I said.

He didn't respond. Lately, he was beginning to do that, which frankly made me insane. I hated being ignored.

I went to the bedroom to gather my things.

"Listen," I said, as I was walking out. "I'm gonna be gone for a while. I think you need some space. Just know I'm here if you need me, okay?"

Flex looked at me, then down at his hands. "You're breaking up with me, aren't you?"

I stood for a moment digesting what he'd just asked. I dropped my stuff and went to kneel in front of him. "Why would you think that, Flex?"

"You've been coming by less and less, and I'm too fucking feeble to do anything but be a nuisance."

I shook my head. "Baby, you got shot. You have a right to be feeble while you're recovering, and who the hell said you're being a nuisance?"

When he didn't respond, I added, "Nobody thinks you're a nuisance. You may be an old stick in the mud from time to time, but nuisance? No."

Flex looked at me out of the corner of his eye. "Are you making fun of me?"

"Nope, just speaking the truth."

I could tell he wanted to get mad, and for a moment I thought he was going to. "You're an ass, Mitch Armstrong. All this time I thought you were some angel, but you're just as big an ass as my cousin."

"Well, best you figure all this out now before we have them children you were talking about before."

"Dear God, I was on a lot of pain medicine when I said all that."

I chuckled. "I liked it, got any more? I'd like to hear more about how much you adore me."

Mitch reached over and pulled me toward him. I could tell it hurt, but he didn't let go. "I don't need fucking pills to tell you how much I care about you."

"Well, prove it," I said.

He put his forehead on mine and rested it there for several moments. When I looked at him, he was crying. "This is no good, Mitch. I feel like I'm holding you back. I'm not even able to make love with you, not like you deserve."

"You know what I want most right now?" I asked, and he looked up at me.

"I want you to stop feeling sorry for yourself. You are strong, Fletcher Henry. That's what attracted me to you in the first place. You survived something that might have killed a lesser man. Yeah, it hurts, but your doctors said, the more you do now the better you'll feel. Seeing you survive all that has made me want you more than ever, so for God's sake, stop your sulking!"

I leaned back, looking at him. "I want you to take your life back and not give up. I want you to let me love you without pulling away, even if it's just letting me touch you. Every day it seems like you drift further and further away, like you no longer want me in your life, so no, I'm not breaking up with you, but it sure as hell feels like you're breaking up with me!"

I didn't know where all this was coming from. I sure didn't mean for it to come tumbling out of me like that.

Flex shook his head. "You're right. I've been feeling so sorry for myself. I can't seem to stop. I know you're busy and the season is picking up, but I still convinced myself you were avoiding me. I just don't think I can sit in this motorhome any longer. It's like the walls are closing in on me."

"Well, I invited you more than once to stay with me, Flex. I can't make you, but I've got a hell of a lot of room at my place. You never *had* to stay in the motor home, you *chose* to."

I could still hear the frustration in my voice, which continued to surprise me.

"I'm sorry, Flex, I'm just frustrated. I haven't known how to manage all this. On the one hand, I want to take care of you, keep you motivated, and fuck, keep you occupied with something other than your own damn thoughts, but on the other, it really isn't my place, is it? We're still just learning to be together."

I stood up and Flex grabbed my arm again. "I didn't want you to have to take care of me, Mitch. Fuck, I've been a damned invalid since that son of a bitch shot me. I've only recently been able to get to the fucking bathroom on my own, at least, not without someone being close by in case I fell, or couldn't get off the damned pot or something. That wasn't your job. *Hell*, it wasn't anybody's job."

"That's right, Flex, everybody here has taken care of you, because we wanted to, because we care about you. I promise if you ask Eddie, Emma Jean, or Jimmy, they're all gonna tell you they wanted you here, wanted to take care of you."

"I should've gone home with my mom. They could've hired a nurse."

"That's bullshit, and you know it, Flex, not to mention, we could've hired a nurse here just as well as there. If that's what you wanted you should've said. I'm gonna go," I said, knowing if I kept going I was likely to say something I'd regret. I never did do well with a pity party. My addict mother was an expert at pulling heartstrings.

"Wait, you're right. I wanna go with you, I need to, and now I'm able to be up and about, maybe I can take on some of the front desk duties when you need to be out working on the property?"

I thought for a moment. That could actually be a great compromise. He could spend time away from the RV, and I could have someone at the desk to help Ruth when guests stopped by.

"I'll make you a deal. You promise to stop feeling sorry for yourself, because I've had enough of that from my mother to last a lifetime. Buck up, and while you're still recovering, I'll put you to work. You can do what you can do, and if you step up, I'll even try to learn how to cook something besides frozen pizza."

When he laughed, I knew I had him.

"Okay," he sighed. "I think I'm done with the pity party. The thought of being able to help you, that gives me hope, something to look forward to, besides sitting here and being out of my mind with boredom."

"Oh, there's no time for boredom at the motel. Trust me, there's plenty to do. Okay, I'll stay, and tomorrow morning, I'll help you pack, and we'll move you to my house. You can take shifts as you feel comfortable."

He smiled and when he got up, he stood there until I came into his arms. He hugged me and smelled my hair. "I've missed this. I was so convinced you were breaking up with me, I couldn't let myself just enjoy you. Now that I'm gonna be cheap labor, I feel confident you won't kick me to the curb anytime soon."

17

Flex

MITCH WAS A TOUGH boss. Well, not really. He was just as likely to force me to go lie down as he was to force me out of bed when I got into a funk. He always seemed to know which was best.

Ruth and he tended to me and Ace, like we'd always been their family. True to his word, Mitch would either cook something, or pick food up from the diner. We only had frozen pizza occasionally. As I began to improve, I took over the cooking, knowing how much he hated doing it, and truth was, I sort of didn't mind.

I steadily got better every day under their care. Ruth and I became close, and I even managed to watch her soaps with her a few times without falling asleep.

Mitch took advantage of my manning the desk and worked in his gardens, or did upgrades around the motel he'd wanted to get to, but said he never had time. "I'll get started on a project, and just as I'm about to make some headway, a guest will show up and need to be checked in," he told me one night when he was bragging about how helpful it was to have me here.

I never knew if he was just saying things to make me feel better, or not, but it did, so I just went with it.

I was recovered enough by the holidays that I was pretty much on the front desk anytime Ruth wasn't. There were two rooms that were still particularly rough that Mitch said he couldn't rent until he refurbished them. He told me he was going to take advantage of the Christmas lull and gut them.

Effie stopped by the motel at least once a week, and brought the boys to see me. Emma Jean and Jimmy even came by regularly to check on me. God, I did miss them.

Eric surprised me late one evening, when he checked into the motel and announced he was staying through the Christmas holidays. He'd shown up at the hospital right after I'd been shot, but I was too out of it to spend much time with him. He was clearly in a funk, but when I tried to push him to talk, he shrugged it off saying he wasn't ready for a heart to heart yet.

So, I just pulled him into a hug, and held onto him so long Mitch cocked an eyebrow, and threatened to kick him out if we didn't cool things off.

"Jealousy isn't attractive, lover," I said, and got a laugh and a wink from him.

Effie and Eric spent the days helping tear out and rebuild the two rooms, and actually finished them before Christmas Day. I could tell Mitch was relieved at having them done so quickly, and I noticed he was more relaxed than he'd been since I'd come to stay.

Everyone, including Ms. Ruth, had Christmas dinner on the big front porch of the ranch house.

Ruth, Emma Jean, and I were on food detail, and when we all got together it was literally a feast the likes of which was a sight to behold.

Even my mother threatened to come down, but she chickened out at the last minute. Besides, I was almost sure she and Mark were spending the holiday together, not that she'd admit that to me. It was Mark who'd let the cat out of the bag, when I called to see if he wanted to come and lead the culling of Barbary Sheep, an invasive species that were literally taking over.

After the holiday, I was able to start back helping at the ranch. Mitch had argued with me about leaving, but I put my foot down.

"Why do you have to go back? I need you here."

"Because, I ain't a fucking mooch," I'd said.

"You ain't a mooch. I have you working almost eight hours a day, and I don't pay you. That more than covers any costs of staying here."

"Bullshit," I said, and walked away.

I knew he was angry, but shit, I was not going to take advantage of him, just because we were sleeping together. A man had to have a little pride.

Lander's article came out, and we'd had several inquiries about hiking in the backcountry. At the moment, we weren't quite prepared for much else, so I sprung for a new ATV with some of my inheritance money. Of course, that wasn't gonna last much longer, but at least with the backpackers coming in, we'd begin seeing some kind of revenue.

As soon as I was back on the ranch, I missed Mitch too much to stay away. As things stood, I could either spend the night with him, or we had to take things as they were, because he was always too busy this time of year to come out to the ranch for more than a quick visit.

"Why are you pouting?" Effie asked, after dinner one night.

"I'm *not* pouting. Leave me the fuck alone," I said, and got up to leave.

"You and I both know you're pouting. In fact, I'm willing to bet I know why."

Jimmy and Emma Jean had come out to join us, and I was sure this conversation was going to get more nerve-wracking before it got better. I tried to shrug so he'd change the subject, but Effie was never one to let something go once he'd started in on it.

"You're pouting, 'cause you miss Mitch, right?"

I sat back down on the swing, and Emma Jean came over and sat next to me.

"Why aren't you staying with him?" she asked.

"What do you mean?" I asked her back. "I belong here, on the ranch."

"You belong with the man you love," she said.

"You ain't doin' nobody any good here pouting all the time neither," Jimmy added.

"What, did y'all plan this, or something? Is this an intervention?"

Emma Jean chuckled. "No, baby, no planning, but we're all of the same mind it appears."

"How can I stay there when you need me here? Aren't we supposed to have cattle by now?" I asked.

"Well, soon enough," Jimmy replied. "We ain't quite ready for that anyway. Need a barn, and need you to be back to full health."

I sighed. "I'm almost there."

"Oh, y'all stop it now," Emma Jean shushed Jimmy and Effie. "You're coming along perfect and that ain't the problem. What is the problem is you got your head being someplace else. You know Jimmy and I lived in Alamito for years before we moved to the ranch. Your grandparents had to add that downstairs room, just so we'd have a place to stay once we got here. So, ain't no reason you can't stay in Alamito and drive in like *we* used to."

I sighed again. "What makes y'all so sure Mitch wants me?"

Emma Jean laughed. "Have you seen how he looks at you?"

I shook my head. "I feel like I've taken too much advantage of him already. Hell, my dog even refused to come back, so he's stuck with him too."

"You ever think that dog stayed put 'cause he knew that's where you two belonged?" Jimmy asked.

I stood up, the conversation making my head spin. "I don't have enough money to pay rent, and I'm done mooching off him. We'll just have to make this work," I said, as I walked out to the lonely RV to try to get a little sleep.

18

Epilogue - Mitch

Fletcher Henry was a stubborn old goat. I tried to get him to stay with me longer, not just because I could use the fucking help, but because I loved waking up every morning cuddled in his strong arms. Even Ace and I had settled into a routine, since I got up long before Flex. I'd take Ace out for a nice walk, we'd come back and he'd fix us breakfast, while I made myself coffee.

After Christmas, when Flex decided to move back to the ranch, Ace had pretty much refused to go with him. At the time I thought it was funny, but Flex evidently didn't.

"He's trying to tell you to stay put. Why do you need to leave?" I asked.

He said some bullshit about not being a mooch. I didn't buy it. He knew he wasn't a mooch. He worked the desk more than

I did, giving me time to get work done that I would never have finished if he wasn't here.

That was our second argument, and unfortunately, where I'd won the one that'd caused him to move in with me, I lost this one. Now his stubborn ass was sleeping miles away, and my bed was too cold without him.

I'd probably have sucked my pride up and stayed with him in that Fifth Wheel, if I hadn't been so damned busy at the motel, I could barely move.

I knew it was also selfish of me, but I missed being able to get so much work done when I had him on the front desk.

I shook my head as the next guest came in. I still had six rooms that needed a refurb. Unfortunately, I had to put this guest in one of them. Even with the steep discount, I usually got a negative review when people stayed in those. I'd tried putting new linens in, had the old carpets cleaned professionally and caulked every hole, tile, well, everything I could find, but those rooms were still ugly 1950s, not even cute retro, just ugly.

The two rooms we'd just refurbished had been so bad, I hadn't rented them out since I inherited the place, so at least I had those now. Thanks to Eddie and Eric. *Damn, I forgot to get them a card when I was in Alpine.* I'd have done something special for them for Christmas, had I known they were gonna show up and give me free labor like they did.

Best Christmas present I'd ever gotten!

I loved Flex's family. Emma Jean and Jimmy had always been people I admired and enjoyed seeing in town. I didn't know Eric or Eddie until recently, but they made me smile when they were around. Flex and the two of them felt just like three brothers the way they cut up and teased each other.

The boys had started calling me Uncle Mitch on their own accord, and I wasn't sure if I was ready to be that for them yet, or not. It seemed to me an uncle was someone you could rely on, someone who'd be there through thick and thin. Flex was moody as shit since being shot, and even while he lived here, I thought the man could leave and go back to Houston at any moment, leaving all of this and us behind. I knew he was just frustrated with the recovery process, but I couldn't help but feel unwanted.

Ruth and I had become family in our own way since the lawsuit. We argued enough to be family. She never hesitated to tell me when she didn't approve of something at the motel, and even though it was irritating, she was right more often than not, which, incidentally, was just as irritating as the arguing.

The fact that Flex's family included her in the Christmas events warmed my heart. After Flex confessed his love to me, I pretty much came to terms with the fact I was in love with him too. I still thought it was too soon to admit it, but living together for all that time, watching him improve and coming back into himself, that all touched my heart a little too much for him to be just a boyfriend. I had to face the fact, I saw myself with him now and far into the future. As much as I feared it, as much as I didn't want to get hurt, I had to accept the truth of it. Fletcher Henry was *my* one.

One week after Flex moved back to the ranch, I was a fucking mess. Ruth came in and took one look at me and said, "Go get him, kidnap him if you have to, and bring him back here."

I laughed. "You really think I'm a caveman, don't you."

"Well, if that's what it takes."

"Ruth, this isn't some romance novel, or in your case, soap opera. People have the right to do what they want. I can't force him to come or go."

"Have you told him you're in love with him?" she asked.

I caught my breath. I hadn't thought of that. "No…" I said hesitantly.

"Well, boy, that's the problem. You do love him, right?"

"It's too soon, but I do love him, Ruth, more than I've ever loved another man… well, besides my grandpa."

"That don't count. If you love him and want him back here, where incidentally he belongs, then you need to go tell him, then beg him to come back. I can't hardly stand the place this week. You're all pouty, and I don't have anyone to fuss at for sittin' around and not cleaning. You know that boy wouldn't clean a damned thing if I weren't on his ass, which I enjoy doing, so I want him back so I can get back to it!"

I laughed at her. She did ride his ass something awful, which he ignored like a pro. The two of them had created some kind of word volley. She'd fuss at him for not cleaning, or whatever she'd find to fuss at him about, and he'd call her a fussy old woman, or tell her to get her hair or nails done like a civilized woman, and the two would end up laughing.

He ended up driving her to Alpine before Thanksgiving and forced her to go to the beauty shop there and even paid for her nails. She showed those nails to every guest that came in, telling them her new boyfriend had bought them for her. Flex would blush over in the corner, which caused her to cackle like one of the hens out back.

"You're right as usual," I confessed. "You willing to take a shift tonight, while I go talk him into coming home?"

"Hell, yeah," she said. "How many are checking in late?"

"Ten," I chuckled, and she moaned. "You owe me another damned pie," she said.

"I have two waiting in the freezer for whenever you want them," I replied, and she laughed.

"I should've never told you those are my soft spot. It really shouldn't be that easy for you to bribe me."

"This was your idea, Ruth," I complained.

"Well, and it's a good one. Go on, get cleaned up and put on some of that pretty smelling stuff you use when you're trying to get laid."

"Ruth!" I chastised, and she laughed.

"Seriously, go get cleaned up, you need to woo him and convince him you need him. Meanwhile, I'm gonna cook up one of those pies for my dinner. I've been dieting all week and lost five pounds. I looked in the mirror this morning, and my chins were about to touch my tits. I'd rather be fat than have skin flapping around."

I couldn't help but laugh. Before I knew it, I'd channeled my boyfriend, and said, "Your tits were down to your knees, you say?"

Ruth turned around, her eyes wide. "Well, well, our boy Flex has been rubbing off on you. Good job, grasshopper, good job!" she said, and slapped my butt when I blushed and turned to escape into the house.

I didn't waste time, and after a quick shower, I dressed and headed out to the ranch. I decided I wouldn't call, I'd surprise him. I liked to keep him off-kilter when I could. Otherwise, that sharp mind of his tended to impede any progress when it came to me convincing him to do something he was opposed to.

When I showed up, most everyone was on the porch. I looked around and there was no Flex. "He's pouting in the camper," Eddie said.

"Did you eat?" Emma Jean asked.

"Yes, Ma'am," I replied. "I had something before I left. I'm gonna go on in and talk to Flex," I said, and blushed, but not really sure why.

"You go on ahead," Jimmy said. "He's been hankering to see you anyway."

I left the group behind and knocked on the door. "Flex, it's me," I said, and went on in.

Flex was lying in his bed and raised up when he saw me. "Damn, you're a sight for sore eyes," he said, pulling me onto the bed with him.

"Mmm, you smell sexy. You put that on for me?" he asked, as he nuzzled my neck.

I giggled as his whiskers tickled me. "Maybe," I said. "Maybe it was for your cousin…"

"What?" he asked, and began tickling me for real.

"Stop that!" I yelled. "Before your family comes in here."

He stopped then and smiled down at me. "I've missed you so much."

I sat up. "Well, that's why I'm here. I'm prepared to belt you over the head caveman style and haul you back to the motel with me. I don't want to live without you, Flex. Please come back."

Flex sat up, the humor gone from his face. "I-I don't…" He put his head in his hands. "Mitch, I don't want to take advantage of you. It seems like that's all I'm good for any longer."

"Stop that right now, Flex Henry," I said. "I'm sick of all this feeling sorry for yourself. I pulled his face around to look at me. "I love you. I know I haven't told you before, but it's true."

Flex looked at me, I think to see if maybe I was just saying that to get him to come back.

"Why now?" he asked.

"Why now what?"

"Why are you telling me now?"

I leaned back onto my legs, kneeling on the bed. "Probably, 'cause it's true, and has been for a while. Flex, I was in love with you when you confessed all that to me months back. I was just too afraid to face it, but having you with me these past few months, working together, living together, and playing together... maybe *especially* the playing together." I winked at him. "It's just made it harder to ignore. My family, we don't fall in love over and over. My grandpa loved my granny 'til he died. My mom, even though my dad was a shit lowlife felon, loved him and never another since he left her. It's scary to me, 'cause I know like them, you're my one. There'll *never* be another man I love as much as I do you."

Flex pushed me back down onto the bed and kissed me hard and long.

"Good, I want to be your one, 'cause you're mine too, and your family ain't the only ones like that, Mitch, mine are the same. I want to continue courting you. Eventually, I wanna marry you and I wanna wake up fifty years from now all old and wrinkly, and still sexy hot for your body."

I smiled. "I want that too, so will you come back home?" I asked.

"This is all a ruse to get me to come back and be free labor, isn't it?"

My grin grew bigger and I hoped looked wicked. "Maybe," I said.

He tickled me again and then reached down and slipped his hand into my pants and around my cock.

I drew in a deep breath. "Okay, maybe that's the real reason!"

Flex chuckled in that deep way he did that made my heart beat faster and the blood rush out of my head.

Before it turned sexual, though, I said again, "I love you, Fletcher Henry, with all my heart and all my soul."

He stared at me and when his face clouded with emotion, he said, "You are my soul, and I'll be yours forever."

Eddie is confronted by a ghost that Alex resembles. Neither trusts the other. Can their unlikely relationship help them survive the imminent danger?

Continue the Big Bend series with ***Love's Heirloom***

Love's Heirloom by Adam J. Ridley and Blake Allwood

Available at your favorite bookstore.

Join Blake's email list to get advance notice of new books and receive his occasional newsletter:

www.blakeallwood.com

MM Romance
By Blake Allwood

Transitions Series
Aiden Inspired
Suzie Empowered (MF Romance)
Bobby Transformed

Chance Series
Love By Chance
Another Chance With Love
Taking A Chance For Love

Romantic Series
Romantic Renovations (1)
Romantic Rescue (2)
Romantic Recon (3)

Melody Series
Melody of the Heart
Melody of the Snow

Road to Rocktoberfest Anthology
Changing His Tune - 2022

Coming Home Series (2023)
A Long Way Home
Family Home
Down Home
…and many more

Novellas
Tenacious
Moon's Place

Romantic Fantasy
By Adam J. Ridley

Big Bend Series
Love's Legacy (1)
Love's Heirloom (2)
Love's Bequest (3)

The Witch Brothers Series
Emerald Earth
Diamond Air
Ruby Fire
Sapphire Water

Blake Allwood was born in west Tennessee, then moved to Kansas City MO after earning a degree in Early Childhood Education from Graceland College in Lamoni, Iowa. He met his husband Shaun in 1995 and they officially married in 2015, once gay marriage was legalized; although they still consider Valentines Day 1995 as their true "anniversary date". Twenty-two years later (2017), after fostering 12 children together, he and his husband sold their home, purchased an RV and began traveling the country with their two dogs.

Typically, Blake can be found relaxing in the RV or by the fire with his laptop and their Jack Russell Terrier, Buddy, curled up between his legs demanding attention. Denver, their Siberian Husky mix is often asleep at his feet or playing tug of war with Blake's husband.

Most of Blake's stories are inspired by the places they have visited in their ongoing travels. His first book, ***Aiden Inspired***, was released in 2019 and he has now written over 20 books. In

2023 he is releasing the ***Coming Home*** series which is comprised of ten-plus sweet contemporary romance novels that are based on a fictional town in his home state of Tennessee.

Blake also writes under the pen name of Adam J. Ridley for his urban fantasy fans looking for stories revolving around gay characters. His first series is The Witch Brothers Saga, starting with ***Emerald Earth***.

bibl, biblio...

bibliopride.com

Books by LGBTQ+ authors

www.ingramcontent.com/pod-product-compliance
Lightning Source LLC
Chambersburg PA
CBHW061053190726
48286CB00006B/1738